A GOOD WALK SPOILED

Recent Titles by J M Gregson from Severn House

Detective Inspector Peach Mysteries

DUSTY DEATH
TO KILL A WIFE
THE LANCASHIRE LEOPARD
A LITTLE LEARNING
MISSING, PRESUMED DEAD
MURDER AT THE LODGE
PASTURES NEW
REMAINS TO BE SEEN
A TURBULENT PRIEST
THE WAGES OF SIN
WHO SAW HIM DIE?
WITCH'S SABBATH

Lambert and Hook Mysteries

AN ACADEMIC DEATH
CLOSE CALL
DEATH ON THE ELEVENTH HOLE
GIRL GONE MISSING
A GOOD WALK SPOILED
JUST DESSERTS
MORTAL TASTE
SOMETHING IS ROTTEN
TOO MUCH OF WATER
AN UNSUITABLE DEATH

A GOOD WALK SPOILED

A Lambert and Hook Mystery

J.M. Gregson

This first world edition published 2008
in Great Britain and the USA by
SEVERN HOUSE PUBLISHERS LTD of
9–15 High Street, Sutton, Surrey, England, SM1 1DF.

British Library Cataloguing in Publication Data

Gregson, J. M.
  A good walk spoiled
  1. Lambert, John (Fictitious character) - Fiction 2. Hook,
  Bert (Fictitious character) - Fiction 3. Police - England -
  Gloucestershire - Fiction 4. Detective and mystery stories
  I. Title
  823.9'14[F]

ISBN-13: 978-0-7278-6666-0   (cased)

All Severn House titles are printed on acid-free paper.

Printed and bound in Great Britain by
MPG Books Ltd., Bodmin, Cornwall.

One

'**B** loody ball! Bastard bloody ball!' Priscilla Godwin found that all ladylike pretensions disappeared swiftly on the golf course. She watched the small white sphere run erratically over the grass, then turn determinedly to the right and disappear with its final roll into the muddy depths of a pond. 'Bloody, bloody, bloody *bastard* ball!'

Her voice rose towards a scream with each repetition, so that heads turned towards her from adjoining fairways. Experienced eyes divined swiftly what had happened: heads nodded sagely before returning to their own concerns. Routine golfing frustration: nothing to get really worried about. The poor woman would no doubt be all right in a day or two.

The three people who were playing with Priscilla knew that she was normally a quiet, reserved thirty-year-old. Even now, in the depths of her suffering, her vocabulary had not lapsed into the vehement obscenities which were familiar to her male companions: only the repetitions and the rising decibel level had marked the intensity of her frustration, the degree to which achievement had failed to meet with aspiration.

The four gathered to stare into the depths of the pond, watching the ripples spread out towards the irises on the far side of the water, as if concluding some unspoken golfing ritual. Priscilla stared malevolently at the spot where her ball had entered the pond. 'Another ball gone. I'll be lucky to complete the round at this rate. Oscar Wilde was right. Golf is nothing more than a good walk spoiled.'

Paul Young glanced sideways at her thunderous face. He knew that it was Mark Twain who had offered that observation, but it did not seem a good time to correct his golfing partner: she still held a five iron in her hand, and she might not miss the larger target of a human head. He said instead, 'Leave this one to me, Pris. I'm almost on the green in two.'

Supercilious sod, thought Priscilla. Smug bastard. No wonder his wife had chosen to play with someone else. 'I don't know what I'd do without you, Paul,' she said, accurately but acidly.

Golf is a great game for cementing friendships.

The other female in the four looked up at the blue sky and flying white clouds. 'This sure beats a day in the lab, whatever we score,' she said cheerfully. Debbie Young was ten years older than Priscilla, with a round face which was still largely free of wrinkles, blue eyes, and blonde hair, which was now a little dishevelled by the wind. She was buxom rather than plump, and the brown and white trousers and yellow sweater she wore emphasized the fact. Men who were not entirely dedicated to this ridiculous game liked to follow her down the fairway and enjoy certain compensations for their golfing trials.

'Even bad golf beats work.' The fourth member of the group stated that axiom firmly, like a bishop iterating an article of faith. Jason Dimmock was tall and lean. He had a handsome face, with a nose which had been bent minimally and interestingly by an adolescent rugby injury. He had been playing golf for only two years, having come to it at thirty-seven when he accepted that his days of serious cricket and tennis were numbered. Yet he was already the best golfer in the four.

Jason decided that it was time to get things moving again. He addressed his ball, which lay to the left of the pond, took a single look towards the green, and dispatched his ball there with a controlled shot and a minimum of fuss. 'Good shot!' said Priscilla Godwin, after a pause to gather the shreds of her sporting resources. 'Looks like this hole will be between the two men.' The sweet smile she directed at Debbie Young was not wholly benevolent.

The game proceeded. Priscilla Godwin, for no apparent reason, played a little better; her colleagues noted even minimal improvements and complimented her upon them, like diplomats nervously accepting every opportunity to avoid the disaster of open war. The two men fought each other steadily as the round progressed, the two women made occasional unexpected and unpredictable contributions to the struggle. Fierce contest was maintained beneath the brittle banter. Bodies strained every nerve and sinew to get that irritating white ball into a succession of holes which were much too small for the purpose.

The non-golfers who proceeded with caution across the footpath which crossed the course thought how pleasant it must be for men and women to relax and take exercise in this carefree and undemanding fashion on a sunny summer after-noon. One wonders what hope there can be for peace among the peoples of the world when such fundamental mis-apprehensions are rife among people from the same nation.

Few people can maintain blinding, blood-curdling anger for longer than a few minutes at a time, and Miss Godwin was no exception. After the crisis of the pond, she became grad-ually quieter, until she was eventually a little embarrassed by her outburst. She was consoled by a volley of curses from her partner on the sixteenth, occasioned by nothing more damaging than a four-putt. 'It's not the end of the world, Paul, is it?' she said cheerfully, with that combination of logic and bonhomie which can cause apoplexy among serious golfers.

Paul Young did not reply, but she expected no response. His thunderous glare into the middle distance was exactly what she would have expected from a committed golfer. She found it comforting, rather in the way that people now accept the news of a moderate overdraft as an assurance of an unchanging world.

Priscilla even managed to win the last hole, with the help of her handicap and her first long putt of the day. The match was over by then, but this small, irrelevant triumph gave her the irrational glow of happiness which is familiar to all practitioners of the game.

They showered in their respective changing rooms, feeling the bad golf wash away from them in the warm jets, watching the imprecations and the tensions swirl away into the oblivion beyond the plugholes. Changed and with drinks in front of them, they sat outside on the veranda and enjoyed the sunset, whilst watching fellow-golfers struggling towards the eighteenth green with patronizing smiles and the charity which stems from alcohol and a pleasant fatigue.

It is not the best time to make balanced judgements or take responsible decisions. That became apparent when Debbie Young said slowly, 'I enjoyed it today. Perhaps we should have a group outing from the firm. Get everyone together who plays golf and make a day of it. Perhaps even stay a couple of nights somewhere and have two or three rounds.'

She expected that someone, probably one of the men, would immediately pour very cold water on such a proposition. But no one did. Priscilla Godwin said that a golfing break might be too ambitious, that they'd get a much better turnout for a one-day competition with a meal to follow. She spoke about the value of bonding exercises, and confessed that she for one found that she tended to become cocooned in her own sphere of work activity, so that she would welcome a day of mixing informally with other people who did very different jobs.

Three people who earlier in the day might have ridiculed such naivety nodded sagely and took sips of their drinks. They were all intelligent people, but this was the wrong time of the day and the wrong place for intelligence.

Indeed, it was the best golfer among the four, Jason Dimmock, who eventually nodded and said, 'A company golf day sounds like quite a good idea to me.'

In fairness to him, it must be said that he could have had no idea at the time of the consequences of this innocent proposal.

Two

Gloucester Chemicals was a good place to work. Most people agreed that if you had to earn your living somewhere, you could do a lot worse. When the British talent for understatement is taken into account, this means that most people felt they were lucky to work there, though few of them would have dreamed of putting it as strongly as that.

It was a prosperous firm, for a start. Forty years earlier, the founders had hoped for a modest but consistent success in the world of pharmaceuticals. They had done much better than that. The burgeoning British National Health Service had vastly increased the demand for a great variety of medical drugs. This lucrative but highly competitive market was made for young men with chemistry degrees and an entrepreneurial bent. They had prospered, resisted takeover bids from the big boys like Glaxo and Beechams, diversified, and floated the company on the stock market during the boom times of the nineties.

One of the key events in the company history had been the acquisition of government contracts in 2000. It seemed appropriate that the new millennium should mark the transition of a company which had begun in a deserted warehouse by the River Severn to a large factory with extensive laboratory facilities on the new industrial estate three miles away.

In national and international terms, Gloucester Chemicals was still a small firm, with a workforce of under three hundred and a profits-per-worker ratio which was among the highest in the world. In this field where new products were the very lifeblood of a firm, a very high proportion of profits was ploughed back into research and development. The laboratories were regarded by everyone who worked in the establishment as the centre of the company. Each year two or three of the brightest of new graduates enlivened and invigorated the work on new products on which the company depended for its prosperity.

Priscilla Godwin had been one of these herself only seven years earlier, arriving with her doctorate proudly brandished and possessing what she now saw as a touching naivety about the world of business and its strange but sometimes exciting practices. Cambridge had been good fun as well as hard work, full of sexual and other excitements after the restrictive world of Cheltenham Ladies' College. But she considered now that the ancient university had been the ivory tower which her less fortunate contemporaries had warned her it would be, as far as the hard lessons of life went.

A series of affairs both fortunate and unfortunate, with two in particular much more life-changing than the others, had left her at thirty both wiser and more cautious. She told herself sturdily that she would not have lived her life differently, that a few scars were necessary to the rounded and effective twenty-first-century woman which she was sure she had now become.

She had to tell herself that a little more often and a little more insistently than should have been strictly necessary. She valued her freedom, and a few scars were surely a small price to pay for independence.

Five days after the golf outing, Priscilla was working late in the lab. She wanted to conclude her recording of the latest of a series of experiments. Writing came harder than science for Priscilla. She liked to have privacy to concentrate upon her sentences and her syntax. There was a skill in making complex scientific information readable and easily understood: she had read enough turgid and inconclusive accounts herself to realize that. She could write crisp sentences, but she needed to concentrate to do it properly.

If her desire to present things in a decent and orderly fashion gained her a reputation for conscientiousness, that would be a useful by-product of her industry. You might feel threatened sometimes by these bright young minds who joined you each year, but if you could show the people who ran the company that you were industrious and diligent, that might well be noticed. Miss Godwin had learned quite a lot about the way the world worked in her years at Gloucester Chemicals.

People who worked in the rest of the firm thought that lab work was glamorous, that you lived your life continuously at the forefront of technology, waiting for the Eureka moment of the next breakthrough. It wasn't like that at all, thought Priscilla ruefully, as she dutifully recorded the negative outcomes of her latest work. Most of the research was routine stuff, investigating the possible side effects of promising developments, checking out the safety factors on the newest drugs, devising the necessary final tests on mice and rats before new treatments were released for human use.

There were small but important discoveries, even the occasional revolutionary new drug treatment which everyone dreamed of. But these were usually the result of patient teamwork over many months, rather than individual brilliance. Indeed, one of the principles of the lab was that you shared new thoughts and new initiatives with those around you. The 'Einstein moment' was a joke among working scientists, including even those with the most original minds and the most creative ideas. If many of the people who worked in the labs had a secret fantasy of emulating Alexander Fleming's discovery of penicillin in 1928, they kept such visions strictly to themselves.

Priscilla Godwin was completing the record of her latest mundane findings when Richard Cullis came into the office she shared with three others at the end of the laboratory. He glanced round the deserted area and said heavily and obviously, 'So the dedicated researcher works on alone, whilst others depart to the concerns of ordinary life!'

Priscilla smiled up at him and said something deprecating. She couldn't set aside a certain satisfaction that the boss had come in here and found her exceeding the calls of duty to complete her work. Richard Cullis was a bronzed, fit man of forty-four. He had a BSc in chemistry, but boasted that he had long since forgotten all he had ever learned about science. He had made his way in sales, rising to become sales manager on the back of the firm's successful drugs programme. He would admit to his intimates when he was feeling charitable that it had been easy in those years: a succession of effective new drugs had left clients eager to buy, so that his main problems had been the welcome ones of ensuring a smooth supply chain.

Two years ago, Richard had taken advantage of the firm's expansion to become a member of the board. He was now Director of Research and Development, which put him officially in charge of the laboratories. His job, as he told anyone willing to listen, was to translate scientific initiatives into working products. He was a link between the research which was the heartbeat of the firm and the commercial concerns of the high street.

Cullis reminded shareholders who wished to maximize gains that the prosperity of the firm lay in research and the continual supply of new products which it would bring. He reminded those people in the labs who liked to see themselves as unworldly boffins that profit was what drove things forward, that without it there would not be the constant updating of facilities and personnel which was the basis of laboratory development.

Richard Cullis was good at banging heads together and making people face reality.

He came across and peered over Priscilla Godwin's shoulder at what she had written. She caught a faint, musky scent from him and wondered whether it was aftershave or some other, more mysterious, male addition. She was suddenly embarrassed at the paucity of her findings, at the humdrum quality of this negative write-up. Cullis must feel that she was giving herself airs and graces, staying behind to record dull stuff like this.

'It's just routine,' she said apologetically to the man whose breath she could feel on the side of her neck. 'Nothing exciting, but it has to be done, to save other people from going off down blind alleys.'

'I know the form,' he said, coming round to where she could see him. 'You can leave me standing on the technical stuff, but I still remember the way we operate, the way all science operates. Throw lots of pebbles and wait patiently for the one that hits the target.'

Priscilla smiled. She had heard the analogy many times. Now she heard herself voicing her usual corrective. 'We hope that what we already know helps us at least to cast the pebbles in the right direction.'

He smiled at her, but said nothing. Probably he had heard this modification before, perhaps even used it himself when explaining their activities to the members of the board who did not have scientific backgrounds. He walked over to one of the other benches, glanced at a page of figures which one of their new bright young men had left there, picked up the ball-pen which lay across the sheet, pressed and re-pressed the top of it to bring out and recess the writing-point, as if this were an aid to thought for him.

Cullis said speculatively, 'There still aren't many women scientists of quality available, are there? We couldn't find a single one worth shortlisting, when we appointed Ben.'

He sounded as if he was apologizing for the fact. Perhaps it was his concession to feminism. In truth, Priscilla liked the fact that she had little female company in here. It made her feel a little special, as if she had won through against the odds, as if she was slightly more remarkable than the bright young men who sometimes seemed a threat to her. She said, 'It all goes back to the schools. Generally speaking, maths and science isn't well taught in girls' schools. And in co-educational establishments, girls seem to think the arts subjects are more feminine.'

She wished immediately that she hadn't spoken. Richard Cullis wasn't a fool. He would know all this: probably he would think her banal and uninteresting. She realized with a little, rather pleasant, shock that she did not want him to think that.

But he nodded slowly and thoughtfully, as if she had offered him a more original thought. He walked over and looked out of the window at the almost empty car park and the equally deserted school playing fields beyond it. Then he walked to the door at the end of the lab and stood for a moment looking into the big, hangar-like room where they kept the rabbits and the other animals on which they tested new drugs.

It was almost as if he was checking that they were the only ones left in the building, Priscilla thought. She concluded the sentence she had been writing when he came in and pushed her completed record to one side, wondering if he thought her stupid because she had not yet learned enough mastery of syntax to put her stuff directly on to the computer.

Richard Cullis turned and came back towards her, stopping by her desk when she thought he was on his way out of the lab. 'I don't get much chance to chat with people individually.

In my job, you're always meaning to do it, but something more pressing invariably intervenes. Do you fancy going for a drink?'

'Now?'

'Why not? Seize the moment!'

She glanced at her watch, snatching a second to think, telling herself that a thirty-year-old mature woman should not be thrown by such a simple proposition. 'I can't. I have to go round to my mother's house. She's not been well.'

It was true. But of course he wouldn't believe it. She could see he didn't as he said, 'You're sure? Not just a quick one?'

'I haven't time, I'm afraid. I should be on my way already, really. Mum will be wondering where I've got to.'

'Lucky old Mum, I say!' He gave her a broad smile which said that he understood everything. 'Well, some other time, perhaps.'

'Yes. I'd like that.'

Priscilla Godwin tried to put conviction into the bland, routine phrase. She was surprised as she gathered her things together how much she hoped that he would ask her again.

May Hill is only about a thousand feet in height, but it commands a view of seven counties and is a well-known local Gloucestershire landmark, a centre of ancient folklore and much affection.

Jason Dimmock and his wife Lucy were making the easy climb, an ideal stroll for fit people with a dog on a summer evening. The first section was steep but short, and Lucy found herself panting a little, resenting her husband's easy stride, which seemed only marginally shortened by the steepest incline. She paused for a moment to get her breath, gazing west at the clouds over the Welsh hills. 'There'll be rain before nightfall.'

'We'll be off the hill and back home by then. And approaching rain means we'll be able to see more from the top. Visibility is always best in the hour before rain falls.' Jason stretched a hand back towards her, offering help over the steepest part of the incline, but she shook her head, preferring the balance and rhythm of her own efforts.

Lucy Dimmock was slim and healthy, with black hair which swung attractively in the breeze, a long neck and large, widely set dark eyes. The effort had brought an attractive colour into her usually pale cheeks. She said, 'I'll be all right, if you let me move at my own pace. I'm just a little out of condition, that's all. It's a while since I had much exercise. I'm not able to spend as much time on the golf course as you do.'

'No. You have other ways of finding exercise.'

It was out before he knew it was coming and Jason regretted it immediately. He had not meant to offer the barb; they had been getting on well together in the last few days. He had hoped that the fresh air and freedom of the hill and the long views of different kinds of country around them would remove tensions, bring them closer together. Now he had thrown in this senseless blow when each of them had least expected it: the jibe had come from somewhere deep within him before he could prevent it. It had been unthinking and instinctive, but that made it worse, not better.

He did not know what to do about it. There was no way he could rescue himself; it wasn't the sort of remark which could be wiped away by a simple apology. He walked on quickly, out of conversational distance, needing the release of hard physical movement, banishing the images of tangled naked limbs which his words had brought with them. He called needlessly to the dog, pretending it needed his attention. The nearest sheep were half a mile away and the golden retriever was docile and obedient.

Jason stayed nearer to the dog than his wife, even when the ground levelled out and they began the long, gentle ascent to the circle of fir trees at the summit of May Hill. They passed a family of children running happily on their way down. The parents spoke to Jason and Lucy in turn, looking back a little curiously at this couple who walked thirty yards apart.

They sat together in silence on the bench by the summit, a careful two feet between them, gazing out over the wide reaches of the Severn as it ran towards the Bristol Channel. After two minutes, Jason said, 'The tide's in. Those last big bends of the river always look better when the water's high and they catch the setting sun.'

She did not respond to his deliberately neutral remark, not because she did not want to, but because words would not come. Simple, innocent, harmless words should be the easiest, yet anger and an absurd sort of pride stilled them in her throat. After a moment, she said, like one picking at a scab she knew she should not touch, 'You can't let it go, can you? I've told you it's over; I've done what I can to make things right with you. But you can't let it go. You have to take every opportunity to rub my nose in it.'

'I'm sorry.' The words had come at last. But they were as useless as he had known they would be, a mere automatic response to her prompting. He turned his face away from her, called, 'Oscar, come and lie down, please.' He pointed at a spot by their feet and the dog came and lay down there with a huge sigh, as if he was conscious that he was merely a diversion for these unnecessarily complex humans. Jason fondled the ears and the warm brown head affectionately. Then he reached sideways and took his wife's hand awkwardly. She did not reject his touch, but she did not respond to it either.

He held her hand for a little when they rose and moved round the clump of firs to look in the other direction, towards the sharp line of the Malvern Hills. 'You're right about the rain coming,' he said. 'You can see more detail on the side on the Malverns than I can ever remember seeing before.'

'Yes.' The lame, useless monosyllable was all she could manage. The wild piebald ponies which roamed May Hill were visible on this side of it. Lucy Dimmock watched them and found herself envying their freedom.

Six miles from May Hill, Detective Sergeant Bert Hook was searching for his lost youth and failing to discover it.

A mixture of persuasion and taunts from his fourteen-year-old son had drawn him out to bowl in the nets at the village cricket club. His presence there excited considerable interest, for until he was thirty-six Bert had been a stalwart of Herefordshire cricket in the Minor Counties competitions, a fearsome seam bowler who had made even the most talented batsmen hurry their strokes.

He had enjoyed the benefits of a powerful, stocky build and a springy action, which had ensured that his bowling was always a little quicker than it looked from the edge of the field. Now he found that muscle had run to fat, that he was panting hard after three deliveries from a shortened run.

Nevertheless, the young batsman in the net was regarding him with a new respect after losing his off stump to a good one.

Now came the real test, the reason why he had been brought here. Time was called on the man at the other end of the pitch and, with a challenging grin, Jack marched briskly into the net. Bert's wife Eleanor had said that he was to go easy on the lad, to remember that he was still only a boy really. Eleanor didn't understand much about sport and only a little more about father–son rivalries. Bert grinned at young Jack and breathed in deeply, pawing the ground like an ageing bull.

He pitched his first ball on a perfect length, but not too fast; he didn't want to embarrass the lad in front of his friends. Jack took a quick stride forward and drove it hard and smoothly through where mid-off would have been, then replayed an imaginary shot, as if concerned only with his timing. Bert muttered a grudging, incredulous, 'Good shot!' but his son was preoccupied with his technique. Then, when Bert pitched his next ball on leg stump, Jack drove it like an arrow through mid-on and nodded to himself, apparently satisfied on this occasion with his execution.

Bert studied him with hands on hips, in a pose which the *Bedfordshire Gazette* had likened to Fiery Fred Trueman's in an earlier era. It was rather wasted, as his son was looking down at his hands and making minor adjustments to his gloves. Bert went back to the end of his full run with single thought: bugger bloody Eleanor and her mistaken view that this was still a child.

He gripped the ball across the seam, sought hard for the old rhythm as he approached the crease, dug it in just short of a length so that it would rise quickly. There was a lot of grass on this practice wicket and the ball did just that. Jack aimed a hook at the ball, but it was too quick and it rose too steeply for him. It hit him on the chest, just over the heart; he winced away and clasped his hand briefly to the spot as his body jackknifed.

Bert was transformed in an instant from opponent to father. He went down the pitch and said anxiously, 'OK, son?'

'No prob, Dad.' Jack was instantly the fit young man, ashamed of the momentary weakness he had shown. 'Quite a good one, for an old man, that!' He rehearsed the shot he had meant to play, dispatching the imaginary ball high over square leg for six, refusing to rub again the spot where he had been hit. Bert Hook made the long journey back to the end of his full run deep in thought.

The old ploy should be good enough for this young and inexperienced whippersnapper. He would show Jack that he had still much to learn and then depart with dignity into the sporting retirement he should not have forsaken. The fast yorker, pitching in the block-hole and taking out leg or middle stump, was the delivery for a batsman caught on the back foot after the short ball. It had been one of Bert Hook's specialities in his day, accounting for better batsmen than this young sprog. Bert took a deep breath and gradually accelerated up his long run to the wicket.

He almost got it just right – for a man who hadn't bowled it for years, it was a very good effort. He was just a fraction short, a mere couple of feet. That was enough to turn his intended yorker into a half-volley. Jack stood tall, scarcely needing to move his feet, and met the ball with a gloriously straight flowing bat. The ball hit the very middle of it and flew back like a bullet at the bowler.

Bert, still off balance in his follow-through, instinctively stuck out an ill-advised foot towards the missile. It hit him just above the ankle and flew away to his left. He found himself before he knew what had happened lying on his back and clutching his leg tight against his chest. Probably he had uttered a cry of pain before the steady groaning which now filled the air, but he could not be sure of that.

He scrambled to his feet as soon as he could, waving aside assistance, setting the injured limb gingerly on the ground with a grimace of agony which he turned into a rueful grin. 'Not quite as quick as I used to be!' he told the concerned faces around him. 'I'd have had that in both hands, twenty years ago!'

That wasn't true, of course, and probably no one believed him. But no one among the crowd around the old warhorse could deny it, could they? Distance lends enchantment to the sporting view; we are all supreme athletes in the golden glow of recollection.

Eleanor Hook noted that both her returning men seemed a

little subdued. Being a wife and a mother and thus blunt to sporting perceptions, she said brightly, 'How did it go, then?'

From Jack, she elicited a grunt and the impenetrable phrases she now realized marked the beginnings of adolescence. From Bert, she had some routine musings about the effects of Anno Domini upon the human frame and the tragic inability to muster the speed and grace which had once been his. Then, with a can of beer inside him, he said with a strange combination of reluctance and pride, 'Your son has the makings of a batsman, if he keeps his feet on the ground.'

Jack Hook shut the door of the bathroom and removed his T-shirt with elaborate care. The bruise at the top of his chest was black and swelling: he winced as he touched it. It would be an impressive wound to show at school, to demonstrate just how fearsome a bowler his dad must have been. He studied it in the mirror, judging that it would be at about its best in either two or three days, when the blackness would still be vivid at its centre, but set off by green and yellow hues around it. He wouldn't show it to his mother until then, would wait through her long wails of tender concern before revealing with apparent reluctance that his dad had done it.

Jack took a last look at it before taking himself to bed. He had to lie on his right side, finding the left too painful. The old boy must have been quite a fearsome proposition, in his day.

A couple of hours later, Eleanor Hook noted the bottle of witch hazel on the shelf of the bathroom cabinet. She had listened to Bert doctoring his ankle inexpertly and trying to suppress little whines of pain behind the locked door. Men weren't good at pain.

She pretended to read her book as he hobbled into the room, holding himself erect and making an absurd pretence of moving normally. He sat for a moment reflectively on the edge of the bed, then levered himself into it with elaborate care. He said good night to Eleanor, held her briefly and tenderly for a moment, then turned away from her and stretched his legs cautiously and experimentally into the coolness of the cotton sheets.

Jack was going to be a cricketer, and a damned good one. Making his way easily over the green fields of England as a batsman, not a toiling, sweating bowler. Bert saw a graceful, commanding figure, with bat held high in the elegant follow-through of a perfect cover drive. His leg throbbed steadily, reassuringly. He was very quickly asleep.

Beside him, Eleanor Hook listened to the first gentle snore and set down her book. Boys will be boys, whatever their age and infirmity. She fell asleep contentedly on that thought.

Three

A lison Cullis was not a scientist. For a great deal of the time, she was glad of that. When she and her husband fought their battles, it was good that she had studied history and philosophy, not science.

It gave her a wider perspective, a knowledge of other civilizations and other ways of thinking. It gave her the knowledge that many of the things she and Richard wrestled over had been discussed many times before, by other and greater minds than theirs. It gave her access to the limitless world of great ideas and great thinkers, when Richard thought that mere facts were the key to everything.

These thoughts intruded upon Alison Cullis now as she knelt in the Church of the Sacred Heart and tried to pray. An onlooker would have seen a composed figure, a dark-haired woman with an oval face of quiet beauty, which might have come from a Flemish painting. The onlooker would have been greatly deceived.

Alison had come here to look for composure, but she had not found it. The more she tried to cool her emotions and direct her thoughts towards spiritual things, the more her mind raced out of her control. You could not pray with your mind in turmoil: more than anything else in life, prayer needed concentration. She gave up the unequal effort and eased herself back on to the pew behind her, staring up at the roof of the church, soaring impossibly high above her in its Victorian neo-Gothic.

Alison's eyes were drawn against her will to the statue of the blue-clad virgin with arms outstretched on the side altar. Away to her left, the image of the Sacred Heart, the cheap sensationalism of a Christ with heart exposed and burning for the sins of the world, stared down the long nave of the church. Images sanctioned by the most intellectual Church in the world to awe its peasant worshippers, she thought. A grand old Church, even with all its shortcomings, her mother had always said. She shut her eyes and bowed her head and tried again to shut out her own petty concerns and address herself to her God.

Instead of Christ, she saw Richard, his lips curled in amused contempt, mocking this tattered, outdated brocade of religion. He maintained that Alison would have discarded the whole elaborate sham years ago if she had been a scientist instead of an out-of-date romantic. When she thrust his face desperately aside, she found her mind filled with an image it had not entertained for years. A nun, her age indeterminate because of her wimple and her habit and most of all because of her serene certainty, talking to a group of sixteen-year-old girls impatient to take on the world. A quiet, confident figure, assuring them that Faith was the greatest of all the virtues, that Faith would conquer all doubts.

Alison Cullis hadn't thought about Faith for many years now. Faith was a Catholic method of cheating, seized on also by other religions when they met queries they could not answer. You could overrule all questions by simply declaring them out of court and telling the doubters that they must have Faith. Alison tried to dismiss such unhelpful thoughts; she was getting further away from prayer, not closer to it. She concentrated on the single red light which burned in front of the high altar, the symbol of the real presence of God in this place, the simplicity which should cut through all the complex layers of confusion and deceit and enable you to speak personally to your Lord.

With her eyes closed, she heard the door of the sacristy open ten yards to her right, caught the shuffling of feet, the muted sound of the door of the confessional opening and closing. In the stillness of the high church, it seemed almost beside her. She was mouthing the words of worship, trying to dismiss the sounds she heard, but prayer would not come to her stubborn mind.

She opened her eyes. The dim light from behind the closed door and the name over it told her that Father Donnelly was now within his private cubicle and waiting to hear confessions. That was irrelevant to her. She did not know Father Donnelly and she had not come here to confess. Why should you need a priest between you and God to obtain forgiveness? This was part of the outdated shambles which she was surely on her way to discarding.

And yet, without any conscious decision to stir her limbs, Alison Cullis rose and moved through the adjacent door and into the confessional.

In the warm darkness within, childhood took over. She knelt easily and automatically, pressed her head towards the grille, mouthed the words she thought she had forgotten. 'Bless me, Father, for I have sinned. It is many months since my last confession . . . '

The old priest's voice was asthmatic, experienced, sagging a little with boredom. She caught a whiff of half-digested food through the holes of the metal, wondered irrelevantly if it was bacon she could smell. Then the stronger smell of stale tobacco took over and the tired voice with the Irish brogue told her to proceed.

Alison had not prepared for this. She concentrated upon the small, half-forgotten, unimportant sins you had to conjure up for this, the losses of temper, the uncharitable fits of impatience. She wondered if you were still supposed to confess the use of birth-control devices, whether this wheezing voice would order her to desist from the instruments of Satan if she told it she was on the pill.

Even here, where the barriers were down and you were supposed to have no shame, she found that she could not articulate those greater sins, those urges which would send her soul screaming into hell. She could not force these things into words, even for herself.

Before she knew that she had finished, the aged, invisible mouth was rasping out the words of absolution. It was time now to rise and to go, but the knees which had bent so automatically to the kneeler would not straighten. Then, as if it was in league with her atrophied limbs, the priest's voice said, 'You did not come here today to confess, my child. God has forgiven you the small sins you have confessed, but your soul has other clouds upon it.'

'Father, I want a divorce.' The words she had been unwilling to voice to any of her intimates came out now to that unseen, alien, surely unsympathetic face behind the grille. 'I've tried hard to make a—'

'Divorce is against the teachings of Holy Mother Church, my child. You know that as well as I do, in your heart of hearts.'

Alison Cullis tried to summon the contempt Richard would have voiced so effortlessly. Instead, she found herself making pathetic apologies. 'I've tried, Father. I've tried really hard.'

'Marriage is a sacrament, my child. The vows you freely undertook when you came to the church to participate in that sacrament were solemn and binding promises, made in the presence of Almighty God and invoking his blessing. They cannot now be subject to the whims of men or women.'

'We are well into a new millennium now, Father. The Church must move with the times.'

The habits of childhood are embedded deep within us: Alison Cullis felt very daring in making even this mild, hopeless protest to the figure of ancient authority she could not see behind the screen.

And it was hopeless, of course. The man who had never been married voiced the platitudes of love and humility, of the willing acceptance of the will of God. She must pray for guidance and rely upon her faith to carry her through. That word again: faith. As it rang in her ears, she realized the futility of this exchange and found herself at last upon her feet again.

Alison Cullis moved away from the confessional, into the main body of the church, where she sat alone and looked up at the high altar. She was still for perhaps twenty minutes, unwilling to re-enter the real world outside, looking unseeingly at the brass and the gold and the ivory in front of her. When she left, she paused at the back of the church to take a last look at the vaulted ceiling and the distant altar. She would not come here again.

If divorce wasn't on, she would have to think of another way out of this.

The man Alison wished to be rid of was full of his own concerns. Six hours later, as the warm summer twilight moved into night, Richard Cullis sat alone in a pub between Gloucester Cathedral and the city's ancient docks on the River Severn.

The Director of Research came here quite often. The beer

was surprisingly good, and you could be anonymous here, among the cross-section of the city's residents which migrated to the dock area in the evenings. They were a strange mixture, but one entirely to Cullis's taste.

There were sales reps staying in Gloucester who came here in search of a little local colour: Richard smiled at his euphemism, picturing what it covered as he looked round the place. The man with a creased suit and hair straying over his collar was no doubt looking for a woman. If he did not pull here he might be cruising in pursuit of the local prostitutes before the night was out. The man with dyed blond hair and Botoxed face who kept looking at his watch was no doubt waiting for a different sort of assignation. Richard, sensing that the male awaited was not going to come here, was seized by a sudden sympathy for the loneliness and desolation of a world which was totally unknown to him.

The rowdy group of youths whose number had grown from four to eight at the far end of the public bar looked as if they were drinking to fuel a confrontation, perhaps with one of the rival gangs which were becoming an increasing city-centre problem. They wouldn't be interested in the likes of him; they were looking for a rumble with roughs of their own age. Nevertheless, Richard would steer clear of them, be gone long before they were tanked up and dangerous.

Richard wondered if they were customers for the drugs which changed hands in places like this, or more likely in the small, dimly lit car park behind the pub. Several men and a lone woman who wore greasy anoraks even on this summer evening struck him as possible pushers, simply because they looked like users with a habit to feed. But this was no more than speculation: apart from a little experimental pot at university, he had never indulged in illegal drugs. When you were in the business, he told anyone who raised the question, you knew too much about the consequences to mess about with cocaine or heroin.

There was a variety of other individuals in here, the flotsam thrown up by the diverse life of the city, people who probably craved anonymity as much as he did. There was a smattering of accents which would never have been heard here ten years earlier, mostly Eastern European, if his inexpert ears could be relied upon. Legal immigrants, he supposed, or they would not have cared to be seen even here, where few questions were asked, and the men and women who served you did not chat across the bar, as they might have done in a village or even a suburban pub with a local clientele.

Richard Cullis had the sudden, unwelcome thought that he too was a loner, that if he continued his present lifestyle he might eventually end up as isolated and desperate as some of the figures who became the detritus of Gloucester society in places like this and worse. The horrifying Fred West and his equally horrifying wife had conducted their gruesome crimes not half a mile from here, with no one thinking such things were possible until it was too late.

Cullis banished such ideas firmly and turned his attention to more positive thoughts. Priscilla Godwin, with her demure air, her face of an old-masters' Madonna, her suggestion of sexual tensions beneath her calm exterior, was beginning to fascinate him. He had made some progress the other night. He would come back to it, use his experience to play the game skilfully. She was there for the taking, if he went about it in the right way.

Then he looked ruefully at the bottom of his glass and wondered if that was the beer talking. He went and ordered a single whisky at the bar, taking care to put plenty of water with it: you had to be careful with your drinking, when you were driving. He smiled at himself and his attack of rectitude. He wouldn't speak to that bitch of a wife of his when he got home. He'd go straight to bed; perhaps what he had drunk would get him off to sleep without the need for a pill, tonight.

Richard Cullis was surprised to find that it was dark when he went outside. He was glad he had not left his BMW in the car park, though there had been space there when he arrived. He did not fancy going into that cavern of darkness, enclosed as it was by high walls. It was dark enough on the narrow street where he had left the car, with the street lamp above it failing to function. He had a feeling that he did not remember experiencing before: he wanted to be out of this place quickly and driving on to the wider roads which led away from the older parts of the ancient city. He pressed the automatic de-locking button on his car keys, was reassured by the familiar bright orange flashing in the darkness.

Richard never knew where the man came from. He might have followed him out of the pub, he might have been waiting for him in the shadows: he might even have been crouched between two of the closely parked cars. Cullis did not hear or see this unwelcome arrival: the first thing he was conscious of was a voice hissing urgently in his ear, 'Don't look round! Look straight ahead and go to your car, if you want to survive this.'

'I don't have—'

'And don't speak a fucking word!'

The obscenity should not have scared him, but it did. It convinced him with its vehemence that this man meant him ill, that violence was only a careless move or a wrong word away. He slid into the driving seat, heard his enemy slide into the back seat behind him, heard the rear door click shut almost simultaneously with his own. So much for the virtues of central locking on which he had just congratulated himself.

Richard felt the coldness of metal briefly on the side of his face, then the sharpness of the knife's point on the back of his neck. He licked dry lips, heard the tremor in his voice as he said, 'You're welcome to whatever money I have. My wallet's in my inside pocket. If you will allow me to take it out, that's the only move I'll make. I won't—'

'I don't want your bloody money, Cullis!'

The man knew his name. This was personal. Just when he had thought the situation could not be worse, the screw had been turned. He could hear the man's breath behind him, almost in his left ear, but he didn't say any more. It was as if he wanted his victim to appreciate the full horror of his situation before he went any further.

It seemed to Richard a long time before he could put words together to frame a question. 'What is it you want of me?'

'You'll find out. That's if I decide to let you live. Drive! And don't try anything fucking clever.'

It took him several seconds to get the key into the ignition, a thing which he normally did automatically and unthinkingly. He was terrified that his assailant would think that he was being deliberately evasive. He turned the key, heard the familiar engine purr into life, rammed his foot nervously hard on the accelerator, so that the engine roared towards a scream in the darkness. 'Sorry!' he said automatically to that hostile presence behind him.

'You bloody will be, Cullis, if you draw attention to us. Now drive!'

Richard eased the car forward, pulling carefully out of the line of vehicles at the kerb without touching the shabby grey van in front of him. 'Where to?'

'I'll tell you where to. Take the road out to the bypass. Then the A38 to Tewkesbury.'

The man knew exactly where he was taking him. That somehow made it even worse. Richard's hands and feet moved automatically, conducting the ritual of driving; his eyes glanced right and left instinctively at the roundabout, looking for other cars. His brain was wondering insistently what this unseen, dangerous, unbalanced enemy planned to do with him. As if to point the question, the sharp point of the knife jabbed at the back of his neck, reminding him it was still there, breaking the skin, causing a trickle of blood to run.

Blood must surely be hot, but it felt cold as ice.

'Left here, then first right. Be careful at the turning.'

They hadn't stayed on the A38 for long. Suddenly Richard wanted to laugh at the mundane injunction to take care, to yell out about the uselessness of taking care when he had a knife against the back of his neck. He realized that he must be very near hysteria.

In fact, the direction to be cautious was well founded. As he waited to turn out into the narrow lane, a car came along it too fast, its brakes squealing a little as the driver saw them and belatedly slowed, its headlights on full beam dazzling Richard and his anonymous assailant. Richard stilled an absurd desire to yell out a useless attempt for aid at the swiftly passing motorist. For a second or two, the night seemed even blacker after the sudden blinding white light of this other vehicle. He felt the insistent pain of the knifepoint as he eased the car out between the high hedges and on to the lane.

They went on for four, perhaps five, miles through narrow lanes. Richard lost all sense of time and location, felt that he might drive thus for hours, until a merciful oblivion overtook him. The man behind him said nothing, apart from occasional curt directions about which way to turn the car at junctions. Richard thought that they were probably deep into the countryside between Gloucester and Tewkesbury, in the flood plains of the Severn. The recent summer floods had still not drained: he caught glimpses of fields beneath feet of water, catching the light from the stars and the crescent moon above, still and sinister in the prevailing darkness.

'In two hundred yards, you'll see a parking place on your side of the road. Pull in there and stop.'

It was the longest order the man had given him. A young voice, Richard decided, more educated than he had thought at first, when the obscenities had deceived him. It was not much, less telling than even a single visual detail, but if he ever got out of this and went to the police, they'd want whatever he could give them. His brain seemed to be working again.

There was another car in the parking spot, its windscreen facing him as he pulled with infinite care off the road. He suddenly didn't want to cease moving, sensing that he had been brought here for a purpose, feeling that stopping the BMW might be his last action in this world.

'Well, Cullis,' said the voice in his ear, its excitement rising.

Richard had the image of a medieval torturer who was going to take pleasure in his work. He said hoarsely, 'Who are you? What is it you want with me?'

'Switch off the engine now. Don't try to turn your head, or I'll enjoy it and you'll regret it.'

He turned off the ignition, heard the soft notes of the big engine disappear into a silence more profound than he had ever experienced before. He could hear the regular breathing of the man behind him, but the voice said nothing for long seconds, enjoying the terror seeping through the pores of its victim. Richard stared at the windscreen of the car facing him. It was no more than twelve feet from him, but he could distinguish no detail of the faces behind it. He thought he caught a movement there, but that could have been his overwrought imagination, or a cloud crossing the face of the moon above them.

'You work at Gloucester Chemicals.'

It was a statement, not a question, so Richard said nothing. He should have been even more perturbed at what they knew about him. Instead, he felt an unnatural, overwhelming relief, rising to his temples, bringing him near to a dead faint. He might not be killed, not here. They wanted something from him.

After perhaps half a minute, the voice said, 'You're the Director of Research at Gloucester Chemicals.'

This time some response seemed to be needed: perhaps the man wanted an acknowledgement of his cleverness. Richard said, 'That is my title, yes.' For the first time, he had an inkling of where this was going. It brought his terror back to him. If he was right, these were ruthless people, quite capable of unthinking, illogical violence.

The voice said calmly, 'You're going to release those animals from your laboratory.'

'It isn't in my power to do that. I'm not a working scientist any more.'

The man went on as if he had not spoken. 'You're going to make sure that all experiments cease forthwith.'

'I don't do any experiments on rabbits or dogs – not even on rats.'

His hair was abruptly seized and his head bent backwards. The blade of the knife was at his throat now; both he and the man behind him knew that his life could cease in an instant with the severance of his carotid artery. 'You're in control there, Cullis. We came for the organ-grinder, not the monkey.' A sudden harsh laugh told him that the man with the knife at his throat was very near the edge of his control. 'We'd rather see monkeys live than scum like you.'

'Even if I wanted to, I couldn't stop the testing of drugs on animals. There are government requirements that we do exactly that. We have—'

'Don't give me that! You're in charge of the labs, Cullis. You're the bastard who can stop this. And you're going to do that. If you want to go on living your miserable life, you're going to do exactly that!'

Richard said nothing, realizing that he could not go on arguing, accepting that reason was something this man and his colleagues did not want to hear. Terror now was sagging into despair. This wasn't a random attack by a hoodlum. The man with the knife at his throat might be demented, but he was part of something larger, which had its own perverted creed to drive on its actions.

He fancied the man's breathing quickened a little in the silence. Then the voice said, 'You got the message, bastard?'

'I've got the message. The problem is that there's nothing I can do about it.'

'No, bastard. Your problem is to find a way of doing something about it. Your problem is to ensure that the torture of innocent creatures ceases. And ceases fast. *That*'s your problem. We shall be watching you. We've got someone in those labs of yours now, so we know everything that goes on there. Just as we know that as Director of Research you're the man who can stop it.'

'That's not true, you know. We're a big international company now, driven by forces which you—'

'Shut it, bastard!' His head was roughly pulled back; the blade of the knife caressed his exposed throat, as if the movement was a prelude to something more conclusive. 'We know all about you, Cullis. We know where you live, who you see, when you come and go. We'll be watching you. If you want to live, you'll produce results. Now get on your way! And don't even think of looking round!'

The man waited until Richard's shaking hand restarted the engine, then slid silently from the back seat and out of the car. Richard kept his head facing rigidly ahead as he turned on to the lane. He stole a glance into his rear-view mirror, but there was no trace of the man who had threatened his life. A quick glance sideways told him nothing about the occupants of the car which had been here when they arrived, the car which presumably contained other animal rights fanatics, who would collect his attacker and receive his report.

Richard Cullis had no real idea of his exact position. He drove until he reached the outskirts of Tewkesbury, then took the main road for Cheltenham and his home. He felt an overwhelming urge to stop and try to recover, to still the trembling he saw in the hands on the steering wheel, but was driven on by an even stronger, irrational fear that his adversaries might still be behind him.

He had never been so glad to turn into the tree-lined avenue where his house lay, never so relieved to press the button which opened the double door of his garage electronically. He pressed it again as soon as the BMW was safely within it, heard the big door lumbering shut on the springs behind him. Then he switched off the engine and plunged his head into his hands.

He remained slumped thus for a long time before he went into his house.

Four

Saturday morning. A soft Gloucestershire rain falling steadily, coming in from the Welsh mountains, which were obscured by cloud to the west. No more than a steady drizzle, but not the sort of summer morning to have you leaping out of bed and springing eagerly into the weekend tasks.

Yet some of the weekend pleasures were still available, if you were open-minded and versatile. Paul Young knew that his wife was awake, though she hadn't yet spoken. He turned on to his left side and slid his arm round her, running his fingers over the perennially exciting curve of her belly.

Debbie Young said sleepily, 'Saturday morning. Things to do, you old satyr.' But she put her hand on his affectionately, moved it up over the waist she thought too ample to the curve of her breasts above it.

'It's raining, love. I won't be able to get into the garden this morning. Maybe not all day. Great pity, that, I was so looking forward to it. Leaves me with all this energy needing some sort of outlet.'

'The children will hear.' She smiled drowsily, feeling very secure as she went through the ritual with eyes still closed and waited for him to make his answers. She moved his hand over her nipple, delighting in the slow, leisured process of marital arousal, in the confidence rather than contempt which was bred by this sort of familiarity.

Paul knew what was going to happen now; understood also his part in the preamble. 'Ellie's away on a stopover. Danny was out with the lads last night: he won't surface before midday, and you know it.'

'Ooh, you've got it all worked out, haven't you?' She mimicked the wide-eyed teenager she had been when they had first known each other, slipping on from that into gross caricature. 'You're going have your wicked way with me whatever I do, aren't you, Sir Jasper?' She stretched luxuriously in the big bed, feeling his member reassuringly urgent behind her.

Paul smiled secretly into the familiar tousled blonde hair at the back of her neck and happily banished his anxieties in a happy, innocent lust. It was going to be all right. He had put off telling her his important news last night and now he was putting it off again. But escapism was surely allowed when you were making love to your wife. Escapism had never been so delicious.

He rolled Debbie over on to her stomach and ran the back of his fingers up and down her spine, as if he needed to search for the familiar cleft at the top of her bottom. Once it was found, he turned over his hand and let his fingers play gently there, a preface to the more vigorous and intimate stroking they both knew would follow in due course. It was good to rejoice in your awareness of each other's bodies, to do what you both expected and still find it exciting and satisfying.

Fifteen minutes later they lay on their backs and looked at the ceiling with secret, satisfied smiles. It was several minutes before Paul said, 'I'll nip downstairs and make us a cup of tea.'

Debbie eased her limbs into a delicious post-coital stretch, straining her toes towards the end of the sheets, planting her forearms luxuriously against the headboard. You didn't need to worry about suspicions of underarm hair and upper-arm flab when your lover was your husband. 'It must be nearly nine o'clock. We must really get the show on the road, you idle man. There's shopping for me to do, even if you can't mow the lawn.'

'Overrated pastimes, shopping and lawn-mowing. I'll get that tea.'

He pushed the boat out and brought toast and marmalade as well on the big wooden tray. Debbie levered herself up to sit with pillows behind her, pneumatic and relaxed, knowing that she had nothing to prove and nothing to hide here. In a moment, she would discuss the children and the differing problems which adolescence was bringing to a seventeen-year-old girl and a sixteen-year-old son. She had borne the children early, but Paul would still tell her whenever she allowed him to that he found the forty-year-old mother more attractive than younger women. That idea was fanciful and its repetition was tiresome, Debbie Young told him occasionally, but she never instructed him to abandon it.

She was completing her second slice of toast when Paul said earnestly, 'I've something to tell you. You should really have known last night, but I had to wait for the children to go out and then the moment didn't seem right.'

'And this morning you had other things on your mind.'

'Yes.' He ran his hand gently over her stomach, this time in simple affection, with no sexual intent. 'I'm being made redundant.'

His news had come out in a rush, bald and direct, almost like a physical blow, when he had finally brought himself to deliver it.

It took Debbie completely by surprise. She stopped for a moment, then continued to munch her mouthful of toast slowly and methodically, as if she hoped that the physical digestion of food might help her to digest this news. Then she said slowly and evenly, 'Redundant?'

'Surplus to requirements. Fired, if you like. That's the word they'd have used in my dad's day.'

'Never mind your dad. Can this be changed? Have you a right of appeal?'

'No. They can show they're cutting back. I've got a month's notice. And minimum redundancy pay. It won't be much.'

'What happened to "last in, first out"?'

'There's no agreement about that at Gloucester Chemicals. They can choose whom they get rid of. In any case, in this particular sales team, they can argue that I was the last one in.'

'Recruited by Richard bloody Cullis.'

'I suppose so. He was in charge of sales then. It was before he became Director of Research.'

'Before he took the job I should have had.'

'Yes.' Paul realized now that this was why he had been so reluctant to give her the bad news: he had known that his own disaster would turn into another diatribe against Debbie's boss.

'That man affects our whole bloody lives.'

'I don't think he was personally involved in this. You'd certainly never be able to prove that he was. As we've both agreed before, I'm not really cut out for sales. I don't know why I took the job in the first place. I have to admit that my record isn't that good, and if they're looking for—'

'It's because you're my husband. Cullis probably took you on with a view to sacking you.'

'That's preposterous, love. You'll see that when you think about it a bit more. You're making this personal when it's just an unfortunate fact of life. I'm sure that Richard is far too busy with his own concerns to—'

'It's personal, all right. Don't make any mistake about that. He'd like me to move on as well, you know. He knows I should have had his job and he feels threatened with me working in the labs. He can't sack me, but he thinks that if he makes life unpleasant enough I might go and work somewhere else. Well, he can get stuffed! I'm going nowhere. If anyone goes, it will be Richard bloody Cullis!'

'Don't let this upset you! I'll get something else, love.' Paul did not sound convincing, because he wasn't convinced himself. Forty-one wasn't the age to be looking for a new start in a different field, especially when you carried the stigma of redundancy from your last post into any application. 'I'll be realistic, not set my sights too high. It might take a little while, but I'll get something.'

'Cullis thinks he can do anything he wants. He's got the job I should have had and now he's put the word in to make sure my man doesn't have a job at all. Someone needs to do something about Mr Cullis.'

His wife's ringing declaration in that quiet bedroom would come back many times to Paul Young in the weeks that followed.

The police are sometimes accused of being too sanguine about threats of violence. The public perception is that they shrug their shoulders, go through the motions of trying to protect the innocent by asking a few routine questions, and then go away. It seems to many people that the guardians of the law wait for something to happen and then react, rather than trying to prevent crime. When someone is threatened, they cover their backs by asking routine questions and offering routine warnings and then disappear.

The truth is that the law often makes it difficult for them to do much more than this, where malice is only suspected and only vague verbal threats have been offered. Especially where domestic threats are involved and evidence is disputed, it is difficult for the police to do much more than offer stern warnings.

But when a man is seized by an anonymous enemy and told what to do with a knife at his throat, they take the incident very seriously.

There could be no real criticism of the service's reaction to the threats offered to Richard Cullis in the darkness of a Gloucestershire lane. The threats, which had all the hallmarks of being from All God's Creatures, were a matter of heavy police concern. All God's Creatures was an organization with much more than its quota of fanatics, and fanatics always spell trouble for the police. They bring extreme forms of protest, which spill over too often into violence. Many of their demonstrations end in conflict, and police officers themselves have often been the targets of attacks.

Cullis's BMW, particularly the back seat, where his assailant had crouched, was subjected to detailed examination by forensic scientists. There were two hairs on the headrest which did not match the sample volunteered by Cullis himself. There were a couple of clothing fibres on the rear seat which might have belonged to his attacker or to some other, quite innocent passenger. There were soil particles in the footwell which were fresh and probably had come from the man who had in effect kidnapped Cullis and made him drive to the prearranged rendezvous with his fellow-thinkers. But the material was loam and clay, which might have come from almost anywhere in the county or its neighbours.

In other words, forensic efforts produced nothing of great significance. These things were carefully filed away as evidence against an eventual arrest: the hairs in particular might provide a useful match with anyone subsequently arrested and charged with a criminal offence, but there was no match with any DNA samples retained by the police.

It had been the wettest summer on record, as the still-flooded fields attested. The place where Cullis had been directed to drive his BMW to meet the car presumed to be occupied by other animal rights protesters was unpaved. Useful tyre-track evidence remained and moulds were dutifully taken and retained by the forensic team. The tyres on the car which had waited to meet the BMW in this off-road spot were much less distinctive than those of Cullis's vehicle. They were typical of the tyres used by many middle-sized mass-produced cars: a Ford Mondeo or a Vauxhall Vectra were the most likely makes, but these were cheap replacement tyres, not the originals, so they could have been fitted to any of ten or a dozen popular models.

However, tyres have distinctive wear-patterns, which can occasionally be almost as revealing as fingerprints, especially when they are expertly photographed so that enlargements can show individual blemishes. If arrests were made and a vehicle driven by suspects was examined, there was every chance of a match being found. But this would obviously depend on swift developments: tyre patterns change swiftly with wear, as a defence counsel would delight in pointing out caustically in court.

Detective Inspector Christopher Rushton recorded all these findings dutifully on his computer. Then he collected DS Bert Hook and went off to interview people at Gloucester Chemicals.

They began with the victim at the centre of all this activity, Richard Cullis. 'You say this man implied that his animal rights group, All God's Creatures, had someone actually working here in your labs.' Rushton looked sceptical; it wasn't common for this group to infiltrate undercover troops, it required too much patience and discipline compared with their normal direct and often violent methods.

Richard Cullis said vehemently, 'The man didn't just imply it. He stated directly that they had someone working here.'

'Can you recall his actual words, Mr Cullis?'

'Yes, I can. When someone drags your head back and holds a knife against your throat, you remember what he says and how he says it. But I don't suppose you've ever had to contend with that, Detective Inspector!' Cullis looked for a reaction, but found the lean and dark-haired Rushton quite impassive. 'This man told me I had to stop all animal testing here. I tried to explain to him that I hadn't the power to do that, even if I wanted to. That just annoyed him – he wasn't interested in reasoned argument. He said I'd better make sure that experiments on animals ceased and then he whispered into my ear, "We've got someone in those labs of yours now, so we know everything that goes on there".'

'You didn't catch a glimpse of this assailant, I believe, even when he finally left your car.'

'No. It was pitch dark. Well, not quite dark, because I could see the floodwaters in the fields as I drove there. I think there was actually a sliver of moon and some stars, but he was away behind the other car as soon as he released me. I was happy enough to get away from that knife.'

'I don't suppose you heard or smelt anything which could be useful? Was he a smoker, for instance?'

'I didn't smell tobacco on him. But there was one thing. I listened to his speech and I'd say he was educated Midlands. His local accent came out when he got excited, when he was threatening me.'

'Birmingham?'

'I think so, but I couldn't be sure. I've no great ear for accents – I couldn't distinguish between Brummie and Black Country.'

Rushton nodded thoughtfully. 'He might be bluffing about having one of the animal rights people under cover in your research section, knowing that he can give you a scare and us a lot of useless activity. But we can't assume that. Is there anyone in your workforce whom you now suspect?'

'No. I've given a lot of thought to this since last Thursday night, as you might expect, but I haven't come up with anyone I could point a finger at with any confidence.'

Rushton sighed. 'You'd better let us have copies of the job applications of everyone you've taken on to work in the labs in the last five years. If you or any other senior person who works in there has any further thoughts, particularly on anyone you've taken on during the last year, please contact me immediately with those thoughts.' He gave Cullis a card with his name and telephone number at Oldford CID section.

Cullis regarded the younger man resentfully: Rushton looked at least ten years younger than him, and members of the public in their forties tend to assume that their problems are not being treated seriously if a younger man is assigned to the case, whatever the rank involved. 'Why isn't Chief Superintendent Lambert handling this? Are threats to the life of local citizens not thought worthy of his attention nowadays?'

Rushton gave him an acid smile. John Lambert had built a considerable local reputation as a result of securing arrests in

some high-profile murder cases over the last fifteen years.
Rushton was quite used to hearing his name mentioned by
the public. He considered John Lambert something of a
dinosaur himself, but you couldn't argue with his results. Even
the Home Office didn't argue with them: they'd recently given
him a three-year extension to his service. Chris Rushton said
acidly, 'Chief Superintendent Lambert is presently fully occupied with a complex fraud case in the north of our area. He
is fully informed about this incident and the threats made to
you, Mr Cullis.'

'And no doubt if they carry out those threats and slit my
throat he'll take charge of the murder inquiry. A fat lot of
good that will be to me!'

Bert Hook said, 'Chief Superintendent Lambert will be over-
seeing our inquiries, Mr Cullis. How many people here have
you told about what happened to you last Thursday night?'

'None. The first thing your uniformed people said was
that I should keep this to myself.' Richard didn't add that
he didn't want his staff wondering just why he had been in
that particular pub at that particular time.

'I understand that you are in charge of research and development but do not work in the laboratories yourself. Can you
give us the name of one of your senior people who has been
here for a long time? It obviously needs to be someone in
whom you have absolute trust, but we'd like to speak to a
person who is in daily contact with the most recently employed
laboratory staff and working alongside them every day.'

'You think I don't know my own people?'

Hook wondered if the man was always this prickly and
whether the people he directed here were happy with their
boss. But perhaps it was fear which was making him touchy:
he had certainly been badly shaken by his experience four
days earlier. He said patiently, 'It's quite possible that this
undercover traitor doesn't exist, that he or she is simply a
mischievous figment of your attacker's imagination, as DI
Rushton suggested. If such a person is working here, any
suspect behaviour is more likely to be spotted by someone
doing the same sort of work alongside him or her every day
than by someone who doesn't spend much time in the labs.'

'Yes, I can see that. I'm sorry. I suppose the person you
should talk to is Mrs Young. She's been here longer than I

have. As a matter of fact, Debbie Young was interviewed with me for my job eighteen months ago.' He might as well tell them that: the woman was pretty sure to blurt it out before they'd talked to her for five minutes. He smiled. 'Debbie's an excellent research worker who knows the sort of work we do in the labs here better than anyone. One of her jobs is to help new research scientists we take on to find their feet here.'

'She sounds ideal. We'll see if Mrs Young has any thoughts on the matter. I trust she can be relied upon to keep this confidential?'

'I'm sure she will. She's a talented scientist and a most reliable member of our staff.' He nodded his approval of her: if Debbie Young started complaining to them about her husband being sacked, let them think her paranoid, not him.

Debbie Young didn't talk to anyone about the questions the CID officers asked her, but the news that plain-clothes police had been in the place asking questions inevitably flew round the factory at lunchtime.

By the end of the day, everyone knew that it was suspected that they had an infiltrator working among them. Rumour being the many-headed sensationalist hydra that it is, the talk by the end of the day was of not one but several potential saboteurs working in various parts of the factory, intent on tampering with products being sold to the public rather than studying what went on during laboratory experiments. Two days later, after the CID's discreet questioning had revealed nothing of note, the firm's press officer had to issue a denial that any such devilish moves had ever been suspected.

Even denials are useful media starting points during the 'silly season', when Parliament is in recess and many people are on holiday. The national and local press reminded the public of the more extreme crimes undertaken by animal rights fanatics, of research scientists being physically attacked and an innocent woman's remains being removed from her grave merely because of a supposed connection with laboratory experiments. The secretary of the animal rights organization, All God's Creatures, refused to comment on the attack in Gloucester, but added the smug generalization that her members were 'committed to fighting the exploitation of animals wherever it occurred and with whatever weapons present themselves'. The company's shares lost ten per cent on the stock market, then began to edge back up as the scare disappeared from newspapers and television.

Exactly two weeks after she had talked with Richard Cullis in the laboratory, Priscilla Godwin again stayed behind to write up the results of her day's work. It was nothing to do with Richard, she told herself. She merely liked to have the place to herself for quiet concentration.

When he walked through the deserted lab and came into her office it was ten to seven: no more than ten minutes later than the time of their brief conversation a fortnight earlier. She couldn't help wondering if he as well as she had been conscious of the day and the time. Cullis had that knowing, humorous look about his features as he said, 'The dedicated scientist pushing back the frontiers of knowledge, working on into the night again.'

'Or the woman who isn't efficient enough to record her dull findings when there is noise and activity going on around her.' She shouldn't do herself down like that: she could hear her mother's voice ringing in her ears.

'And still too busy with other things after work to come for a drink with her boss, no doubt.' He gave her the roguish smile which showed her that he didn't take either his own or her words very seriously, that he had other and more exciting fish to fry. He did it well, perhaps because it was such a habit with him that he was scarcely conscious of it now.

'I wouldn't mind a drink, Richard.' With her daring use of his first name, Priscilla felt a blush rising and was furious with herself. People with her dark hair and eyes and pale complexion shouldn't suffer from the condition; educated, experienced thirty-year-old women should in any case have moved beyond such things years ago. Nevertheless, she was sure that she felt her cheeks reddening. She made a belated attempt to recover her ground, to show that she and not he was controlling the situation. 'Not tonight, though. I think I told you that I go round to my mother's on Tuesdays. She'll have a meal ready for me. I could do tomorrow or Thursday, though.'

'Let's make it Thursday, shall we? And why not let me treat you to a modest meal?'

'Oh, let's not do anything like that, anything as formal as

a meal.' He might be attractive, but he had a wife tucked away somewhere. Priscilla was playing with fire and she didn't quite know why she was doing it. Yet she didn't want to put him off. 'We could always grab a sandwich or a snack in the pub, if we felt like it.'

'Very well. The lady shall call the shots. The modern lady shall as usual be in charge. What time?'

'Seven thirty?'

'Seven thirty it shall be. Give me your address and I'll pick you up at exactly that hour.' He made a mock bow to show his subservience to her wishes. And then, with another smile which promised much to come if she wished it, he was gone.

Five

Whilst Richard Cullis was making his play for Priscilla Godwin in the laboratory, Jason Dimmock was playing golf with his wife. That was an unusual event in itself, but there was an even more remarkable accompaniment to the activity. He was being patient with her shortcomings at the game.

'Just keep your head still and take the club-head through the ball,' was all he said after Lucy Dimmock's third topped iron in a row sent the ball trundling hopelessly along the ground in front of them.

Lucy glanced at him thunderously before she stalked after her ball without a word. An experienced golfer like him must surely know that it was dangerous to offer advice to an infuriated woman with a six iron in her hand: she might miss a golf ball, but a human target offered much greater scope. She sighed, then took another, deeper breath, trying to control her raging emotions. He was doing his best to be friendly, so she must bear that in mind. The fact that he was so good at this game no doubt made it more difficult for him to understand the frustrations of lesser players.

As if they wished to reward such charitable thoughts, the capricious gods of golf now smiled upon her. She took no great trouble over her next stroke because she had ceased to expect success. But the very middle of her club-face descended upon the back of that elusive white ball, seemingly from the perfect angle, because the ball soared high and straight, hung for a delicious moment against the blue of the evening summer sky, and then descended gracefully towards the short grass of the fairway.

It was going on to the green! The ball bounced once, twice, three times, and then rolled obligingly to within six feet of the distant flag. Lucy stood very still and tried to look as if she had expected this amazing thing.

'Good shot! Wonderful shot!' said her husband. Jason could not keep the incredulity out of his voice, but Lucy did not mind that. She smiled a modest, superior smile and walked after her ball with head held high and shoulders back. It was a little late in the day for skylarks, but she was sure that some sort of birdsong was ringing through her head.

It didn't last, of course. There were some bad shots on the remaining three holes, and desire still outstripped performance by a good deal. But the confidence of that stroke she had hit on the fifteenth was still with her. If she could not quite replicate the beauty and perfection of that moment, there were still several quite respectable strokes, which ensured that the ball rose into the air and stayed there for a second or two.

Jason seemed genuinely pleased with her, even though he appeared to think it was his tuition which had prompted the improvement: men were gullible creatures, and nowhere more so than on the golf course. He even managed to convince her that her efforts pleased him more than his own game, which as usual was highly competent. Yet both of them were conscious that he was on his best behaviour: the last time they had been out in the fresh air together was when they had had that row on May Hill, and neither of them wanted a repeat of that.

'You can sleep with me tonight if you get down in two putts!' he called to her when she reached the edge of the eighteenth green. She looked hastily towards the clubhouse to make sure that no one had overheard, then putted too hastily, so that the ball pulled up seven feet short of the hole. 'Give you that one!' he said with a mischievous grin. He picked up her ball and gave her the ritual small kiss with which mixed golf is expected to conclude, holding her a fraction longer than was necessary, to show his real affection.

Lucy hugged him back, wanting to reciprocate, to tell him that she only wanted him, that he should put that insane, dangerous jealousy behind him because there was no reason for it. But she found that she was too careful of her actions to behave spontaneously. She was glad when they went to the car and began the mundane distractions of stowing clubs and shoes away.

When they sat with a drink on the veranda in the warmth of the setting sun, Lucy was happy to let Jason purr on about the improvement in her golf, because she could not trust herself to lead him into any more meaningful thoughts about their relationship. She wanted to reassure him that the affair which so troubled him was no more than history now, but she was frightened of any subject which might trigger his jealousy.

She was quite glad when the golf-club steward asked him to go to the phone.

The steward spoke discreetly to Jason in the hall. This was a situation he had handled many times before. 'It's Mr Cullis's wife. Apparently he told her that he was playing golf here this evening. I thought that as a colleague you might be able to handle it.'

In other words, lie to save a friend's skin. Tell his wife that something had cropped up at work, that Cullis had had to entertain an unexpected and important visitor. Even say that you've seen him and he's still out at the far end of the course, if you can't think of anything better. Jason Dimmock smiled knowingly at the steward, said, 'All right, Chris, I'll handle this,' and watched the white-coated man depart gratefully to resume his position behind the bar.

Then he went across to the members' phone and picked up the instrument. 'Mrs Cullis? Oh, hello, Alison, it's Jason Dimmock here. I'm afraid there must have been some misunderstanding. Richard certainly isn't at the golf club and hasn't been here.'

Take that, bastard.

'You don't normally have Thursdays off.'

Bert Hook's sons were being curious when he least wanted them to be, as is the habit of children everywhere. 'In CID, you take time off when you can, build it round the work you're doing.'

Fourteen-year-old Jack was appropriately sceptical. 'I think you're still suffering from that straight drive of mine you tried to stop in the nets. I thought you were limping when you came in yesterday. You're not going to see the doctor, are you?'

'Of course I'm not. And don't you get above yourself, young Jack. I'll whistle one through and take your middle stump out, when I'm fully fit.'

'Mr Dalton says dads who can't accept their age are one of the banes of this country. They keep pulling muscles and providing work for doctors and osteopaths.'

Bert glared at his son, wondering how one small frame could absorb so much food so quickly and stay so lean. He said heavily, 'Mr Dalton is twenty-three years old and a PE teacher. You should not look to such people for pronouncements on the mysteries of life.'

'Shall I tell him that, Dad?'

Eleanor Hook removed the smile from her face as she set more toast upon the table. 'Get on with your breakfast, boys. Don't forget your dad won't be dropping you off: you've to catch the school bus today.'

They'd been told this the night before, but twelve-year-olds tend to forget such details in their struggles with the greater themes of school and life. Luke finished the Shredded Wheat which the advert told him would make him as strong as Sir Ian Botham and said, 'What are you doing today, then, Dad?'

His mother said briskly, 'Ask no questions and you'll be told no lies, young Luke. Your dad's got a day off, that's all. Have you got everything you need for school in your bag?'

'Not suspended, are you, Dad? Not being paid in kind for turning a blind eye to dubious ladies?'

The papers had yesterday made delighted reports of a copper in Birmingham who had turned a blind eye to prostitution in return for personal favours rendered to him by the offending ladies of the night. Eleanor Hook said sternly, 'Get on with your breakfast and keep an eye on the time, Luke.'

'What's payment in kind, Dad?' Luke turned wide and innocent blue eyes upon a father struggling with his muesli.

'I'm taking a day off. Can't I do that without suffering the Spanish Inquisition?'

'No one expects the Spanish Inquisition!' said Jack, throwing back at his father one of his own favourite catchphrases. He took a large bite of toast and said calmly to his younger brother, 'I expect he's taking time off to work for some exam. It will be something to do with his Open University degree.'

It was one of those occasional totally accurate, totally unexpected hits which are among the many disconcerting aspects of teenagedom. Before she could prevent herself, his mother said, 'How did you know that?' Then, aghast at her gaffe, she added uselessly, 'It won't be a proper examination, though, just a practice laid on by his tutor: the real exams are later in the year.'

'It's true, then.' Jack nodded with immense satisfaction, then demolished the rest of his toast whilst the other three at the table watched him open-mouthed.

Bert recovered first and snapped, 'Don't talk with your mouth full! How did you know that?'

'That's what they call a non sequitur, Dad. I know that because I did one at school and Mr Lewis said I must produce reasoned chains of argument. But I expect you've covered that with the Open University.' Jack took a leisured drink from his mug of tea, enjoying the incomprehension around the breakfast table. 'If you want to know how I guessed you were taking study time for your exam, I played a hunch. I expect you do that all the time at work, when you're being a detective.'

'We do nothing of the sort. Mr Lambert is a man for facts and logical deductions, not hunches.'

Jack nodded thoughtfully. 'How's this for a logical deduction, then? A parent who normally downs his food like a hungry horse is pushing his muesli around his bowl as if he can't raise an appetite. Ergo, he is nervous. Ergo, he has something to be nervous about. Not many things put Dad off his fodder, so it must be something out of the ordinary. One of the few things he does which are not ordinary is to take occasional exams, which we all know make him nervous. Ergo, it might be the prospect of an exam which is making him want to throw up this morning.' He beamed round the table, enjoying the effects of his little speech.

'What's ergo?' said Luke.

'You've got five minutes to get out for that bus!' said his father.

Ben Paddon watched the way the CID officers went about their investigation with interest. He had never seen anything like this before and he prided himself on being open to new experiences. A man and a woman in plain clothes, who someone had told him at lunch were a detective sergeant and a detective constable, were working their way methodically through the people who like him worked exclusively in the labs. They seemed to have begun with the people who had most recently arrived. Ben waited his turn with interest.

Ben was twenty-seven now. He had worked in the laboratories at Gloucester Chemicals for two years; it was his first job doing pure scientific research and he had no intention of moving on. He knew he was not the kind of figure who normally impressed at a first meeting, as you had to do in an interview. He was a gangling six feet five, with legs which were a little too long even for such a frame and limbs which did not seem well coordinated. Because of this unpromising physical equipment, people were often surprised by his sporting skills: he had a good eye and used his reach well as a batsman on village greens, and he showed an adept touch where opponents expected him to be cack-handed on tennis courts.

Sport, however, had not recently played a large part in Ben Paddon's life and he felt that it was no longer a major interest for him.

It took the police officers some time to work their way back to those people who had been here as long as him. Ben had the idea that they were not treating this too seriously now. They seemed to him to be rather going through the motions: he wondered if they had isolated a suspect among the people they had talked to earlier, or whether they had merely decided that the people who had been here for as long as two years were not real suspects.

It was the detective sergeant who did most of the questioning when Ben Paddon accompanied them into the office they were using for interviews at the end of the biggest laboratory. Dark-haired, sallow-cheeked, scrupulously polite; probably Jewish, Ben decided, even before she told him that her name was Ruth David. He felt a little spurt of satisfaction at his cleverness when she gave him her name.

They told him that there was nothing personal in this, that they were going through a routine which had to be observed whenever someone gave information to the police. He nodded sagely, replied earnestly, gave them his impression of the reasonable man personified. He did it rather well, he thought.

This was not a situation he had ever been in before and he found himself rather enjoying it.

The young detective constable, who had so far watched him closely but offered very little in the way of words, now said, 'You have access to some of the most deadly and least detectable poisons in the world in this place, don't you?'

'We do indeed, yes.' Ben smiled as he might have done at an intelligent child. He could surely afford to be a little patronizing to one who was so young and of such a low rank. 'Any one of us could probably wipe out twenty or thirty people, if we had a sudden inclination to do so.' He leaned forward a little. 'And as you say, the most deadly of the recent poisons are sometimes the most difficult to detect in the human digestive system. If one of us planned things carefully, it might be difficult to find the evidence to pin the crime on him, however desperately the long arm of the law might try to encircle him.' He giggled a little at such a ridiculous concept. 'But of course, what occupies all of us here is saving life! A great deal of our work is devoted to producing new ways of healing people.'

DS David thanked him for his patience and cooperation and he gave her the boyish smile which women had told him they found attractive. 'When you've nothing to conceal, there's no pressure, is there? I only hope that you catch the person you're looking for. If there really is such a person, that is!'

She gave him an answering smile and then said quite suddenly, 'Are you married, Mr Paddon?'

'No. Never have been. And no children.'

'Are you in a serious relationship?'

'Is this really necessary? Is this sort of question going to help you to find the person you want?'

'Very probably not. A lot of our questions prove in the end to be unnecessary, but we like to have the fullest possible picture of everyone we investigate. Sometimes the people they associate with can be quite significant, you see. In the case of terrorist investigations, that has certainly proved to be so. But of course, these things would be obvious to an intelligent man like you.'

She suddenly reminded Ben of a girl who had taunted him

at school, who had made his life in the sixth form a misery for a time. That girl had been tall and dark-haired like this woman: he hadn't thought about her for years.

He hadn't anticipated them talking to him about his private life and he certainly didn't want them prying into his associates. His smile and his certainty had gone as he said, 'I'm not in a serious relationship at present. I have to say that I still cannot see the relevance of this line of questioning.'

DS David smiled, becoming more urbane as Ben became more rattled. 'Neither can I, at the moment, Mr Paddon. But as I explained, what is pertinent to this matter and what is not may only become clear with time. Perhaps I should point out that there are no constraints upon you here: you are a member of the public helping us voluntarily with our inquiries, offering us the kind of helpful cooperation which we expect from all good citizens.'

'But if I refuse to answer your questions, you will draw your own conclusions.'

'We shall certainly be free to do that, yes. That is a fact of life, isn't it? They might be totally the wrong conclusions, of course. But that possibility would be avoided if you gave us honest answers. Which would be in confidence, of course.' Ruth David gave him her broadest, most innocent smile. He was reminded again of that girl who had taunted him cruelly all those years ago.

'Look, I think I know what you're getting at. I'm not gay. All right? I keep myself to myself because that suits me. But I have girlfriends, not boyfriends. So far, I've never wanted to get married. That's probably one of the reasons why my relationships don't tend to last.'

'Your sexual orientation is of no great interest to us, sir. But any sort of crisis in your private life might be. If you were a man going through a divorce, a man with a dying child, or a man in any one of a dozen pressure situations, you might behave irrationally. If you had secrets you wished to conceal, you might be at the mercy of someone who threatened to divulge them, and thus perhaps driven to criminal conduct. The personal backgrounds of people constantly influence the actions they take.'

Ben realized he was attracting unwelcome attention to himself by his prickliness. He took a moment to compose himself before he said, 'All right, I can see that, now that you explain it. I've never been through this sort of thing before.'

'And you may never have to go through it again, with luck. I hope it hasn't been too uncomfortable for you.' She paused, managing to imply that if he was uncomfortable he must have something to conceal. Then, when they seemed about to finish the exchange, she said abruptly, 'What do you know about this animal rights movement, Mr Paddon?'

Ben wondered if he looked as shaken as he felt. 'Nothing, nothing at all. Well, only what I've read in the press. Like everyone else.'

'And seen on the television, no doubt.'

'I've seen items about their protests on television, I suppose. I don't watch the news very often.'

'What about the local All God's Creatures people? Do you know any of them?'

He scratched desperately at his brain for inspiration. Did they know something? Had they been spying on meetings? Was this a trap for him to walk into? 'I don't know any of these people, no. Unless I've met them unwittingly – I don't suppose they go around trumpeting their ideas until they're sure of their ground.' He shrugged his shoulders, which seemed to have suddenly become very rigid. 'They've always struck me as rather a crazy lot.'

'We'd probably agree with you there. You've been here two years and you strike me as an observant man. Are there any of your colleagues you would suspect of having sympathies with these people?'

'No.' The monosyllable had come too promptly and certainly, and Ben realized it immediately. 'I've given the matter some thought already, you see. You're probably aware that your investigations over the last two days have not gone unnoticed.'

They released him then, with the injunction that he should get in touch with them if any useful thoughts on the matter occurred to him. Ben took note of the people who were interviewed after him. The last of them was that paragon of scientific virtue, Debbie Young. She had been here as long as anyone, Ben thought, so he must surely be a long way down on their list of priorities.

He found he needed that reassurance, for he was more shaken than he had ever expected to be by his half-hour with the police. Perhaps he should not have taken it so lightly, should not have dared to enjoy the experience at the start.

Still, the main thing was that they had not rumbled him. Ben Paddon was pretty sure of that.

Six

Priscilla Godwin dressed carefully for her little outing with the boss. The days were steadily getting shorter, but it was still a mild evening.

She was trying to treat it lightly, but found herself taking more care than she had done for years over the selection of her high-necked ivory blouse and simple blue cotton summer skirt; the fact that she had recently been complimented on both of these was quite incidental, of course. Her new off-white sandals with the raised heels set off the blouse nicely, and made her shapely legs look just a little longer, she thought, as she studied them from front and rear in the full-length mirror of her wardrobe.

She sat down on her sofa to wait for her escort, then found herself within two minutes on her feet and back at the mirror in her bedroom. A little too plain, perhaps. She opened the lid of her jewellery box, studied the contents for a few minutes, then extracted the Victorian amethyst brooch which her grandmother had left her, which was too valuable to be worn except on the most special of occasions.

The sun had already disappeared over the Welsh hills and darkness was dropping in early, reminding them autumn could not be delayed for much longer. Yet the night was still warm enough for Richard Cullis to have the sunroof slightly open on his BMW. 'We should make the most of this,' he said cheerfully. He followed the words with a slight, confident smile, but he did not take his eyes off the road ahead.

Priscilla couldn't be sure whether he was referring just to the weather. She said, 'It's certainly a perfect evening for early September,' and immediately felt leaden and obvious.

Richard laughed but did not say anything, turning the big car off the road and negotiating the lanes towards the quiet country pub he had used many times before. It wasn't very far from here that his unknown assailant had forced him to drive on that night he was trying to forget.

As if she divined his thoughts, the woman beside him said, 'Everyone in the labs has had the third degree from the CID this week. Did anything come out of all those interviews?'

'Not as far as I know.' The police had told him to say nothing, but this pretty woman with the demure air which so excited him could surely not be involved in any animal rights nonsense. 'Maybe there isn't anyone. Maybe the man who kidnapped me was just throwing out random threats about an infiltrator to cause us and the police a lot of trouble. They tell me that's the sort of thing these people do.'

'Looking round the labs and the people who work with me, that certainly seems the likeliest explanation.' She found herself trying to reassure this man who was usually so confident.

'Anyway, we're here to enjoy ourselves, not worry ourselves about idiots like that.' Richard spoke firmly as he swung the dark-blue BMW into the car park of the country inn. He smelt the perfume of the woman next to him as he switched off the engine, shut his eyes for a moment before he slid from his seat. More than he could remember for months, he was thrilling to the heady excitement of the chase.

Priscilla asked for a gin and tonic and he bought her a double when he went to the bar: no harm in helping things along a bit, even when you had confidence in your charms. He set the drinks down on the little table, then slid in beside her on the leather bench behind it, feeling her thigh warm against his beneath the summer skirt. 'Priscilla's rather a mouthful, for a simple chap like me. Do you have anything shorter available for your intimates?'

She smiled, wondering if she looked as nervous as she felt. 'Most people go for Scilla, but I don't like the association with Cilla Black. You can call me Pris if you like.'

'I do like, so Pris it shall be! I shan't call you that at work, needless to say. I'll be careful not to embarrass you there.' Best to let them know that it wasn't anything long term, however good they were between the sheets. The gradual realization that you were experienced, that you'd had plenty of shags in your time, was one of the things which attracted women, in Richard Cullis's view.

Like many determined womanizers, he knew very little

about women in general and only minimally more about most of the ones he had bedded.

They talked a little about work, both of them picking their way carefully through the beginnings of a conversation they hoped would become more interesting. He said 'That's a very pretty brooch,' and leaned forward to look at it more closely on her breast.

She said, 'I've always liked it. It's got sentimental value, too, because my grandmother left it to me.'

Then the waiter came out from the dining room and announced, 'Your table is ready when you are, sir. Would you care to look at the wine list?'

Priscilla took a nervous pull at her drink and stared hard at the table until the man had gone. She said evenly, still without looking up into the features which she knew would be carrying that knowing, man-of-the-world smile, 'I distinctly recall saying that we weren't having a formal meal tonight.'

'Ah, but you did say that we'd indulge ourselves with a bit of pub food. I merely took the liberty of making that a little more formal and bringing you to a place where I know the food is good. Take it as a compliment to a charming companion. Don't be offended, Pris.'

She did look at him now, and he had the look not of a roué but of a little boy who might have unwittingly offended and was anxious about it. She knew it was an act, but it made her want to laugh, so that she knew she could not carry on the argument. She said as firmly as she could, 'What started out as a quick drink seems to have grown like Topsy. I think I'd like to go Dutch on this.'

'We'll see.' He moved his hand across the table and put it on top of hers. 'Let's just enjoy the evening, shall we, with no strings attached. It's only a fortnight since I was forced to drive through lanes not far from here with a knife pricking into my neck. I'd certainly like to forget about that. And you should forget all about the cares of work and let your hair down, Pris.'

She made no further protest and he led her through into the dining room. The low hubbub of conversation and sporadic outbreaks of laughter from other tables soon made it seem to her that she had probably made too big a deal of his presumption in booking a table for them. She determined to show him that she wasn't an impressionable adolescent, nor even some ingénue who was unversed in the ways of the world. When Richard offered her the wine list, she chose a claret which would nicely complement her lamb fricassée and his beef, enjoying the little flutter of surprise across his tanned features when he found that he was with a woman who had the confidence to choose the wine.

She became less careful during the meal, telling him more about herself and her opinions on life than she had envisaged doing at the beginning of the evening. He kept her glass filled and she was aware that this had something to do with her relaxation, but she felt well in control of herself. She wasn't driving, so there was no need to be cautious with the claret, as he reminded her twice. A good reason, too, to be cautious with his own imbibing, he reminded her, as he poured the last of the wine into her glass.

At the very back of her mind, a tiny but insistent voice kept telling her that this man was married, that she wasn't, and that she had no need of complications in her life. Priscilla gave a small, secret smile at herself for having such old-fashioned inhibitions. This was the twenty-first century and she was a modern woman. She had a burgeoning career, a job she liked, and the education and experience to control her own destiny. She might be with a man of the world who had a certain reputation, but she would show him that she was herself a woman of the world. She might even enjoy pointing that out, if the necessity to show that she was in control should ever arise. An attractive woman of thirty didn't reach that age without being able to brush off men. And she was not at all sure that she wanted to brush off this particular one.

She had fruit salad for the sweet course, then allowed him to talk her into a brandy with her coffee. They were chatting happily now and she said suddenly, before she knew that she had formed the thought, 'I'm glad you ordered this meal. It was a good idea after all. It's been a most pleasant evening.'

'And it's not over yet!' said Richard Cullis, with a mellow, slightly predatory smile.

At the moment when Priscilla Godwin was looking round at the other diners and sipping her brandy, Ben Paddon was meeting a quite different set of people.

He was in a crowded room at the back of a decrepit Victorian house in Cheltenham. It was in an area which had once been highly desirable, but which had gone down rapidly in the last twenty years. Most of the houses had now lapsed into flats which were little more than bedsits, with a constantly changing and often dubious occupancy. The front gardens, which had been filled with geraniums and lobelia in the heyday of these houses, had long since been covered with concrete, which disappeared at nights beneath a variety of ageing cars and vans. The high windows which had once had velvet drapes were covered now with a variety of ill-matched and some-times ill-fitting cheap curtains.

The curtains in this room were old and fading, but they covered every square inch of the glass against any prying eyes. The single electric light bulb had a cracked and dusty shade, so that the illumination from its already inadequate hundred watts was further diminished. The room was crowded; there was no heating, and when they had met here during the winter, the place had been cold and clammy. Tonight, on a September evening, it was too hot, mainly because of the number of bodies crammed within it. Someone had tried to open the sash window, but the swollen frame had not moved more than an inch.

All God's Creatures were working to an agenda, of sorts. But because no one had seen it in writing and they were most of them inexperienced in the protocol of meetings, disorder was constantly threatening. The assembly roared its approval of what pleased it and dissolved into hisses and boos when something displeased it, so that the man at the centre of things was constantly calling for silence to enable the meeting to proceed.

He had tried to conduct the meeting from a sitting position, in the interests of democracy. That hadn't worked because there weren't enough seats for all of them and because of the rowdy nature of the assembly. It was good to have such a good turnout, but the numbers made it more difficult to control things. The leader had been on his feet for some time now and was abandoning his gestures towards equality in the attempt to drive things forward. Belatedly, he realized that they had spent too long and allowed too many contributions on the evening's first items, so that he now needed to press ahead quickly if chaos was to be avoided.

He looked at the scribbled notes in his hand and called out. 'Direct action: Scott Kennedy to report on the initiative taken two weeks ago, please.'

Kennedy stood up, stroking the stubble on his chin, waiting until an expectant silence fell upon the people packed so closely around him. He was a little nervous, but nevertheless determined to enjoy his moment of prominence. His dark eyes glittered with a heady sense of mission.

'Following the approval expressed at our last gathering for such action, I conducted an abduction of the Research Director of Gloucester Chemicals from the dock area in Gloucester on that Thursday evening.' He wasn't sure he had got exactly the right word, but 'abduction' sounded better to him than a simple 'kidnapped'. He had them quiet now, wanting the first-hand account from their own man of the exploit most of them had read about in the papers or heard described on radio and television. Scott said portentously, 'I am confident he will not be able to identify me, even though I forced him to drive his own car for twenty-five minutes to the place where I had arranged to meet Tony and Wayne.'

There was a little stir of movement as people looked sideways at their neighbours, trying to identify the supporting cast in this pleasing little drama. Scott Kennedy raised his hands unnecessarily in front of him, enjoying the feeling of control as he felt the hush descend upon his listeners. 'I can report to the meeting that the Research Director in question, a man by the name of Richard Cullis, was shit-scared on that night.'

There was laughter and delight at this sudden descent from formal language into mild obscenity, even the beginnings of a ragged cheer. As someone tried to begin a round of applause, Scott held his right hand up imperiously and said modestly, 'I had a knife pressed against the back of his neck and eventually against his throat. I flatter myself that I sounded as if I meant business at the time, so the bastard had every reason to be scared! I warned him that we wanted all animal experiments and all testing of drugs on animals at his place of work to cease immediately.'

There were rumblings of approval of this. Then a white-faced, intense girl at the back of the room said, 'And what has happened since then? Have they stopped torturing animals?'

Scott looked deflated. The man in charge of the meeting took the opportunity to regain his control. 'We await developments. The gauntlet has been thrown down. Scott Kennedy's mission was to issue this injunction, not to cause any physical harm to Richard Cullis at this stage.'

'So what happens next?'

The question the leader had not wanted. 'Nothing' was the answer, but he could hardly say that. 'We've made our gesture.' Hearing rumblings of support for the woman's question, he went on hastily, 'That is for this meeting to decide. Scott Kennedy has carried out the brief we gave him and is surely to be congratulated upon his success.'

Someone shouted, 'Hear! Hear!' and this time there was a sporadic round of applause. Another voice from the back of the room called, 'One of the reports on the radio said that we had claimed to have someone working within those laboratories. That wasn't repeated in subsequent bulletins.'

The leader glanced down at Ben Paddon, who gave him a little nod and then stood up, feeling his pulses racing as he looked down from his six feet five inches. 'I am the person in position there. The police suppressed the information after that first bulletin, probably because they wanted to come up with a big announcement that they'd discovered our undercover man. Well, they haven't! They spent two and a half days questioning people, including me, but I'm quite confident that the pigs haven't a clue. They seem to be spreading the word that Scott's warning to them was an empty threat. I know it wasn't and now you know it wasn't!'

He sat down again to cheers, feeling his cheeks burning with excitement and pleasure, whilst the leader warned the meeting about the absolute importance of keeping his identity secret. Then the white-faced, thin-lipped woman at the back spoke up again. 'So where do we go from here? What action are we going to take at Gloucester Chemicals?'

There was some support for her question, but the leader sensed that the meeting wanted to enjoy the heady excitement of their successes, without pressing too hard at the moment for more tangible achievements. He said firmly, 'I think you should leave that in the hands of your committee. We shall review the situation and decide how best we may build on the undoubted advantages we have gained. You may be confident that we shall take action, but that action needs to be derived from a day-to-day knowledge of the situation and the opportunities which may offer themselves. I don't think it can be determined by a general vote at this juncture, which would tie our hands.'

There was a little hubbub of discussion, which generally seemed to support this strategy. He said, 'Speaking of direct action, we have to decide tonight on our tactics towards the hunt at the weekend.' There was immediate animation at the prospect of more immediate excitements, as he had known that there would be. He emphasized that though the hunt officials were now claiming that this was just a drag hunt following a scent laid by human runners, there was reason to suspect that foxes were still being pursued and killed illegally. A chorus of disapproval followed and many hands were raised eagerly in support of an organized demonstration against the riders.

Scott Kennedy, still thrilled with his earlier moment of prominence and disappointed that it had passed so quickly, said, 'We've had a lot of publicity out of our efforts against Gloucester Chemicals. The television cameras will be at the hunt and the media will be out in force if we let it be known that we propose to be around. We should take full advantage of this situation to get our message across. We need some direct action against these buggers poncing about on horses and I'm prepared to lead it.'

If one or two people suspected that there was a class element in this, perhaps even a suggestion of jealousy, they had more sense than to voice the thought amidst the exhilaration which was dominating the warm and airless room. Most people offered their support for the hunt protest and they agreed to meet together to coordinate their efforts half an hour before the stirrup cups which still signalled the beginning of the hunt. There was much excitement as the meeting broke up. The leader had to remind them these proceedings were secret, that they should depart quietly through the streets outside and keep a low profile around the centre of Cheltenham.

The room seemed more squalid after the main body of the protesters had left. The leader waited for the excitement to seep away with them, for reality to reassert itself amongst his small committee. Then he said to Ben Paddon, 'I don't think you should have revealed your identity to the meeting at large tonight. The fewer people who know about it, the easier it is for you to operate to our advantage. Sooner or later your cover will be blown, now that everyone knows about it. We may need to bring forward our plans for direct action.'

It wasn't until they went out into the open air that Priscilla Godwin realized that she was much drunker than she had thought. She staggered a little, looked up at the almost full moon emerging from the clouds, and then wished that she hadn't done that. The gable end of the pub span for a moment among the stars above her. She snatched at her escort's wrist and found Richard Cullis's arm instead round her waist, holding her hard against him; he giggled sympathetically with her as she stumbled, taking the chance to slide his hand up and over her breast.

'Oops!' she said. 'Thank God I don't have to drive! Are you sure you'll be all right?'

'Quite sure. You can rely on me, Pris.'

Her head steadied after a moment and she recovered her balance. She extricated herself from his grasp in slow motion and made her way uncertainly to the passenger side of his car, moving round the BMW with her hands placed on the roof to support her. 'Home, James, and don't spare the horses!' she commanded, then fell rather than slid on to her seat, laughing as hard as if she had offered an original and highly witty remark.

Promising, thought Richard. Pleasantly pissed, without being too drunk to enjoy herself in bed. And even more attractive, now that she had relaxed: he had always known that something hot and earthy lurked beneath that prim exterior. He wanted her here and now, in the car, but he controlled himself, knowing it would be better and more prolonged if he waited. He started the engine, left it running softly as an assurance that there was nothing to fear, whilst he pulled her gently towards him and kissed her upon the lips, quite chastely, without letting his hands go where they wanted to go. As he ran his lips softly across her brow, he could smell her perfume and the warm scent of her body and her hair, heavy with the promise of the more abandoned coupling to come.

They did not say much on the journey to her flat. Richard had drunk much less than her, but he was near enough to the limit to ensure that he took great care with his driving. Priscilla Godwin fingered her grandmother's amethyst and smiled happily to herself. She was enveloped by the drowsy euphoria which comes with the gentle movement of a comfortable car at the end of an evening of good food and wine in pleasant company.

She jerked back into full consciousness when he stopped the car at the entrance to the small block of modern flats. 'Safely home!' she said a little stupidly. 'Are you going to come in for a coffee, Richard?'

'Just try to stop me!' he said with a laugh. He was out of the car and round at her side to assist her whilst she was still fumbling for the door handle. Her skirt had folded beneath her and he had a generous glimpse of the top of her thigh as he helped her out. He felt a hot, almost overwhelming, craving, telling him to run his hands up beneath that blue cotton skirt, to have her here and now, with the stars above and the warm night air around them.

But this was not the place, in the streets of suburbia with some late dog-walker likely to surprise them. That was for randy schoolboys who could not control themselves. Men of the world waited for the right moment, even when the urges returned to them as strongly as they had ever burned in youth.

Priscilla did not need his assistance to move through the entrance and up to the door of her flat. She found the lock with her key at the very first attempt, though it needed the elaborate, slightly comic concentration of a child. He watched her with a smile and his hands thrust deep into his pockets: all her movements now were kindling to his lust.

Priscilla switched on the lights and directed him when he requested it to her neat little bathroom. Then she moved with deliberation into the kitchen, absorbed and single-minded in her task, anxious to show him that she was not really drunk but just pleasantly tiddly. 'Make yourself at home!' she called over her shoulder. 'It will only be instant, but it won't take a moment.'

She heard the lavatory flush as she set out china beakers and reached up for the jar of coffee. She did not hear him arrive in the kitchen and leapt with the shock when she felt his breath on her neck. 'Forget the coffee! We can do better than that for ourselves, can't we?' He was behind her, his hands round her waist, holding her body tight against him, feeling the soft curve of her buttocks intoxicatingly close to him through the thin material.

'Richard, I don't think—'

But she could not get her rejection out. He was turning her torso towards his, crushing his lips against her mouth, thrusting his tongue urgently after hers. Then he lifted her, sliding his hands under her bottom, forcing his knees between her legs, carrying her out from the kitchen into the sitting room, hesitating there as he tried to decide which door led to her bedroom and the delights which awaited them there. 'I've wanted this for months!'

She felt the hot words in her ear, breathy, animal, terrifying. 'Richard, you've got the wrong idea. It's probably my fault, but—'

He swallowed the rest of her protest, his lips hard, brutal, bruising. 'It's all right, Pris, I've got a condom on. You know you want it too. You know you're a hot bitch beneath that cool exterior. And believe me, you're going to enjoy it, girl!' If she was going to play hard to get, that was all right by him: her modesty was fanning the flames of his lust even higher.

She knew now that she was in trouble. The drink had fuddled her, delayed her realization of what was going on and her reactions to it. She must not panic, or what was going to be embarrassing for both of them might become something much worse. 'Richard, this is silly! Stop this at once, please, before it goes any further and leaves us both regretting it.' She was suddenly very sober, very prim, more prim than she could remember being since she was a teenager. But she had never had to contend with anything like this before.

His voice was loud and harsh, as she had never heard it before. 'You want this as much as I do, you horny little hussy! Don't come the Little Miss Muppet stuff, you're all the same with your pants off! I bet prudish Priscilla shouts as loud as anyone when she comes!'

He bore her backwards towards the deep-pile rug in front of the fireplace, and she lost her balance even as she realized what he planned. She was on her back and he was on top of her, shouting words she could not hear, did not want to hear, in her ears. She tried to scream, to twist her body and throw him sideways and off her. But he was stronger than her and exulting in that strength. Every move she made seemed only to excite him more.

Her skirt was round her neck, in her mouth, as she tried to shout at him. He was sliding her pants down. She needed hands everywhere, and still she would not have enough of them to fight him, to stop him from doing this unthinkable thing which had so abruptly become reality. He was on her, in her, grunting, shouting at her to enjoy it, yelling words at himself as his thrusting reached a climax. She wanted to faint, to lose all consciousness of what was happening to her, yet she could not. She saw herself and her sufferings from the side of the room, as if it were some other person who was enduring this.

He stayed on top of her for what seemed a long time when it was over. Priscilla was too exhausted to try to move. She had an obscure fear that he might turn violent, that he might swing the back of his hand hard against her damp face, if she tried to move.

Eventually he levered himself up on to his elbows, looked down at her face beneath him, muttered some coarse phrase she did not want to catch. She breathed in, felt his hips heavy and loathsome on hers, exhausted with their efforts, pinning her still to the rug. She had her eyelids shut still as she whispered her first hoarse words in twenty minutes. 'Get out!'

He levered himself off her, heavy and uncoordinated, all energy spent now. She kept her eyes closed, made no move after a single sweep of her right arm to move her skirt back to her knees, lest he should review where he had been and what he had done to her. He continued to talk, but she would not listen to what he was saying; she shut his words out without needing to cover her ears. She divined from the rhythm of his phrases that he was trying to soothe her, to rationalize what he had done, probably to talk about work and what they must do there.

She took in all the breath she could and this time she shouted the only two words she had for him. 'GET OUT!'

After she had heard the door shut, she lay still for a long time, feeling the silence creep back into the flat and over her, like a weightless blanket. It was an effort to move, to rise eventually to her knees and rest her shoulders against the sofa which no longer felt familiar.

It was minutes more before she lifted her head and looked round the flat. She saw the open door to the kitchen and the beakers which had never been used. She made herself look behind her and see the crumpled rug where he had taken her. She felt a stranger, as if this was someone else's flat, with furnishings which had set themselves up to help the creature which had done this to her and now was gone.

Her blouse was torn beyond repair. Her grandmother's amethyst brooch lay beside it on the carpet. A little while later, she began to weep. She found that even the tears were painful, rather than the release they should have been.

Seven

Bert Hook was making nervous jokes. Nervousness came oddly from this stolid frame, this village policeman whose presence was an assurance of normality to his fellows in a rapidly changing world. But Bert Hook was this morning not a detective sergeant but a student, suffering the anxieties which beset such beings when the crisis of an examination looms, suffering them much more acutely in fact because he was a mature student.

The Open University is a splendid institution, offering people opportunities for study and personal development in later life which most of them had never anticipated, bringing the delights of learning to adults. Mature people are usually much more appreciative of the joys of higher education than the adolescents who have poured straight from school into universities, perhaps after the advantage of the now-fashionable 'gap year'.

But every pleasure has its price. The time of reckoning for most students is examinations, and the anxiety brought by these trials is much greater for those who have been away from their tortures for twenty years and more.

This morning Bert was off to a practice examination, a trial run, as the tutor called it. She had arranged it in answer to her students' repeatedly expressed fears over the real examinations in November. As she continually reminded her group, their work and grades had been good throughout the year: because they already had excellent grades for course-work, they had nothing to fear from the more formal testing to come.

The commonly expressed view among her students was, 'We're not too bad when we've plenty of time, but we can't work under pressure. That's where we'll never measure up to the young 'uns, when we have to compile answers under the pressure of time in examinations.' They pronounced the five syllables of the dreaded word as if it were some dragon lurking within the cave of academia, waiting to emerge at the eleventh hour as success beckoned and incinerate them with long spouts of fire from its destructive nostrils.

The tutor recognized an argument she was not going to win. 'I can't alter the OU system. But I can give you practice in this dreaded ordeal, if you want it. The eight of you can have a trial run in my front room. I'll set the questions and I'll mark your efforts. There'll be strict adherence to time and no concessions. I'll put my chiming clock on the mantelpiece and drive you to distraction!'

They had welcomed her offer delightedly, thanked her for her understanding, agreed secretly among themselves that she was a brick and that they were going to take her to the Royal Shakespeare Theatre at Stratford-on-Avon as a small reward for her efforts to accommodate them.

Now, as Bert picked at his breakfast and Eleanor made ready to drive him to the tutor's house, this practice exam did not seem such an excellent idea. For the second time this week, their sons were full of invention on Bert's behalf. 'You can produce an excuse and they'll take it into account,' fourteen-year-old Jack volunteered, full of the knowledge derived from GCSE rumours at school. 'You could say Oscar died this morning and you were stricken by grief.'

The golden retriever looked up enquiringly from his basket at the mention of his name. 'But he's only three. It wouldn't be convincing,' said Luke.

'Dad could say he'd been run over. But he'd have to weep buckets and be very convincing. And Mum would have to write a note to say what had happened and how Dad was very sensitive and very attached to Oscar and how it had devastated him and would ruin his exam performance.'

'I'll be writing no notes,' said Eleanor Hook decisively.

'It's only a practice for the real thing,' said Bert. 'I'm not at all worried about it. And you two will be late for school if you're not out of here in five minutes.'

Jack examined his father critically with his head on one side. 'You look pale, Dad. Not nervous, are you?'

'No, I'm not. And if you don't—'

'Because you won't do yourself justice if you're nervous,

you see. Mrs Fogarty told us that during geography. It's elementary psychology, she said.'

'Get out!'

'All right, Dad, don't throw your toys out of the pram. It's only natural you should be a bit on edge about an exam. At your age, I mean. Only natural.' Jack avoided his father's huge lunge at him across the table and was gone with a bright farewell smile.

Eleanor Hook tried not to smile at the recollection of her boys' banter as she drove her husband to his experimental exam. The lads were growing up fast, but it probably wasn't the time to mention that to Bert.

Her husband had just noted the first yellow leaves on the chestnut trees and hoped that wasn't an omen of his own decline into autumn. 'It's only September,' he said, suddenly and resentfully.

Eleanor wondered how to react to this abrupt temporal observation. She glanced sideways at her normally relaxed passenger. 'You do look a little pale, as a matter of fact.'

He looked at her resentfully and sank deeper into his seat. 'Not you as well. I thought higher education was supposed to broaden your horizons. I suppose it might, if you had the support of your family.' They journeyed another mile through the forest and then he said reluctantly, 'You've all been quite good, really, haven't you? You in particular have been very supportive.'

She grinned. 'We're all very proud of you, actually, Bert Hook. The boys think it's tremendous that you're going for a degree at the ancient age of forty-three. But you can't expect boys to say that, can you?'

He smiled his first smile of the day, which disappeared abruptly as his tutor's house came in sight. 'We're there.' He gave her a brief, unexpected kiss and then disappeared without looking back at the car. He was walking very stiffly, she thought, as he did when he went to give evidence in court. He always lost his natural roll when he was nervous.

If Bert Hook had known what Priscilla Godwin was feeling, it would have put his anxieties about a dummy-run examination into a proper context.

She knew what she must do, but it nevertheless cost her a

great effort of will. She sat by the phone for several minutes before she rang the police station at Oldford at eight o'clock on Friday morning. It was a man who answered. Of course it was a man: she had known it would be a man. Priscilla said as calmly as she could, 'I want to report a rape.'

The young uniformed officer had been well trained. He spoke as calmly as if it had been the enquiry about a missing dog which he had just dealt with. 'You want the Sapphire Unit. Hold the line for a moment, please.'

For an absurd moment, Priscilla thought there must be some connection with her grandmother's antique brooch, which lay still where it had fallen last night after it had been torn from her blouse. Then she heard a woman's voice, calm, deep, re-assuring as treacle. Like a large middle-aged bosom in which you could bury your face.

Priscilla said again, 'I want to report a rape.'

'Are you the victim?'

'Yes.'

'Name. Please.'

She gave it them. It sounded like someone else entirely.

'When did this assault take place?'

'Last night.' She thought she detected a sigh, but she might have imagined it. 'I know I should have reported this sooner, but my mind was in splinters. I suppose I couldn't believe what had—'

'That's all right. We'll take it from here. Are you speaking from the place where this incident took place?'

It had been reduced to first an assault and then an incident. She wanted to yell into the phone that this was rape, that she had the cuts and bruises to prove it; that the mental cuts and bruises were bleeding still within her skull. Instead, she said dully, 'Yes, I am.'

'Is this a domestic incident?'

For a moment, she could not think why the calm voice was asking that. Then she said with a start, 'No. I'm not married. I live here alone.'

'And you are alone there at the moment?'

'Yes.'

'And what is your address?'

She gave it, spelt out the address of the road, her brow furrowing with impatience at the delays of bureaucracy. 'I'll come in to the station straight away. I can be with you in twenty minutes.'

'No, don't do that. Stay where you are, please. There may be evidence we can collect to support a prosecution.'

She didn't want a prosecution. She wanted someone to go round and beat Richard Cullis insensible, or, better still, to do what he had done to her, while he screamed as she had done. But she knew that was impossible even as she thought it. 'All right. How long will you be?'

'We'll be there just as quickly as you said you could come to us: in twenty minutes.'

She began to give directions, but the woman said they knew the way. The calm voice said, 'We'll be on our way within a minute, Priscilla. Please don't touch anything at all. People tend to tidy up when they know we're coming, but that's the worst thing you could do. Have you washed yourself?'

'Yes, I had a shower. Some time during the night, I couldn't say exactly when. I shouldn't have done that, should I?'

'It would have been better if you hadn't, but people often do. It's a natural reaction. Don't worry about it, what's done is done. But please sit still and don't touch anything at all until we're with you. Don't even go to the toilet: we shall need a urine sample from you.'

'All right.' Priscilla Godwin put down the phone and stared at it for a moment. Then she sat stiff and unmoving on the upright chair beside it, obedient as a schoolgirl.

Ben Paddon was weighing out granules of a new diabetes drug when Richard Cullis came into the lab.

They exchanged good mornings and then conducted a staccato conversation about the experiment Ben was conducting. He was cautious after the excitements of the All God's Creatures group meeting on the previous night, knowing that he should not really have announced himself there as the mole at Gloucester Chemicals. He would need to be more careful than ever now not to give anything away to the people around him at work.

The normally urbane and articulate Cullis was not able to carry the dialogue forward as easily as he would normally have done, preoccupied as he was with what had happened between him and Priscilla Godwin on the previous night. After another long pause, when he knew he should have been moving away, he said, 'You haven't seen Miss Godwin this morning, have you?'

'No. She's usually around by now, though. Have you tried the other lab?'

'I was in there earlier, but I didn't see her. Perhaps she's taken a day's leave. I wanted a quick word with her about the work she's doing on the Alzheimer's drug, but it's nothing that can't wait.'

Ben, aware that the boss was about to move off, said, 'Have those detectives finished their work here now?'

'I think so, yes.'

'Can't think they're going to find any saboteurs in here. Bit of a wild-goose chase, I thought.'

'Apparently the CID thought that, too. But you can't be too careful, I suppose.'

'No. Well, I'm glad it's been cleared up. We can get on with our work without interruptions now. Will you be taking any notice of these threats? Will there be any adjustments to the testing of drugs on animals?'

'Emphatically not. Legislation requires that we measure the effect of drugs thoroughly on animals before there is any question of them being approved for human use. And we certainly don't want to be held to ransom by idiots like the All God's Creatures crew, do we?'

'Indeed we don't!' Ben put all the enthusiasm he could muster into his agreement. Privately he was telling himself that this pompous twit hadn't been so brave with Scott Kennedy's knife at his throat.

Cullis wanted to tell him to ask Priscilla Godwin to come into his office, if and when she arrived. But he decided it was best not to look too anxious in front of this junior researcher. He turned away, then thought of a less suspicious reason for his presence here. 'I hear you're a bit of a sportsman, Ben.' He looked dubiously at the tall man's lanky and uncoordinated frame.

'I play a bit of cricket and tennis. Had quite a good innings for our midweek limited-overs team last month.'

'Yes, I remember now.' Richard didn't, of course, and he doubted whether Paddon believed that he did, but that scarcely mattered. 'I don't suppose you play golf, though, do you?'

'Not regularly. But I played quite a bit when I was younger. My dad was rather a fanatic.' Ben didn't admit to that when he was with his animal rights friends: golf wasn't a game that many of them approved of.

'You might be interested in the company golf day in October, then. There'll probably be a note round today to give everyone the details. It was originally just seven or eight of us going off for a day's golf, but it's grown like Topsy. The board has approved it as an official outing and I've managed to persuade them to subsidize it handsomely. It will cost you hardly anything and be a day away from the trials of research.'

'You can count me in then, Richard.' Ben felt rather daring: it was the first time he could remember addressing his boss by his first name, though others did it all the time. 'I'll get out my clubs and go to the driving range for a practice.' He joined in every works activity he could: the more normal you looked, the more you became one of the crowd, the less anyone was likely to suspect what you were really planning.

'You do that. I expect we shall have a fun competition between the different sectors of the firm on the day, so you'll have to come up trumps for research and development!'

'I shall hone my limited skills, Richard.'

Ben watched the Director of Research as he went off to the other end of the lab to speak to someone else. He wasn't surprised by Cullis's view that they should take no notice of the threats about animal experiments. And Ben knew enough about life to realize that it had been a major mistake to reveal his identity to the All God's Creatures group meeting. Now that they all knew the identity of their undercover man at Gloucester Chemicals, it was only a matter of time before his cover would be blown. The cross-section of people involved all believed passionately in what they were doing, but discipline wasn't their strong point.

His tenure here was thus now limited. It might be time for drastic action, for some big gesture which would bring things to a head.

The forty-year-old policewoman and the medic she brought with her were in Priscilla Godwin's flat within twenty minutes, as she had promised. They saw a woman moving with the stunned calmness which was familiar to them in rape victims.

Experience made them aware that hysteria might not be far beneath this veneer of self-control.

They asked her to provide the urine sample they had warned her they would need and Priscilla moved wordlessly into her bathroom, like one in a trance. She handed them the little plastic container without the nervous joke with which most people clothed their embarrassment. The black woman whose phone voice she had found so deep and comforting now introduced herself as Sergeant Fox. She was older than Priscilla, and considerably larger. Priscilla asked, 'Why do you take a sample?'

'Standard practice, love. It can show up a drug, providing traces of it remain. Do you think you were drugged last night?'

'No.' It had never occurred to her. 'Unless you count alcohol as a drug.'

'You'd be surprised how often drugs are used. You've perhaps heard of Rohypnol; there's also one called GHB.'

She gave them the beginnings of a smile. 'I know about drugs. I'm a research chemist at Gloucester Chemicals.'

'Then you'll probably know that any evidence of GHB is gone within twelve hours, but traces of Rohypnol can be found up to three days after its administration.'

'I don't think you'll find evidence of drugs in my urine.'

'That's a pity. The administration of a drug without the recipient's consent is the strongest evidence we can have in a court case.'

Priscilla was silent. Her thinking, which had been dominated by a wild desire for revenge upon the man who had violated her, had not got as far as a court case. She tried to speak rationally, to get inside the mind of the man she now hated. 'I'm sure he thought he wouldn't need drugs. He works with me at Gloucester Chemicals and he would know all about them, but I think he thought he'd charm the pants off me without the need of date-rape drugs.'

'We'd better have your account of exactly what happened last night. Take your time and don't leave anything out. If Dr Haslam or I stop you to ask a question, it will be because we need to clarify our own understanding of what took place, so bear with us.'

Priscilla began by trying to describe her relationship with Richard Cullis before last night, of the friendship and the working relationship which had led her to consent to going out to a pub for the first time with him. The thin woman whom she now knew was Dr Haslam had been watching her very closely. Now she said, 'You knew this man quite well, then.'

'Yes. I'm sorry if the facts aren't convenient. I can't help it that it wasn't a stranger who snatched me off the street, can I?'

The policewoman's dark face nodded understandingly at this little surge of pique. 'You can't alter the facts, dear. Ninety per cent of women who are raped do know their attacker. It's just that juries tend to take attacks by strangers more seriously and convict more readily in those cases. It's a fact of life, I'm afraid.'

'I'm sorry for flaring up like that. I'm not being very helpful, am I? I don't quite know where I am at the moment.'

'You've taken the first step. You've recognized rape for what it was and reported it. Forty per cent of women don't even report rape. A lot of them blame themselves. And you've come to the right people. The Sapphire Unit is specially set up to deal with rapes and is staffed by experienced people like Dr Haslam and myself. It's important that you are totally honest about what happened. Nothing you can say will shock us.'

'Why do so many women not even report it?'

The big, consoling shoulders shrugged. 'A variety of reasons. Sometimes it's fear of reprisals. The commonest one is that they think if they've drunk alcohol no one will believe that they didn't consent to sex.'

'I'd been drinking. I wasn't drunk, though.'

A wry smile crept on to her sympathetic black face. 'It might be better if you had been, love. The law now considers that a woman who is drunk is incapable of consenting to sex.'

'I wasn't drunk. And I didn't bloody consent. No way.'

Dr Haslam said quietly, 'How much had you drunk when this assault occurred, Priscilla?'

This was one question she was prepared for. She been thinking about it through the long hours of the night. But she still hadn't the precise answer which as a scientist she felt she should be able to give them. 'I had a gin and tonic when I got to the pub – we'd originally arranged just to go out for a drink. It wasn't until later that I found he'd booked a meal for us.'

'And no doubt you had wine with the meal.'

'We had a bottle of claret. I couldn't say how much of it I drank, but I think now that it was considerably more than he did. He was driving, as he reminded me, but I think now that that was the excuse he offered for making sure I had most of the bottle.'

'Anything else?'

'A brandy with the coffee at the end of the meal.'

Dr Haslam made a note, her face professionally impassive. 'I realize, as you will, that there can be nothing objective about this. But how much would you say that your normal reactions were affected by drink?'

Priscilla frowned with concentration. She found unexpectedly that this request for detail was some sort of consolation, perhaps because it treated her as a scientist and an intelligent woman rather than the dumb and stupid victim she had seen in herself until now. 'I'd definitely have been over the limit for driving. I suppose the best and totally unscientific description I can give of my condition was that I was pleasantly pissed. Pleasantly because at that stage I had no idea of what was coming. God, how could I have been so stupid?'

Dr Haslam gave her a thin smile and made no comment. 'Would you say that your capacity for decision-making was affected?'

'No. If it had been, I wouldn't be accusing the bastard of rape, would I?'

'Please just answer as honestly and fully as you can. It's a question which would certainly be raised in court, and we need the fullest possible picture if we are to prepare a case. Were there any recreational drugs involved?'

'No, of course not.'

'We have to ask. Cannabis and cocaine in particular are now involved in a high percentage of rape cases. It's one of the things we need to know about from the outset. Now, please tell us as fully and as calmly as you can what happened at the end of the evening.'

'It was a pleasant evening, until we left the pub. Until the moment when we came in here, in fact.'

'Did you invite him in?' This was Sergeant Fox taking over

again, looking as if she wanted to put an arm round the victim
even as she asked the most searching questions.

'Yes. I asked him if he wanted a coffee. I think he said,
"Just try to stop me!" '

'A lot of men take that invitation to mean more than a
coffee. Sometimes the women who make the offer do, too.
Did you?'

'No. I suppose I wouldn't have rejected a goodnight kiss
as he left, but I swear I never intended more than that.'

'You may need to swear to it, in court, if this goes the full
distance. What happened when you got in here?'

'Everything happened very quickly. He asked for the loo
and I set about making coffee whilst he was in there. He –
he must have put a condom on whilst he was in there, according
to what he said later.'

'Did you drink the coffee?'

'No. I never even made it. He grabbed me from behind
whilst I was waiting for the kettle to boil. I told him to lay
off, but he twisted me round and kissed me very hard. Then
he slid his hands under my bottom and carried me in here.'
She glanced automatically towards the rug and the brooch
with the broken clasp which still lay beside it.

'Did he at any time ask for your consent to what he was
doing?'

'No. He told me that I was quite safe because he had a
condom on. He – he said that I was a hot bitch under my cool
exterior and that I knew it. That I was going to enjoy it.'

'You're sure he used these phrases?'

'Yes. I can still hear him shouting them into my ear when
he was lying on top of me on that rug!' Her whole body shook
with a sudden, cathartic shudder, and Sergeant Fox reached
out and put a large hand on top of hers, the first and only
time she touched her during the whole exchange.

'Did you try to stop him?'

'Yes. I know that the advice is to go along with it if you
can't stop it, to be passive and complain afterwards, but I
didn't even think of that at the time. I screamed at him to stop
and tried to throw him off.'

'And he took no notice?'

'No. If anything, it seemed to make him more excited.
He said I was a horny little hussy who wanted it as much

as he did. That I was going to shout as loud as anyone when I came.' She was surprised how accurately she could re-member the phrases, how she wanted to repeat them now and then never again.

'He was on top of you?'

'Yes. I struggled as hard and as long as I could, but he was too strong for me. It was on that rug there.' She waved at it, as if its rumpled state would testify to her struggle.

Perhaps she looked worse than she felt, because Sergeant Fox said gently, 'The worst is over now, Priscilla. Tell us how it ended.'

'He lay on top of me when he'd finished. It seemed a long time to me before he moved and let me out, but it may not have been. I told him to get out. He started trying to talk to me, using words and phrases which I don't remember – I don't think I heard them, even at the time.'

Dr Haslam produced a small digital camera. 'It's a good thing that you struggled, from the point of view of evidence. I now need to examine you and to record the details of any injuries sustained.'

She was a slight, intense figure, far less attractive and acceptable to Priscilla Godwin at this moment than the more motherly Sergeant Fox. Perhaps she sensed this, because she said unexpectedly. 'It's got to be done, I'm afraid. It may help you to know that I was raped myself. It's a long time ago, but I remember what it feels like as if it were yesterday. Shall we go into the bathroom?'

There was a lot of bruising on the insides of her thighs, a small cut on her hip where he had wrenched at her clothing, a long scratch she had never felt just below her breasts where the brooch had been torn from her blouse. All good stuff for a jury, Dr Haslam assured her: they were colleagues now against this attacker she had never seen. 'There'll be no semen,' said Priscilla as she stood patiently with her legs apart. 'He wore a condom, and I told you, I washed myself hours ago.' The condom had been a tiny relief to her as she cleaned herself; even now, she was glad that he had worn it.

'He'll have left enough of himself behind to be identified,' Haslam consoled her. 'In any case, I expect he won't deny that you had sex. He'll probably try to make out that it wasn't rape. That's what most of them do.'

When they went back into the lounge, Sergeant Fox had parcelled up the rug into a big plastic bag. 'He'll have left enough of himself on this for a DNA sample, I'm pretty sure,' she said by way of explanation. 'I've bagged your brooch, too. We may get his fingerprints from it. We'll need a sample of yours, too, for elimination purposes.'

Priscilla watched them recording their findings. She was surprised that it was only at this stage that they asked for Richard Cullis's name and added details of his background to what she had already given them. 'People are always devastated by this crime, usually much less in control of themselves than you've been,' Sergeant Fox explained, with a smile of congratulation. 'We let people talk. We fill in anything else we need later.'

'What are the chances if it comes to court?'

'Difficult to say, love.' She glanced sideways at Haslam, who nodded and smiled. 'You've convinced the pair of us, but we don't have to be objective, you see. We've got the evidence. Now we've got to persuade the Crown Prosecution Service that they have a case worth talking to court.' Her big lips wrinkled in distaste at the pusillanimity of lawyers.

'Drink always complicates things,' sighed Haslam. 'He'll probably argue you consented, and then some clever young male defence lawyer will try to show that because you were "pleasantly pissed", you went along with it at the time, maybe even that your resistance was all part of the sexual game.'

Sergeant Fox smiled her big, compassionate smile and said in a voice as dark and sympathetic as evening cocoa, 'We should ask you at this stage if you're sure that you want to proceed with a possible court case against Mr Cullis.'

'Unless he admits what he did to me last night, I do.'

'I'm glad to hear that. But it won't be easy. Because you knew your assailant, because before this action he was a friend of yours and of the people who work with you, things might be difficult. You know the truth, but, human nature being what it is, some mutual friends might even suggest that you've invented the whole thing, or suggest that you permitted it at the time and are only doing this because you now regret it. You'll need to ignore all the gossip and stick to your guns, but don't imagine it's going to be easy.'

'I don't. But I won't let this go.'

Dr Haslam fastened up her big leather bag with the evidence within it. 'Good. If you feel you need any counselling or care in the next few days, you should contact the Rape Counselling Centre.' She wrote down a phone number and an Internet address and said wryly, 'You may find there's a waiting period.'

'I don't think I shall need them, but why would that be?'

'Because they see nine times as many people as we do. Four out of five rape victims never report the fact that they've been raped to the police. You've done the right thing and we'll now set things in motion.'

As they stood up and turned towards the door, Priscilla said with sudden urgency, 'Don't wrap things up to be kind to me. I'm a scientist, used to handling facts. What are the chances of success?'

Sergeant Fox turned back to her, gave her that wide, motherly smile, and then was suddenly serious. 'You said don't wrap it up. I won't. In 1977, a third of people charged with rape were convicted. Today it's one in twenty. And half of those are because the accused admits the crime. Our first hurdle is to get past the Crown Prosecution Service and persuade them to go to trial with this. We've got supporting evidence, so we have a chance. Cullis will be interviewed and I can't deny that the impression he makes there will influence CPS decisions. It's another fact of life, I'm afraid. We'll be in touch as soon as we have any news. You've been commendably frank, but if you remember anything else you think might be useful don't hesitate to get in touch with me at this number.'

Priscilla held the card in her hand for a long time after they had gone. She didn't feel that she would ever be able to resume her life, the life which she had been so content with before the horror of last night.

Eight

It was early afternoon when the Chief Constable rang Chief Superintendent Lambert, the Head of Oldford CID section.

'John, we've got a tricky one. There's been an allegation of rape against Richard Cullis.'

'Yes?' It wasn't the crime but the name which was puzzling John Lambert. It was vaguely familiar, but he couldn't pin it down for a moment. He'd remembered names for months, even years, when he'd been a young CID sergeant, but in your fifties it took you longer. 'That's the man at Gloucester Chemicals that the All God's Creatures people threatened.' He tried to keep the relief out of his voice.

'That's the one. He's a director of the company, responsible for the research and development laboratories: that's why he was threatened by the animal rights lot. It's a sensitive one, this. I don't want a whiff of it in the press, unless it's taken forward and he's formally charged. All hell will break out if he is, but there's nothing we can do about that.'

'Or would want to do, if he's guilty.'

'Of course. But you know as well as I do what the chances are of this even getting to court. He'll have to be interviewed, of course, but I want it kept as quiet as possible until we have the full picture.'

And swept under the carpet if at all possible, in the interests of PR, Lambert thought. He said, 'I understand, sir. I'll do the interview myself.'

There was a pause at the other end of the phone. The CC didn't really want that, but he didn't know how to turn the offer down. 'Are you sure you've got the time, John?'

John Lambert smiled grimly, understanding perfectly the dilemma he had given the chief; Lambert would be as discreet as a reclusive owl, but he would also be thorough. The CC wasn't certain he wanted thoroughness: that might lead to a charge. High-profile rape cases rarely bring kudos to the police service. Worse than that, they can be a public-relations disaster, if evidence is not gathered fully and clever lawyers make fun of leaden police officers in court. 'I'll make the time, sir, if this is as important as you say.'

He remembered after he had volunteered himself for the job that Bert Hook had taken the day off. He would have preferred to have the down-to-earth, unthreatening, but deceptively perceptive Hook at his side. Instead, he collected Detective Inspector Rushton from the CID room.

'Be good for you to get away from that computer for an hour,' he said, with a sour glance at that innocent machine. He knew that Chris Rushton thought he was a dinosaur and he rather enjoyed playing up to the image. He outlined the delicacy of this mission as Rushton drove him out to the industrial estate, knowing his DI would be rather flattered to be entrusted with this delicate commission from the CC.

Chris was happy to tell him that he already knew about the case. 'I've just opened a file on it on the computer, as a matter of fact, sir. I've printed out a copy of the woman's statement for you to look at now. You'll find it in my document case.' Let the old bugger know that the technology he so despised was more on the ball than he was. 'I've been entering the full information from the Sapphire Unit's interview with the victim. Quite full and very interesting. The photographic evidence of the injuries will be available later today.'

Richard Cullis had been in and out of the labs for most of the day. He'd decided now that Priscilla Godwin was not coming in, but he was listening for any scraps of conversation or puzzled looks in his direction, which might tell him that she had spoken to one of her colleagues. He feigned complete surprise when the CID men arrived. 'A chief superintendent and a detective inspector. We're honoured indeed, today.'

'Is there somewhere private where we can speak, sir?'

'You'd better come through to my office. We won't be disturbed there. Is it about those animal rights ruffians? You haven't turned up their undercover man after all, have you?'

'Not so far. We're keeping an open mind on that issue. This is something else entirely.'

They told him what he was fearing to hear, whilst he feigned again the astonishment he had rehearsed all day in his mind. 'I can't believe this. It's quite preposterous.'

Rushton who had his notebook at the ready, said, 'You deny the allegation, sir?'

'Indeed I do. Most emphatically!'

Rushton nodded, professionally impassive, conscious of Lambert's eyes upon him as well as those of this suave, good-looking man whose facility with words he secretly envied. But Chris knew enough about rape to know that this man in his forties, with his tan and his expensive haircut and his lofty position in the firm, was as likely a candidate for the crime as those shadowy men from doss-houses who were desperate for sex and careless of the consequences.

Chris Rushton was a handsome man who did not see himself as such, a thirty-two-year-old whose confidence with women had been severely dented by divorce, a trauma even more common in the police than in other callings. But he could no more have committed a rape than leap over the moon. He said, 'A very serious allegation has been levelled against you, Mr Cullis. You will understand that it has to be investigated, just as the notion that a saboteur had infiltrated your laboratories had to be investigated.'

'I understand that. I know you have a job to do. I hope you will do it discreetly, so that when you accept that I am totally innocent there will be no damaging rumours left behind here.'

'The lady in question is a Ms Priscilla Godwin.'

'I can't say that I'm surprised at her identity. What appals me is that she could even think of accusing me of something like this.'

'You were out with her last night, I believe.'

Richard gave them the urbane smile which he hoped completely covered the turmoil within him. 'That much we can agree upon. Look, let's get this out of the way as quickly as possible. I've known Pris for years as a colleague: she's been a reliable member of my workforce here for quite some time now. A few days ago I invited her out for a drink and a meal. She was only too happy to accept. Quite eager, I'd have said, if we leave modesty aside.'

'Let's do that, sir, if it enables us to get to the truth. You're sure you invited Ms Godwin out for a meal, are you, rather than just for a drink?'

Cullis shrugged elaborately. 'Pretty sure. I told you that she was eager. I may have suggested a drink and divined that she would welcome something a little more extravagant – as she did quite emphatically when it was offered to her. It's hardly important, is it?'

Rushton was happy to spend some time recording the gist of this; silence could be a very effective weapon, if you had a nervous subject. Then he said, 'It could be crucial, sir, if you translated something casual and brief into an evening out together. We don't know what is important yet, sir, and neither do you. If we decide that we agree with you that this is an unfounded allegation, none of this will be important and it will be expunged from our records.'

He stopped for a moment to savour his verb. Richard said a little too quickly, 'That will undoubtedly be the outcome, after the expenditure of a lot of expensive police time.' He glanced significantly at Chief Superintendent Lambert, who had said not a word since they had entered his office, but had studied him throughout with an intensity which was becoming unnerving.

Rushton said, 'We have the lady's account of the evening, as you would expect. Would you please now give us yours?'

Richard had been over this many times in his mind during the day, had even spent an apprehensive half-hour in the privacy of this office at lunchtime rehearsing it. Now he said, 'This is really rather unnerving, you know. I haven't even thought about it until this moment, and now I'm frightened of making mistakes of detail and being picked up on them. I'm beginning to wish I'd never seen this ridiculous woman. I'm certainly wishing I'd never been foolish enough to ask her out for the evening. But she so patently wanted my atten- tion that I suppose I took pity on her. I've always been a bit of a sucker for a pretty face, but I never thought it would land me in anything like this.'

'Indeed, sir. I still need your account of what went on last night. From the beginning, please.'

'Well, I picked her up and took her out into Herefordshire, to the pub where I'd ordered the meal. We had a drink when we got there. I was being careful because of driving, but Pris had a gin and tonic. A double, if I remember right.'

'Ms Godwin ordered a double, did she?'

Richard realized that he was going to have to be very careful indeed. 'I think so, but I really couldn't be certain. We went into the dining room and ordered food. Pris selected the wine: rather a nice claret, actually. I remember thinking that she must be quite a drinker, which I hadn't expected. She had quite a lot more of the wine than I had, too. She was coming on strong to me during the meal, making it quite clear that she had the hots for me. I admit that I found that quite flattering. Of course, it may have been the wine which was removing her inhibitions!' He smiled in self-deprecation, but received no answering mirth from the men on the other side of his desk.

'Your impression was that Ms Godwin was anxious to take your relationship further?'

Richard laughed out loud. 'I suppose you have to use language like that, don't you? I mean that she was giving me come-on signs from the starters onwards. I have some experience of these things, and I can assure you that I was not imagining it.' He was trying to get them on his side as fellow males, to see his side of things, but neither of them responded. Professional detachment, probably. It seemed likely to him that they had every sympathy with a man put into his position, but weren't allowed to show it.

He wished he could see what this starchy young DI was writing. Rushton made another note before he said stonily, 'Carry on, please, sir.'

'Well, we finished the meal and had a coffee. Pris had a brandy with that. She was reeling about a bit when the fresh air hit her, I can tell you! She put her arm round my waist and I got her into the car. She kept touching me as I drove back through the lanes. I had to concentrate hard to do the driving, but I managed to keep her in order long enough to get her back to her place. I'm sure if I'd pulled in somewhere on the way, she'd have had my trousers off in a flash, but I'm getting a bit too old for sex in the car!'

'Best to confine yourself to what happened, sir, don't you think, rather than indulge in hypothetical conjectures?'

Lambert liked this strain in his inspector. Rushton was coming along nicely, he decided.

Cullis thought he realized now what was going on. These men had to take the official, politically correct line, but he was sure they understood his account of things beneath the professional veneer. 'I stopped the car outside Pris's block of flats. She was all for a passionate smooch in the BMW, but I said something like, "Let's go somewhere more private, shall we?" I think she said something like "Just try to stop me!" but I couldn't be sure of the actual words.'

'I see. Your memory is that the lady and not you said that, is it, sir?'

Richard tried not to look as ruffled as he felt. 'She certainly said something encouraging, but I can't be sure of the actual words. I'd like you to try to picture the scene. I'm only flesh and blood and frankly, I was a man about to get his oats. I had a hard-on after the signs she'd been giving me and I knew she was gagging for it: I wasn't worrying too much about the nuances of conversation, was I?'

'I see. Now tell us what happened inside Ms Godwin's flat.'

'I think I said I'd like coffee. I slipped into the bathroom and put a condom on, as a responsible man should. When I came out she grabbed hold of me and the coffee was forgotten.'

'You say Ms Godwin took the initiative in initiating sex?'

He smiled his modest, man-of-the-world smile. 'Who can say who takes the initiative when the blood runs hot? I wouldn't like to say who undressed whom, but I can tell you it all happened at great speed. I was looking for a bed, but I think she'd been without a shag for a long time. She had me down on the rug with her legs round me in ten seconds flat. And I wasn't holding back, I can tell you!'

He looked for some sign of approbation or envy, some grinning male acknowledgement of his luck or his skill in the sex game. But all Rushton said was, 'Did you feel that there was resistance at any stage from the lady, Mr Cullis? Did she ask you to desist?'

Richard was getting thoroughly pissed off with this strait-laced young man, but he knew that he could not afford to lose his temper. He said, 'There was no resistance. On the contrary, she couldn't get enough of it. It was a pretty rough encounter, I can tell you, but that was all because of enthusiasm, not resistance. She's about fourteen years younger than me, is Pris, but I flatter myself that I kept up with her. Kept my end up, as you might say!' He sniggered at his little joke, but failed again to draw them into his mirth.

'And afterwards?'

'I left fairly quickly. Love 'em and leave 'em, as you might say.' He made his final attempt to nudge his hearers into a male conspiracy, then sighed. 'I didn't want her to think this was going to be something serious and ongoing. I uttered a few of the usual platitudes, thanked her for a lovely evening and that sort of thing, and then I was on my way.'

There was quite a long pause. Richard watched Rushton's pen racing over the paper, finding it had an almost hypnotic effect. Lambert, on the other hand, kept his eyes on the face of the Director of Research as unblinkingly as he had done throughout. Then he said slowly, 'Ms Godwin's account of last night's events differs substantially from yours, Mr Cullis.'

Richard raised his eyebrows extravagantly. 'Really? I must say that—'

'You needn't pretend to be surprised at that. You know that we wouldn't be here otherwise.' Lambert let some of the revulsion he felt for the man creep into his tone, then controlled himself. 'I am reminding you of this in case you now wish to modify anything you have said to us.'

Richard knew that he must be careful. 'I've told you what happened. I can't make it other than what it was.'

'Priscilla Godwin will maintain that she at no time consented to sex. On the contrary, she will say in no uncertain terms that she tried to stop it proceeding, that you ignored her pleas, that you penetrated her against her will and in spite of her physical efforts to prevent it.'

'And I've told you that—'

'My colleagues from the Sapphire rape unit at Oldford have interviewed Ms Godwin and taken her statement. They have also taken photographs of certain injuries to her person.'

Richard licked his lips, trying to lubricate a smile which would not come to them. 'I told you, the sex was rough because we couldn't wait to get at each other. I could probably show you the odd scratch on my back, if you wanted to—'

'You have been accused of rape, Mr Cullis. It is a very serious charge. If it comes to court and you are found guilty, the consequences also are serious. A custodial sentence would almost certainly be the outcome.'

'I have told you what happened and I have told you that her trumped-up version of the facts is preposterous. I don't think I should say anything else without having my lawyer present.'

Lambert gave him the first smile he had allowed himself since they had entered this office. It was a grim one. 'That is certainly one thing on which I would agree with you, Mr Cullis. It is our job to collect evidence, not to take sides, in matters like this. We shall present our findings to the Crown Prosecution Service, who will decide whether legal action is appropriate. We shall require a formal statement from you in due course. I remind you again that no charges have yet been preferred and there is still time to change your account of things in that statement.'

Detectives do not need small talk. It can be a distraction from clear thinking. Lambert and Rushton had driven a full mile from the Gloucester Chemicals factory before the chief superintendent said, 'You've seen Richard Cullis before, haven't you, Chris?'

'Yes. I interviewed him after he'd been abducted and threatened by the All God's Creatures mob. I had sympathy for him then because he was a victim, but I can't say I liked him much. I like him even less after today.'

'You think he's guilty?'

'I know that it's our job to gather evidence and be objective. Between the two of us, I think he's as guilty as hell.'

'He won't be easy to pin down.'

'There's evidence. Cuts and bruises on his victim, torn clothing.'

They drove another half mile, reviewing the contrasting stories in their minds, needing to say little because they were used to weighing the chances in situations like this. Then Lambert said, 'He's a slippery customer. He'll do well in court, once he's been prepared for it by his brief.'

'If it ever comes to court.'

They drove the rest of the way back to the station in silence, their minds united by the copper brotherhood against the cowardice of the Crown Prosecution Service and the short-comings of the law in general.

Bert Hook was more exhausted after three hours of exam frenzy than he would have been by a full day's work. He was looking forward to a quiet beer and an evening slumped in front of undemanding television. The last thing he wanted was to be quizzed on the day's events by insensitive teenagers. Family life being what it is, the teenagers were what he got.

He suspected that Jack and Luke had compared notes in preparation for this inquisition over their evening meal. It was the younger of the two who said innocently, even solicitously, 'How did the exam go, Dad?'

'Not too badly, thank you, Luke. For someone whose sons think he is barely literate, I think I did all right.'

Jack pursed his lips and weighed those words. 'All right, eh? Did you select carefully which questions you were going to answer?'

'Of course I did, son. Elementary examination technique, that.' Bert smiled patronizingly at the elder boy, deciding to play a straight bat and enjoy this. He had in fact seen a question which appealed and been so relieved that he had plunged straight in, only later bothering even to read the rest.

'Space your time out properly, did you, leaving yourself as much time for the last question as for the first?'

'Indeed I did. I flatter myself that I kept a proper sense of balance and was aware of the time throughout. I was rather pleased about that.' Bert had spent an hour on the first answer of the four and left himself only fifteen minutes for his last, very hurried, answer. He'd told Eleanor in the car on the way home that this had been his greatest mistake, that he thought he'd get very few marks indeed for his last hurried scrawl. Now he had to ignore his wife's astonishment on the other side of the dining table.

Jack pursed his lips again, in that annoying, quasi-judicial, gesture he had picked up from television. 'Hmmm. I can't think that an arthritic old has-been like you would handle things as well as that. I should have thought your ignorance of the time factor would be your biggest handicap, myself.'

'Well, now you know it wasn't!'

Luke decided that it was time he fired another shot in this intriguing game. 'Mrs Fogarty says it's important you write legibly. She says that your calligraphy affects examiners, even though it's not supposed to.'

Bert, who'd abandoned his fountain pen for a ball-pen after half an hour in the interests of speed as panic had set in, tried to blot out the memory of his almost indecipherable scrawl in the latter stages of his ordeal. He said sarcastically, 'And I suppose Mrs Fogarty knows all about these things, does she?'

'She seems to, Dad. She's a chief examiner for A levels.' Luke's face was a vision of unwrinkled innocence.

Jack came back in, as if he had been waiting for his cue. 'Did you plan your answers properly, Dad? Mr Johnson says three minutes spent planning is well worth it in the long run. It gives you a properly balanced answer, you see.'

'I planned.'

'That's good. And I expect you left yourself time to read through your work and check for errors at the end. Saves a multitude of lost marks through carelessness, Mr Johnson says.'

'Does he? Well, I expect he knows, then. Don't you have any work of your own to do?'

'Just trying to be helpful, Dad,' said Jack, with a face full of hurt.

'Just trying to be helpful,' echoed Luke, as they scrambled through the door. A chorus of boyish laughter echoed at the other end of the hall.

Bert Hook sat down gloomily with the paper. On the way home from his practice exam, he had voiced a fear to Eleanor that he might have made rather a fool of himself in the eyes of his tutor. Now he felt he'd better don his jester's cap and bells before he collected the results next week.

Nine

It was a cool, crisp morning. There were no clouds, but the sun was still low in a clear blue sky. There was no frost, but the sharpness in the morning air reminded both hunt and spectators that autumn was at hand.

The dogs had already caught the scent; they were barking in impatient anticipation of their release. The horses were less excited, but there was the occasional whinny and pawing at the ground as their riders made them wait for the off. Over the horses' heads, a variety of accents now cut through the clean air, where thirty years ago there would have been only the cut-glass tones of the English upper class. But the hunters were clearly distinguished, not only by the fact that they were mounted upon expensive horseflesh, but by the hunting jackets and spotless fawn jodhpurs which most of them wore.

The Master of Hounds rode over to speak to the owner of the ancient house behind them. 'The sabs are out,' he warned quietly.

Lord Elton looked towards the woods and the shadowy movements evident there. 'Don't these people have anything better to do with their weekends? We're observing the law: this is a drag hunt.'

The MOF shrugged. 'They don't believe that – don't want to believe it. The police are here. I'm not quite sure in what numbers.'

Lord Elton looked round at the expectant people on horseback around him, who were conversing with their neighbours and finishing the last of the stirrup cup. 'We'll go ahead as planned. We can't allow our conduct to be dictated by a gang of deluded ruffians.'

The MOF blew the preparatory blast on his bugle to announce that the hunt was about to begin.

It was a signal to others as well as to the riders. Thirty-eight protesters emerged from the woods on this signal from the enemy. They were mostly in jeans, anoraks, and baseball caps or bobble hats, a shabby contrast to the traditional costume of the hunt. They advanced in a ragged line towards the horses, which were preparing to gallop.

Scott Kennedy felt the surge of adrenalin released by action after the long minutes of waiting. 'Bloody redcoats,' he murmured automatically to the woman at his side.

'They call it hunting pink,' said the woman. She spoke precisely, almost primly, in an accent which might have come more appropriately from a rider on one of the expectant horses.

Kennedy glanced sideways at the white, taut face beside him. You got all sorts, nowadays: this one looked like a hunter turned sab. 'Those coats are bright bloody red as far as I'm concerned. Come on, you guys!'

A voice through a police megaphone said, 'Peaceful demonstration, that's what's allowed. No violence on either side, please.' A horse reared in fright at the strange, distorted noise but was instantly, expertly, controlled by its rider, a woman who looked to be at least sixty.

Kennedy and his followers formed a line in front of the horses, denying them access to the scent trail which had already been laid. The MOF said, 'We're conforming to the law. You lot must do the same.'

A voice behind Scott shouted, 'We all know you're planning an old-fashioned hunt. You'll be after the foxes as soon as you get out into the country. Tearing them apart. Blooding the faces of children. You're the barbarians you've always been, or you wouldn't be out here meeting like this!'

There was a ragged cheer, a chorus of similar insulting phrases. Lord Elton, recognizing a face he had seen several times before, rode forward a pace or two until his mount towered over Kennedy. 'You heard what the Master said. We're a drag hunt. The dogs will follow the scent that's been laid, you fool! Now get out of our way and take the rest of your scum with you!'

Scott reached out and took the horse's bridle. They were big animals, when they were almost on top of you. He kept a wary eye on the horse's mouth and determined not to flinch as a gobbet of its spittle brushed the arm of his anorak.

He mustn't show apprehension, with a crowd of expectant followers behind him.

Things happened very quickly then, faster than any of the principals could cope with. The invisible police megaphone voice called from somewhere behind the riders, 'Take your hand off the horse's bridle, please.'

The horse shied at the alien sound, its front feet narrowly missing Scott Kennedy's trainers as it descended. Lord Elton raised his riding crop above the head of his opponent, a gesture of menace which he probably intended only as a warning.

Scott Kennedy, terrified of injury by horse or rider but determined not to retreat, struck upwards at Elton with the stout stick he had brought from the woods. The ranks behind him moved forward in support of their leader, raising sticks, chanting ritual phrases of protest, alarming riders and mounts alike.

There was a skirmish, no more than that, with riding crops and weapons raised but scarcely a blow struck in anger on either side. Then the hunt was through a gap in the ranks of the protesters, riding quickly away after the hounds, the Master's bugle blowing in what sounded like triumph.

And Scott Kennedy was lying with his face in the dust, with a police knee in his back and a young constable's hurried, breathy words in his ears. 'I am arresting you for causing a breach of the peace. You do not have to say anything, but it may harm your defence if you do not mention when questioned something which you later rely on in court. Anything you do say will be recorded and may be given in evidence.'

As Kennedy and three of his friends were shepherded into the big police van, they could still hear the increasingly distant, triumphant shouts of the hunters through the still September air.

Priscilla Godwin was absent from the factory for only one day. She insisted on resuming her research and testing work in the laboratories at Gloucester Chemicals. She told herself that work was the constant in her life, the factor most likely to restore its normal rhythms. More importantly, she was determined to show Richard Cullis that she was whole and functioning, a dangerous opponent for him rather than a helpless victim.

The Sapphire Unit, accustomed to such distressing but inevitable situations, warned her not to engage in any argument with Cullis. She was to treat him with distant politeness and to avoid seeing him except for the unavoidable exchanges of the working day. Above all, she was to avoid being left with him in a one-to-one situation.

This kind of phoney war was easier to engineer than she had thought it would be, principally because Cullis's lawyers had advised him to pursue exactly the same course. After an initial attempt to pretend that she had completely distorted the incidents of that fateful evening, Cullis left her alone. For many days, they did not speak to each other at all. Some of the people who worked closely with Priscilla Godwin noticed the cooling of her relationship with the boss, but thought little of it. Priscilla was by temperament a little withdrawn, a woman who did not easily reveal her emotional state. No one felt inclined to pry and no one was given any encouragement to do so.

The canteen preferred lighter themes at lunchtime, and there was much talk during September of the first Gloucester Chemicals Golf Day. What had at first been a plan for an outing by a few friends had now received the official imprimatur. More important, the company had decided to finance the enterprise and a free outing always stimulates enthusiasm. Even people whose golfing experience was minimal and sporadic emerged from obscure corners of the firm to take up this exciting opportunity.

In more private situations, some of the golfers had crises to negotiate.

Richard Cullis and his wife had spoken increasingly little over the last few weeks. This might be an opportunity to get at least a little closer. Richard, eating one of his infrequent evening meals with his wife, said, 'The company is running a golf day in October. I think you should come and play.'

'So that the Director of Research and Development can play happy families and present a cosy picture of domestic bliss to the firm at large? I don't think so.'

As she did much too often for his comfort, Alison had identified the idea behind his offer. Richard said uneasily, 'It wouldn't do any harm from that point of view, I suppose. I was thinking rather that it would be nice for us to do something together.'

'I see. Something together, but in the public eye. Something which might help to allay the rumours that my sainted husband is shagging everywhere except at home. Is that it?' She enjoyed the coarseness, which he found more disturbing because it was uncharacteristic of her.

'Do you have to be so bitter?'

'And do you have to be such a shit? What did the police want to talk to you about?'

'Nothing. Routine stuff about work.' Richard had been hoping that she'd forgotten about that: he tried to evoke an area where he deserved sympathy. 'They're still trying to catch the All God's Creatures man who held a knife at my throat.'

'One of many who would like to do that. Me included. I want a divorce.' She relished the sudden brutality of that announcement.

'Alison, you know your Church doesn't allow that.' The Catholics had always saved him in the past.

'Maybe not, but that doesn't matter to me any more. I should have started to make my own decisions a long time ago.' She thought of the high-roofed church with the scent of stale incense and the priest who had told her she could not do these things, and congratulated herself again on her belated emancipation from Church dogma.

'It wouldn't do me any good at work. I know you don't give a damn about that, but you should. It's where the money comes from. You can't just pretend such considerations don't exist.'

'I can tell you to stop giving me such shit. Half the company directors in the land are divorced. It would probably get you sympathy and allow you to play the field with a free hand.'

And it would give you a settlement which I can't and won't afford, Richard thought. He reached across and put his hand on top of hers. 'I'm still very fond of you, Alison. I think you know that. I freely admit that most of the faults are on my side. I think we should put the past behind us and make a real attempt to make a go of our marriage.'

His touch made her realize how much she now hated him. She slid her hand from beneath his warm palm. 'That might be more convincing if I hadn't heard it too many times before.'

He didn't want this talk of divorce now, especially with the prospect of a rape case hanging over him. He said stubbornly, 'We need to think about this, about what we'd both be giving up. Then we could discuss it again.'

She smiled, enjoying having the upper hand. 'We'll do that. I doubt whether my own feelings will change, but hopefully you'll get a better grip on reality. In the meantime, yes, I'll attend your precious golf day.'

Jason Dimmock, in contrast to his boss, did not want his wife to attend the golf day.

'It's a company jamboree. There'll be lots of noisy hilarity and free booze. Not your sort of thing, really.'

Marital psychology being what it is, Lucy Dimmock's interest was immediately aroused. She pursed her lips, pretended to think about this. 'It would be a chance to meet some of your colleagues again. I might quite like that.'

'I'd be on unofficial company duty, I should think, having to talk to lots of people from other divisions, not able to give my attractive wife the attention she deserves. You'd be left with people you hardly know exchanging noisy in-jokes about work. Not a situation you normally enjoy, is it?'

'You don't want me to meet him again, do you?'

He tried not to be thrown by her abruptness. 'It's not that at all. I hadn't even thought of that aspect.'

Jason had never been a good liar. That was one of the better things about him, Lucy thought. 'He'll be there, won't he?' She noticed with wry amusement that neither of them was prepared to mention his name.

'I expect he will, yes. He plays golf and as a company director he'd be expected to show the flag.'

'I'm over him, you know. I've told you that often enough.'

'I know you have. And I accept it.' But he didn't, really. Couldn't, although he dearly wanted to.

'I think I'll come, just to show you that your ridiculous jealousy is totally unwarranted.'

'There's no need for you to demonstrate that. I have to go, but you don't.' He sought desperately for some unemotional argument. 'You haven't been playing much golf lately.'

'Enough. In any case, I'll make sure I get a couple of games in before the October date.' Lucy smiled grimly. 'I shouldn't like to let you down.'

Jason smiled determinedly, recognizing that he was not going to change her mind. 'You could never do that, Lucy.' He wished as soon as he had said it that he could snatch the words back. She had let him down, in a big way, or they wouldn't be having this conversation.

Lucy Dimmock knew exactly what he was thinking, as she often did. 'Let's not go down that road. But I'll do my best not to make you ashamed of my golf.'

In another household on the same evening, a reluctant golfer was being pressurized to participate in the company outing.

Debbie Young said firmly, 'You're still an employee of the firm. You're entitled to be there.'

Her husband shook his head. 'I'm serving out my notice. I may even have done my last day's work and finished with the place by the time of the golf meeting – I've got some holiday allocation left and I'm sure both sides will be happy for me to take it.'

'I think in an ideal world you would turn up and win. Show the bastards they can't grind you down.'

Paul Young smiled. 'This is not an ideal world, love. I doubt my golf's up to winning anything. And I'm not sure that many men who've been sacked would want to parade themselves in front of those still working for the firm.'

'Most people won't even know you've been sacked.'

'It gets around, faster than you'd think. Lots of people have offered sympathy to my face. Lots of people will be having a quiet gloat behind my back.'

'I don't think that's true. Even if it was, it would be all the more reason to turn up and show the bastards they can't grind you down.'

They both knew they were going round in circles. Paul tried something more optimistic. 'I might not even be available by that time. I might have found myself a new job!'

Both of them knew that was most unlikely.

Scott Kennedy was never charged with causing an affray or with assault. Thanks to prompt police intervention at the hunt starting point, no one had actually been hurt. Even Lord Elton, who was initially anxious to see the saboteurs prosecuted, was eventually persuaded that he would lose face by an appearance in court in pursuit of so insignificant a quarry.

Kennedy endured an uncomfortable interview before this decision was reached. He quickly found that the comfortably built, avuncular-looking DS Hook was not the soft touch he anticipated. Scott leaned forward, trying to introduce a cosy democratic intimacy into the sterile confines of the small, square interview room. 'Those toffs deserve all they get. They think they can ride roughshod over everyone. It's the job of us sabs to show them that they can't do that.'

'By appearing on the scene with offensive weapons, causing a breach of the peace, and trying to collect yourself a charge of actual bodily harm? Come off it, lad. Get real!'

'They were off hunting foxes, breaking the law you lot pretend to be so concerned about.'

Bert smiled. The tape wasn't on. He knew that Kennedy was going to be released with a caution, but the unshaven young man in the anorak wasn't aware of it yet and Bert saw no reason to enlighten him. 'You're a daft young bugger who's going to get himself into serious trouble before long, Scott Kennedy. You should check your facts, lad. The scent for the drag hunt had been laid. That's the one the hounds and the horses followed. There's no evidence at all that the law was going to be broken. You and your mates wasted a lot of police time. And if it wasn't for our lads being sharp on the job and arresting you when they did you'd be facing very serious charges.'

'Which I'm not. So let me out of the pigsty, copper.'

Bert controlled his anger easily: it was a part of the job he had learned long ago, in a less violent world. He saw in this intense twenty-three-year-old a mistaken idealism and a love of drama which were dangerous but not wholly bad. This might be his own son in a few years' time, if the boy took a wrong turning in adolescence. He sighed dismissively. 'We've proper villains to attend to. You'll get off with a caution: I just hope you realize how lucky you are to do that. You and your friends are small fry, Kennedy. Go away and keep your nose clean.'

'That wasn't what the bloke from Gloucester Chemicals said!' It was bravado, pique at being treated so disdainfully by this man with the village-bobby exterior who had the temerity to call himself a detective sergeant. As soon as he had said it, Scott knew that his tongue had lured him into a disastrous error.

Bert Hook, who had been standing up to leave, signalled to the uniformed constable who was opening the door to sit down again. 'We may have a serious charge here after all,' he said with satisfaction. He set the cassette running in the tape recorder, announced that DS Hook and PC Gordon were present at this interview with Scott Alfred Kennedy, which was beginning at three fifteen p.m.

'Now, tell us about your abduction of Mr Cullis,' Bert Hook said with pleasant anticipation.

Priscilla Godwin decided she did not need counselling.

In the days following her rape, she kept in touch with Sergeant Fox at the Sapphire Unit in Oldford. It was from her that she learned that the photographs of her injuries taken by Dr Haslam had come out well: 'Full range of glorious technicolour for the bruises and cuts. They came out a treat, m'dear!' In three days, she heard that Cullis had been interviewed to obtain his story of the incident, in four that the evidence had been passed to the Crown Prosecution Service, with a firm recommendation from the Sapphire Unit for a rape action.

Priscilla got used to skirting Richard Cullis at work, with each covertly observing the other whilst pretending not to be aware of their presence at all. She did her best to resume the life she had enjoyed before that fateful night. She signed up for the golf day, even went out with a friend to play nine holes after work in preparation. She was glad she had done that: fresh air, exercise, and a calm autumn twilight in the Wye Valley were good therapy.

Priscilla felt the absence of a close friend, a confidante to whom she could reveal the full horrors of her ordeal, but her oldest friend was now living in Leeds and this wasn't something you could talk about on the phone. She said nothing to her mother: it wasn't fair to burden an ageing lady with an experience which would only give her nightmares and make her anxious for her daughter's welfare whenever she went out in the future.

It was a week after she had been raped that Sergeant Fox

rang Priscilla Godwin at work and arranged to see her that evening. The physical presence of the big black woman with the comforting voice was as reassuring as ever, but she refused both coffee and a stronger drink. She sat on the edge of the armchair opposite Priscilla and seemed for the first time in the younger woman's experience ill at ease.

Sergeant Fox hated the news she had to give, hated her own part in it, hated her inability to break things gently. She said, 'It isn't good news, Pris.'

'They want more evidence from me? But I was quite open. I told you everything I—'

'It's worse than that. Those cowards at the CPS have decided they haven't got a case worth taking to court.'

'No.'

'Yes, I'm afraid. We're still arguing with them about in-decent assault, but—'

'I don't want that. I was raped.'

'You know that. We know that. He knows that. I think even our officers who interviewed him feel that they know that. But he's a clever bugger, your Mr Cullis. He's convinced the CPS that he'd make a good impression in court. Probably he would, especially with a predominantly male jury, even though we know he's as guilty as hell. And he'd have the best brief available, of course, a smooth sod from a London chambers who's built up a reputation as the defence counsel in rape cases and become a very rich man as a result. They won't admit it, of course, but I think they're frightened of his lawyers.'

'I was raped.' Priscilla repeated it dully, as if she could change the decision by her resolution.

'It's the drink factor. I told you, it always complicates things. The defence will argue that you were half-pissed and gave your consent at the time, even if it was against your better judgement.'

'He forced me. You could see that from my injuries. You said the photographs were good.'

'They were.' Fox reached out a hand towards the forlorn woman three feet away from her, then thought better of it. 'But they're not conclusive, m'dear, unfortunately. A lot of women as well as men like violent sex nowadays and minor bruises and scratches occur in the course of it. The brief would argue in court that there was nothing conclusive about what we have to show. No doubt Richard bloody Cullis would smirk and say that you enjoyed a bit of rough.'

Fox stood up. She could think of no consolation to offer to the woman in front of her. There was no point in prolonging this. 'Will you be all right on your own? I can stay a while if you like, but I'll quite understand if—'

'I'll be all right. It's bad news, that's all. I wasn't expecting this.' Priscilla spoke like one in a dream. 'I'll deal with it, once I've accepted that this is what's going to happen.'

Fox made as if to say something, to conjure up some phrases of consolation, but found that there was nothing she could offer. She stepped forward impulsively and put her arms round Priscilla, hugging the younger woman against her own much ampler frame, holding her until the first tearless sobs shook the slim body. The rule book didn't allow you to touch people these days, whatever the circumstances. Bugger the rules!

'Bloody lawyers!' she said. She gave Priscilla a final smile as she released her, but did not speak another word before she left.

Priscilla Godwin sat absolutely still in her armchair for a long time after her visitor had gone. The law had let her down. She would have to take her own measures against the man who had violated her.

Ten

After indifferent weather through most of July and August, the country enjoyed an Indian summer of settled dry days as the year drifted into autumn.

Gloucestershire and Herefordshire are splendid places to be in such weather. They have some of the finest trees in Britain. They tower not just in the Forest of Dean but in the soft and fertile valleys which are a feature of the area. The country's longest river, the Severn, which can be a source of major floods in other conditions, flows amiably through rich meadows and ancient cities in settled spells such as this. Its tributary the Wye is fringed by steeper sides and presents more dramatic reaches, as it runs towards the high-stoned ruin of Tintern Abbey and its confluence with the Severn beneath the cliffs of Chepstow.

This is generally a quiet area now, but the ancient cathedrals and abbeys, with their tombs of kings and dusty medieval power brokers, remind us of the importance of the area in those times when powerful barons struggled with kings for the control of the country. Quiet towns like Tewkesbury are more famous now for flood plains than power struggles, yet the turf here was soaked with blood, not water, in the bloodiest battle of the War of the Roses.

The warm but shortening days stretched themselves unhurriedly into October, with still no sign of a break in the high-pressure zone over the south of Britain. The eighty-four golfers from Gloucester Chemicals watched the skies, congratulated themselves on their luck, and came to a course beside one of the loveliest reaches of the River Wye, some two miles above the ancient cathedral city of Hereford.

They took over Belmont Golf Club and all of its facilities for the day. The manager welcomed their trade with eager, professional enthusiasm. He was delighted that the splendid weather had held: good golfing conditions always made things easier for him. Parties were always less grumpy, more prepared to accept any minor glitches in the course of their day, when the sun shone steadily and there was no need for waterproofs or umbrellas.

He liked days like this, when a large group took over the course for a whole day. You had only one master to answer to, not a series of people with different requirements and different temperaments to fit into their day. This chap Richard Cullis, who had conducted most of the negotiations and made the preliminary arrangements, seemed to be pleased with what had been provided for his group. The manager knew that the weather was going to be his ally.

The Wye, flowing blue and serene beside the lower sections of the golf course, was at its very best on this cloudless autumn day, as the heavy dew burned slowly off the fairways and greens. The majestic trees were still virtually in full leaf; these were their most glorious weeks of the year and this one of their most glorious days. There was scarcely a breath of wind, so that the leaves hung motionless in their developing shades of orange and gold.

Even in such idyllic surroundings, this is still an imperfect world. There is still golf to mar the sublimity of the setting. 'A good walk spoiled': Priscilla Godwin knew now that it was Mark Twain who had called it that. She decided on this day of brilliant sun that anyone who walks beside a golf course will hear ample support for Twain's view. The benign autumn morning was rent by imprecations which combined the blasphemous with the obscene.

And the men seemed to be very nearly as bad as her own sex. Only a marginally greater emphasis on the scatological distinguished male from female in this battle against a common foe.

The enemy was the golf course and it was unrelenting. No sooner had you given yourself hope with a lucky putt than the trees swallowed your next drive. When you did get the ball away well from the tee, you found that not only had a pond which you had never seen swallowed it, but that you were forbidden to cross the perimeter of the offending water to retrieve your ball because you might damage some rare and delicate flora or fauna.

Yet Priscilla Godwin, not normally noted for her patience on any golf course, today took all this in her steady and unexpectedly affable stride. She had been delighted to walk straight past Richard Cullis in the reception area of the hotel, ignoring his greeting and snubbing him with considerable elan in front of an audience. She knew she would not see him on the course, for he had taken care to place her group well away from his. A day like this and a setting like this put even rape into perspective, she told herself firmly. There were people lying in hospital who would love to be playing indifferent golf at Belmont. So get on with it, girl, and stop feeling sorry for yourself. Cullis hasn't got away with it: he'll find that you have your own way to take revenge, in due course.

One of her two companions on the course was the gangly youth she had known for several years in the labs but had scarcely spoken to before. Once his shyness disappeared, as it quickly did in the face of the common stresses of golf, she found Ben Paddon an agreeable companion. They laughed together over their mistakes, only the more amused when they heard semantic explosions from golfers on adjoining fairways who had not got the sport into perspective as they had.

And Paddon, who should have been unable to coordinate the movements of his long and seemingly unathletic limbs, was a surprisingly proficient golfer. He hit the ball high and generally straight; moreover, he had the good grace to seem as surprised as she was when she totted up his points for nine holes and saw how well he was scoring. He was three years younger than Priscilla, but he was intelligent and modest, two qualities she had always liked in men. More importantly, he could hardly have made a greater contrast with Richard Cullis. Ben was very diffident; he seemed to take a smile and a word of encouragement from her as a welcome windfall, rather than his right. He complimented her shyly upon her unexpectedly good chip which ran to within two feet of the flag on the twelfth.

'You should call me Pris,' she said to him firmly on the fourteenth.

Alison Cullis was not playing good golf, but she was philosophical about that. She had other things in mind: she was looking around the golf course and wondering which one of these women Richard had raped; wondering indeed if that unfortunate woman was here at all. He had said nothing to her about the police interview, but the rumour factory being what it is, she had soon known that something serious was going on.

A phone call to Richard's PA about the police interviews had discovered that unfortunate woman thinking the wife must know much more than she did. She had unwittingly revealed the fact of the police visit to Richard. A second call to the Sapphire Unit at Oldford had revealed nothing more than that officers had been in touch with her husband, but that was enough: Alison knew exactly what Sapphire Units dealt with. Her husband had refused to say anything when she had confronted him. Richard was going to regret that very soon, as he was going to regret so many other things in this marriage that was over.

Alison Cullis played a delicate eight iron from the elevated tee at the very short tenth hole. She watched it pitch quite near to the flag, accepted the compliments of her companions, and congratulated herself that she felt so completely in control of herself.

Against his better judgement, Paul Young had been persuaded by his wife to attend the golf day after all. He was not enjoying it much, though he repeatedly agreed with his companions that they were all lucky to be out here on such a splendid day. Everyone in the clubhouse and the hotel areas had been carefully polite to him before they began, as you would expect with a man who had lately been made redundant. But it was a surface politeness: they would be happy when he was gone and they no longer had to endure the embarrassment of his presence. In truth, he would be glad himself: he knew he had no real aptitude for sales and he fancied that his sacking was probably justified. He wouldn't have been here without his wife's insistence.

He loved Debbie, had loved her since their last days in the sixth form at school. He loved her brilliance as a scientist, loved the fact that her own job in the labs at Gloucester Chemicals could never have been in jeopardy. In truth, he lived a little in the shadow not only of his wife's talents but of her will. She was a formidable woman, Debbie, Paul thought admiringly. He whacked away an unusually solid three wood and watched it rise, appealingly distant against the blue sky.

He congratulated himself once again upon his choice of life partner.

Jason Dimmock was playing well, but he had far more complex feelings about his wife than Paul Young. He rifled a long iron two hundred yards to the edge of the twelfth green and acknowledged the praise of the two strangers playing with him. This par five hole runs beside the river for the whole of its length; Jason strolled along and gazed thoughtfully into its depths, watching the small eddies in the water and the flies which fluttered over its surface in this final heat of the year.

His companions were far less competent than he was; he had ample time for rumination before they arrived at the green. Lucy, who had seemed to him a little preoccupied and quiet in the early stages of the day, was playing thirty minutes behind him, but the configuration of the course meant that she would be quite near him at this point. He pretended not to notice his wife leaving the tenth green above him as he studied the line of his putt, but he knew from the distant laughter that she was more relaxed now than at the beginning of their day.

Jason Dimmock took an uncharacteristic three putts and was not relaxed at all.

There is something very satisfying about being pleasantly fatigued in convivial company and having a drink in your hand.

The sun drops early behind the Welsh mountains in October, even during an Indian summer. But the eighteen holes of the golf tournament were well over before it disappeared. Even the players at the back of the field were showered and changed and pleasantly perfumed by six o'clock. The day was still warm and cloudless, but the blue of the sky was getting ever deeper and the first bright stars of evening were about to appear. Many people stood or sat and chatted on the terrace outside the Belmont hotel and clubhouse, sensing that there would be few more days in the year when you could relax outside without a coat.

The Wye played its part below them, its waters darkening to blue-black as the light dropped away. On the long, straight reach of water below the hotel, the surface was still enough in the breathless air to reflect the sky above it. The water was undisturbed save for the occasional trout leaping after an evening fly. A few minutes earlier, a woman with five black Labrador dogs had come to the water's edge on the opposite bank, and there had been excited canine barking and splashing as they had twisted and plunged into the river after sticks. But now all was calm again. With the course now empty of golfers, fishermen were the only human presence by the river, and they were so still and difficult to detect that they might have been part of the landscape.

The company was paying for all the drinks, so naturally the bar was extremely well patronized. By the time the crowd moved slowly into the dining room with the announcement of the meal, there was much noisy hilarity. With the early evening thus already pleasantly lubricated, it would have been difficult for the meal to fail. It did not do so.

Both the roast beef and the alternative salmon were expertly prepared and served. The vegetables were plentiful and freshly cooked, rather than the sad collection which has often been waiting too long for diners in such circumstances. The wine flowed freely, so that those who had taken the precaution of coming as passengers congratulated themselves and solemnly warned their drivers not to overindulge. The decibel level rose steadily, the golfing stories became more outrageous, and the laughter became more uninhibited.

With just a very few exceptions, a good time was being had by all.

The tables had been allocated according to the divisions at work, so that the diners could relax with people they worked alongside and compare notes on the golfing disasters and triumphs of the day. The table where the laboratory staff were sitting together was the only one where there were any obvious tensions, though with the general hilarity and noise in the big dining room this was scarcely noticed.

Richard Cullis had taken care to place himself at the opposite end of the table from Priscilla Godwin, who ignored him completely and engaged in close conversation with Ben Paddon, her golfing companion of the earlier part of the day. Paul Young was being determinedly cheerful, an effort helped considerably by his consumption of alcohol. His wife was keeping a wary eye upon him whilst conducting a desultory conversation with Jason and Lucy Dimmock on her left. Alison

Cullis made valiant attempts to join in the general mirth, though her responses to her husband were consistently monosyllabic and dismissive.

There were prizes, of course, and the rule that no person was to receive more than one meant that they were widely distributed. There was copious but polite applause for Jason Dimmock, who had produced the best scratch score of the day, then rather more surprised and enthusiastic cheers for Ben Paddon's winning of the handicap section. Few people in the firm at large knew Ben, but his gauche, blushing acceptance of his trophy and the clumsy movements of his gawky frame, which seemed to belie his sporting achievement, brought him much acclaim.

The cheering became more raucous as unexpected winners were called up to claim the lesser prizes. The last man up, a plump and elderly receiver of the booby prize for the worst score, made a good job of the conventional speech of thanks to the organizer, then complimented the course and catering staff of Belmont Golf and Country Club as the providers of perfect weather, a fine golf course, and excellent fare to conclude the day.

Richard Cullis made the modest, deprecatory speech he had planned for this moment. He concluded with the triumphant announcement that, subject to the board's agreement, he was sure that after the great success of today, the Gloucester Chemicals Golf Day would become an annual event.

There was a final great cheer and he sat down amidst much applause. People were preparing to depart, exchanging their final jokes and farewells, when the commotion came from the research and development table.

Richard Cullis did not even rise from his chair. Instead, he gave a small grunt and opened his eyes very wide in panic for two seconds at most. He half rose, then fell sideways to the floor, with no more than a sigh of distress.

His form twitched for a moment on the carpet, hidden from most of the people in the room by the table where he had been sitting for the last hour and a half. He ended flat on his back, with his sightless eyes directed at the ceiling. Only those closest to him realized that he was dead.

Eleven

Detective Sergeant Bert Hook organized his leisure time very carefully. You had to do that, when you were in the final stages of study for an Open University degree.

He had this Tuesday evening minutely planned. Half an hour with the boys after dinner, collecting their news, offering unsolicited advice on their homework. His thoughts on batting and bowling technique would be rejected even more brusquely than usual, now that the football season had irrefutably taken over; he would have to wait for the winter tour of New Zealand to revive cricket conversations. This would leave him two hours for his studies: with his final examinations looming, he should now be confining himself to revision, but he had still not completed the syllabus. Then there would be a final hour of relaxation with Eleanor and possibly the television, if there was anything worth watching. Then a drink and bed. It was an unexciting but wholly satisfying schedule, he thought.

Eleanor answered the phone. That was their evening arrangement: Bert's precious study time must be disturbed only by the most urgent of concerns.

This was apparently one of them.

Eleanor handed him the portable phone and said simply, 'It's John Lambert.' In the unspoken codes of husband and wife, that meant she accepted this was something that needed his immediate attention and could not wait until the following working day.

Bert heard his chief superintendent's familiar tones in his ear. As usual, there were no preliminaries, no small talk. 'We have a possible suspicious death, Bert. At Belmont Golf and Country Club. It may be no more than a heart attack, but if it isn't, it needs immediate investigation. I can handle it without you if—'

'I'll be there. It's no more than six miles from here.'

'I'll pick you up, then. I have to come almost past your house.'

It was settled as quickly as that. Bert set the books back unopened on his desk, trying to regret the time lost for his studies. But he felt only that adrenaline surge which is familiar to all CID men when there is the prospect of the greatest crime of all to investigate. He seized his new blue anorak from the back of the door, called a quick explanation to Eleanor, and was gone.

The hunter had scented prey.

At Belmont, the big dining room had been cleared and the scene of crime cordoned off. The corpse lay where it had fallen. The police doctor had certified the man as dead, that absurd but necessary piece of ritual which is part of the legal safeguards against corruption.

The mortal remains of Richard Cullis looked sombre but untainted: there was no visible evidence of attack. The photographer had already photographed an unremarkable scene from every angle he could think of. The civilian scene of crime officer was sketching a table plan, detailing who had sat in each chair on the dead man's table from the place tags which were still in place on the cloth. Two of his assistants crawled methodically about the floor with tweezers, laboriously gathering each hair, each alien fibre, each small piece of detritus, which had fallen on to the carpet around the table where the dead man had been seated for his final meal.

'This is probably all irrelevant,' the SOCO said to Lambert as he and Hook came into the room. 'If this is natural causes, none of this will matter. Let's hope it is. If it isn't, you've got a mishmash of stuff in those plastic bags.' He gestured sourly towards the efforts of his staff. 'There'll be stuff from God knows how many of the eighty-three people who were eating in this room, plus the waitresses, plus whatever wasn't vacuumed up efficiently after yesterday's use of this room. I don't envy you trying to sift through that lot!'

'Forensic will do the sifting,' said Lambert tersely. 'We might know what's relevant when we've questioned a few people and lined up possible suspects. Or we might decide the poor chap's collapse was from natural causes and go back to our peaceful lives of burglaries and fraud and domestic violence.'

The pathologist arrived at that moment. He was in evening dress and a thoroughly bad temper, having been extracted from a function he was enjoying. Lambert left him to it and went out into the reception area of the building, where uniformed police were conducting brief preliminary questionings of all the eighty-three people who had been transformed by this event from happy golfers into subdued and resentful people who wanted only to get away to their homes and their beds.

Lambert recognized that he could not keep a gathering of this size together for very long. He announced that anyone who had seen anything he or she thought unusual in the evening's proceedings should speak to Detective Sergeant Hook. The rest, once they had given their names and addresses to the uniformed officers, could depart, apart from the people who had been sitting on Mr Cullis's table. The calmest of these appeared to be a man call Jason Dimmock. For humanitarian reasons, Lambert selected him rather than the widow to go back with him into the anteroom next to where the corpse lay.

The pathologist had become professional rather than irritable from the moment when he knelt beside the body. He looked up at the returning Lambert and said, 'There's no visible cause of death. This may still be natural causes.' He realized that Lambert would be preoccupied with the people who had seen this death and decided that he would not indulge in further speculation. 'I've got the body temperatures I need from here. I don't want to disturb the clothing any more than is necessary. You can get the meat wagon in and remove him as soon as you like. I think this one should go to Chepstow.'

The Home Office pathology laboratory at Chepstow: that itself was no doubt significant. Lambert glanced at the man waiting for him in the anteroom, then made the standard detective's plea to the pathologist. 'This man was threatened by All God's Creatures very recently. His death will be all over the media very quickly. We need to establish the cause of death as soon as possible.'

'I'll emphasize that. With any luck, he'll be on the slab first thing tomorrow. Will you be attending the PM yourself?'

There was the first smile since his evening had been disrupted upon the man's lips: for a man who had been attending them for thirty years, John Lambert was notoriously squeamish about the blood, gore, and scents of post-mortem examinations. Stomach contents were usually of great interest to the chief superintendent, but not at first hand.

Lambert said gruffly, 'One of my officers will certainly be there,' and watched the pathologist make his departure.

He turned to the man beside him. 'Do you think this death was from natural causes, Mr Dimmock?'

The man was tall and lean: late thirties, Lambert's experienced eye told him. He had narrow, watchful brown eyes and a nose distorted a little, probably by some adolescent sporting injury, so that from this angle he seemed for a moment to be observing the police procedures with a slight, detached contempt. He was still carrying his winner's silver cup rather absurdly in his left hand, holding it a little behind him, as if anxious to conceal it. Before he answered Lambert's question, he set it down on the carpet near the door, as though it was necessary for him to divest himself of his trophy to give the police queries his full attention.

He looked coolly into Lambert's grey eyes and said, 'Natural causes? I've no reason to think otherwise. But I'm a scientist. I suppose you could say that I was trained a long time ago to keep an open mind until I have all the necessary facts at my disposal.'

'I understand that all the people at your table were scientists.'

'That is correct, I think. I understand that even Mrs Cullis knows something of science, though she is not a trained professional.'

He picked his words very carefully, thought Lambert. With a kind of prim efficiency, like a man eating cherries with a knife and fork. The precise enunciation came oddly from a man with the hard, spare frame of an athlete. 'But the rest of you are practising scientists?'

'Very much so. Most of us work in the laboratories at Gloucester Chemicals. Apart from Mr Cullis, who was in charge of research and development but had long since ceased to practise.' Lambert was sure he caught a whiff of disapproval in the phrasing, but he did not want to follow that up now. He wanted an answer to the single question which had been troubling him since he had known of this death, though subsidiary queries must precede it.

'Mr Dimmock, I have been told that Mr Cullis did not show signs of distress earlier in the meal. Is that correct?'

'I wasn't watching him closely, of course, but I certainly saw no evidence of discomfort. Indeed, it was only just before he died that he delivered the final speech of the evening. It was no doubt a prepared effort, but he delivered it perfectly competently.'

This fellow definitely hadn't liked Cullis; there was not even the conventional warmth accorded to a dead man in the period immediately after his decease. 'This would be only seconds before his death?'

'Yes. He sat down and there was the usual polite applause for his speech. I think we were all getting ready to go, because Richard's speech plainly marked the end of what had been quite a long day. Then he simply slumped forward without a word and fell where you found him beside the table.' Dimmock looked at Lambert, who said nothing, and decided something further was expected of him. 'I don't think any of us could believe what had happened for a moment. Then someone felt for a pulse and we decided that he was dead.'

'Who was that?'

'Who was it who felt for his pulse? Debbie Young, I think. I couldn't be absolutely sure.'

Both of them knew that this precise man was in fact very sure indeed. Lambert would have liked to shock him out of his assurance, but knew that it would not be easy to do so. 'Mr Dimmock, one thing puzzles me about this. Most people's instinctive reaction to a sudden collapse of this kind would assume it had a natural cause. A heart attack, for instance?'

He was right about Jason Dimmock's self-control: the man did not appear to be shaken at all by his question. 'It's an interesting point, that. I'm sure we all thought for an instant that it was a heart attack. But only for an instant. We are all scientists, of course: that probably had a lot to do with it.'

Lambert shook his head. 'Even scientists would look for the most usual solution first. Statistically, the overwhelming probability was some sort of cardiac arrest.'

'Yes, you're right.' Dimmock nodded slowly, and looked

for a moment as if he would like to enter into a debate about the matter. Then he said, 'I suppose our thinking was probably coloured by the reaction of the person who got to the fallen man first. After Debbie had felt for his pulse, I mean.'

'And what was that person's reaction?'

Dimmock frowned, as if it was important to him to get this exactly right. 'I believe she said, "I think he's dead. Someone should inform the police. And we'll need a doctor." '

'The phrases came in that order?'

'Yes. Yes, I'm sure they did.' Dimmock made a show of reluctance to cast this shadow over his fellow-diner. 'But I don't think the order of words is significant, do you? The lady was speaking in shock. At that moment, I'm sure we were all in very severe shock.'

'You think the natural impulse when you bend over a stricken man is to think of the police before medical attention?'

Jason Dimmock smiled. 'I don't know. I've never been in this situation before, have I?' He made a show of dismay. 'I didn't mean to imply anything against the person concerned, Mr Lambert. It could have been any one of us who reacted like that, in the shock of the moment. I feel that there is a danger of you making more of this than I intended.'

'Who was that person, Mr Dimmock? You've already told us that it was a woman.'

'Yes. Debbie Young felt for his pulse, as I said. But the person who said we should send for the police was his wife. Alison Cullis.'

Twelve

Bert Hook was up soon after six the next morning. He was determined to put in at least an hour with his books, as a partial compensation for the time he had lost on the previous evening when greater things intervened.

This was the time when the brain was at its best. This period of stillness when most of the world was still asleep was not only the best time for original thinking but the easiest time for concentration. The medieval monks in their monasteries had known that; they had set aside the hours between five and seven to do their best work and their best thinking.

It didn't work today for Bert Hook. He found himself thinking about the monks at Tintern Abbey, reconstructing in his mind those stone cells where they had once worked quietly and contentedly. That wasn't concentration, was it? That wasn't helping to penetrate the mysteries of George Eliot and the later nineteenth-century novel. The image which kept returning to his mind was not that of the Mill on the Floss but that of the corpse with the startled expression on the floor of the big dining room at Belmont.

DS Hook was relieved when the noisy descent of his boys signalled that his period of study was at an end.

When he arrived in the Oldford CID section, he found Chris Rushton already busy at his computer. 'John's gone out to Chepstow,' the detective inspector called, when he noticed Bert's arrival. It had taken Rushton years to bring himself to call the chief superintendent by his first name, as Lambert demanded in their private exchanges, but he seemed now to be able to do it without being too self-conscious. 'I'm opening files on all the people who were at the table with the deceased. They were the nearest but according to John apparently not the dearest of Richard Cullis.'

'We're not even sure this is murder yet,' Hook reminded

him sourly. Efficient young bugger with his computer files, his team coordination and his searches for previous criminal records. Hadn't this cheerfully alert young devil got an inefficient or a lazy bone in his body?

Yet Hook, like Lambert and the pathologist and all the other professionals who had been at Belmont last night, was already privately sure that this was murder. A curious assumption, among people who had trained themselves to keep an open mind to every possibility. Perhaps they had picked up something from the people who had sat with the dead man at his final meal, who all seemed to have tacitly accepted from the start that foul play was involved.

Rushton said, 'The *Gloucester Citizen* and local radio have already been on the phone. The press officer's dealing with them at the moment.' He typed 'Deborah Young' into his PC, looked at his monitor with satisfaction, and began another file.

Hook, caught in the phony-war situation where he wanted to get on with things but could do nothing until murder had been declared, went into the canteen and got himself coffee and a flapjack. Once the inner man was happy, he'd check that the formal machinery of a murder inquiry was in place and ready to go. Assuming, of course, that that efficient young sod Rushton hadn't already done it.

At the Home Office forensic laboratory in Chepstow, Lambert was trying to be patient. The staff there had made the examination of the corpse of Richard Cullis their top priority, and he was grateful for that. They'd come up with some interesting results, so the least he could do was listen to a short dissertation on their findings. You need to know about these technical details, even at this advanced stage of your career, he told himself firmly. If nothing else, you will be able to impress your uppity junior officers by retelling nonchalantly what you learned here.

At quite an early stage of the dissection, the post-mortem had excited interest even among the hardened professionals of forensic crime, who had seen most forms of death before. The man speaking his findings into the mouthpiece fastened to his head had suddenly suspended operations and paged one of his colleagues, a balding man whose long face seemed even longer under his domed forehead. The two had conferred in low tones, excluding the laymen like surgeons confronting some complication in an already delicate operation. The difference here was that the thing beneath their trained fingers was beyond saving: there was no need for haste, no obstacle to the most thorough cutting of muscle and tissue. Corpses have no defences against men and women determined to discover whatever is peculiar to a particular case.

It was this second forensic scientist, Dennis Bryden, who now sat in an office with Lambert. He did not seat himself behind the desk, but lifted himself instead to sit on the edge of it, swinging his feet gently beneath it and looking down on Lambert as if he were an expectant student. It was a pose which one might have expected of a younger man with a younger audience. Lambert thought a man of sixty with a long, cadaverous face and very little hair left above it looked slightly ridiculous swinging his legs beneath him as an aid to thought.

His informant was conscious of none of this. Bryden was an academic, working in an environment where he wrote a lot of reports but got few opportunities to address a live audience, even of one person. 'It's an interesting one, this,' he informed his audience with satisfaction.

'I thought it might be,' said Lambert drily. 'In what way interesting?'

Bryden smiled the superior smile of the man with knowledge. 'How much do you know about poisons?'

Lambert felt again like a student whose ignorance was being probed. 'I know that it's not a usual method of killing. I know that there are many fewer poisonings than the public imagines there are. I know that of nineteen thousand murders in America which occurred in a particular year, only twenty-eight were caused by poisoning.'

Bryden nodded his encouragement to this promising learner. 'That figure, of course, does not include cases in which poisoning was never suspected. We shall never know how many of those there were. I suppose it is my job to ensure that there are very few of those in Britain.' He nodded sagely, as if accepting a welcome thought.

Lambert, striving to drag his man back from the general to the particular, said a little desperately, 'I know something about arsenic and strychnine and prussic acid. Apart from that, very little.'

'This isn't one of those,' said Dennis Bryden with satis-faction.

Lambert sighed mentally. 'Let's begin at the beginning. You're telling me that the corpse who was cut up this morning was poisoned.'

'Sorry. Yes, that's what I'm saying. When you've known it yourself for a couple of hours, you tend to assume that everyone else knows. That's why I've been asked to speak to you, Mr Lambert. Whatever the pathologist may suspect, confirmation depends on the knowledge and skills of the toxicologist. That's me: that's why I was called in.'

'I'm strictly an ignorant layman here. Give me the cause of death in the simplest terms, will you? I need to know all I can, since it is obviously going to affect how we proceed from here.'

'Yes. Well, this is one of the newer poisons. You remember Georgi Markov?'

Surprisingly enough, Lambert did. 'Wasn't he the man assas-sinated by a Bulgarian Secret Service agent in London?'

'That's the chap. 1978. Doesn't seem like thirty years ago, does it?'

'Indeed it doesn't.' Lambert remained outwardly affable, but his heart was sinking. Wasn't this the so-called perfect poison? Well, this clever if slightly irritating boffin seemed to have tracked it down. 'You're saying that ricin is what killed Cullis? Isn't it supposed to be untraceable?'

'Not yet, I'm not. And there's no such thing as an "untrace-able" poison.' The man in his sixties chuckled at his own ingenuity like a clever schoolboy. 'The principal problem facing the modern toxicologist is what to look for. There are hundreds of poisonous substances, and more appearing on the scene with each passing year. Ricin is a constituent of the fibre of the castor bean. Markov was assassinated by means of a ricin-filled pellet fired from the tip of a modified umbrella. That caught the public imagination, because it might have come straight out of James Bond. In this case, the method of administration of the poison was not so sensational.' Bryden showed his first sign of disappointment.

'But you think ricin was the method used.'

'Privately, I'm sure that this man died from ricin or some poison very like it. But I couldn't yet go into court and swear that I'm certain. We've retained the brain, the lungs, and the stomach for analysis; during the next few hours I hope to be able to give you definite details of the substance and of the quantities involved. It's very difficult, but that's what we're here for.' Dennis Bryden rubbed his hands together in eager anticipation of problems to be solved.

Lambert repeated through clenched teeth, 'But you think this man died from ricin.'

'That or something very similar. I'm sure we shall be able to give you more details very quickly. We have all kinds of tools at our disposal here, including chromatography and mass spectrometry. Not that these will necessarily be the methods of choice in this case.'

Lambert said grimly, 'I'm glad you feel that you will be able to confirm it. How was the poison administered in this case?'

'Ah! Interesting, that. It is at its most swiftly lethal when injected, as in the case of Markov. But we found no signs of injection on this corpse. Nevertheless, death would have been almost equally swift by other methods. Ricin is one of the most lethal poisons known to man.' Bryden nodded his satisfaction that a case involving it should cross his path like this.

Lambert forced himself to remain polite as he said, 'So how was it administered in this case?'

Dennis Bryden pursed his lips, then threw his hands suddenly wide in a startling gesture. 'Impossible to say! It could have been inhaled through an aerosol spray, but it is much more effective when ingested internally.'

'You think it was added to his food.'

'That seems the likeliest method, wouldn't you think?'

'I would, yes.'

Bryden leant forward confidentially, a difficult feat for a man perched on the edge of a desk. 'Mustn't teach you to do your job, Superintendent. But it seems this must considerably ease your task of detection. Ricin is a rare poison. Not many people would have access to it. Probably only one, indeed. Find that person, and you have your killer, eh?'

Lambert smiled grimly. 'You've obviously been given no details of the people at last night's gathering, Mr Bryden. The dinner tables were made up on the basis of the sectors where people worked in the firm at Gloucester Chemicals. Cullis

J.M. Gregson

was sitting on the research and development table. With the exception of the dead man's wife, everyone sitting round that table was a scientist. Most of them were engaged in work in the research laboratories. I fancy that every one of them would have not only known about ricin but had access to it.'

Thirteen

Alison Cullis stood a little way back from the front window of the big detached house on the outskirts of Cheltenham, so that she could study the arrival of these visitors without being observed herself.

They did not look too threatening. A tall, rather gaunt man, with plentiful greying hair, looking older than she had expected. This must be the Chief Superintendent Lambert, whom the local papers had made into something of a police celebrity over the last few years. Alison could remember one or two of his more dramatic cases, though she had never expected to meet him, let alone be interviewed by him. She supposed that an interview was what was to come, though they had not used that term when they had phoned to arrange the visit.

The other man was more rotund and cheerful-looking: he did not look threatening at all. As if to confirm this, he paused as they came up the path and drew the taller man's attention to the splendid multicoloured display of dahlias which ran up the long border beside the lawn. When she opened the door and gave them a guarded smile of welcome, Chief Superintendent Lambert introduced this man to her as Detective Sergeant Hook.

Lambert apologized for intruding upon her grief so soon after her husband's death and explained that they wouldn't be here long, that it was a necessary part of the routine in a case like this. Alison nodded her acceptance of the intrusion almost peremptorily, shaking her head to terminate his apologies, finding herself calmer than she had expected to be in the hours when she had waited for them. She was almost impatient to be done with these preliminaries: she would have liked to put an end to what she felt was her hypocrisy, to come out and tell them what sort of man Richard had been.

But that would neither be seemly nor good strategy. Alison said, 'It's murder, isn't it?'

Lambert studied her for a moment, no doubt estimating whether she was likely to break down in some sort of emotional outburst. 'It is, yes. That was confirmed to me late this morning.'

Alison nodded. The first hurdle had been negotiated. 'I felt it was, from the start.' She wondered if they expected her to be crying: was it more distressing for relatives when they found that someone had died like this, or was death just death, even if you had loved the dead one?

'Why did you feel this was murder, Mrs Cullis?'

'I don't know. I've asked myself that a few times today, but I haven't come up with anything definite. Richard had no history of heart trouble, of course. As far as I know, he was a perfectly healthy man.'

'As far as you know? Surely you would have known of any medical history, as his wife?'

Alison thought she caught just the trace of a smile as the tall man said this. Lambert was perfectly polite, but she was finding the way he studied her disconcerting: he seemed to have been watching her every move and her every reaction since she had brought them into her dining room. People would never have done that in an ordinary social setting; intense study of a person's face would have seemed rude. She supposed CID people did it all the time as part of their job.

Alison said as lightly as she could, 'Don't they say that no one knows any human being completely? From the moment when we leave infancy, we all keep some part of ourselves back, even from those closest to us. But yes, you're right, of course you are. I'm sure that if Richard had had any serious medical condition, I'd have known about it.'

'That still wouldn't explain why you immediately assumed that this death was a murder.'

For the first time, she felt tense. It seemed this wasn't just routine, after all. She was being challenged here, despite the man's quiet, reasonable manner. 'I'm not sure I did. Not immediately.'

'Our information is that you did, Mrs Cullis.'

They'd talked to a lot of people, last night, but she hadn't heard anything significant in the snatches she'd overheard.

But this man had taken Jason Dimmock, the golfer who'd won the cup, to one side, hadn't he? She scarcely knew Dimmock. Surely he couldn't have tried to implicate her?

Alison took a deep breath, forcing herself to speak calmly. 'I think you're right, that I did assume pretty quickly that someone had killed Richard. It might have been something to do with the atmosphere round that table when he fell forward on to the carpet. I'm sure I wasn't the only one who immediately assumed that he hadn't died from natural causes.'

'That is interesting, the more so now that we know that you were right. Do you think you led the other people to think that?'

This tall, intense man was like a dog with a bone: a very polite, non-growling dog, but also a very persistent one. 'No. I'm sure it was a mutual feeling. I don't know why you should want to suggest that I was the leader in it.'

A slight, almost apologetic, smile crept on to the long, lined face. 'Probably because of your first words after he fell, Mrs Cullis.'

Alison wanted to respond with a smile of her own, but found that she couldn't muster one. 'You'll need to enlighten me, Mr Lambert. It may surprise you to know that I can't recall exactly how I reacted to my husband's death.'

'Our information is that you said, "I think he's dead. Someone should inform the police. And we'll need a doctor." '

'So I was calm. Or appeared calm. I don't think that is significant.'

'The calmness may not be, Mrs Cullis. DS Hook and I are more aware than most people that there are many different and entirely innocent responses to death. But when there is no immediate evidence of the cause of death, it is unusual, perhaps even unique, in our experience, for someone to suggest the police are required before they call for medical assistance. Almost before they can be sure that the man is indeed dead, in this case.'

Alison felt the silence stretch as they waited for her reply. She could think of no immediate response. Instead, she said, 'The wife is always the first suspect in a murder case, isn't she?'

'Not necessarily. Talking to the next of kin is standard

procedure, as I think DI Rushton will have told you on the phone when he arranged this meeting. When there is a wife, we like to see her first, because she might know things about the dead man which others do not.'

'What sort of things?'

'Things about his lifestyle, his personality, his habits. About the sort of enemies he might have had.'

'But in this case you think I killed Richard. Simply because of something I said in a moment of extreme stress.'

Lambert gave the slightest shake of his head, without taking those intense grey eyes off her face for an instant. 'It is our duty to follow up these things. To ask for an explanation of anything we find unusual. We found your immediate reaction to your husband's death unusual.'

Alison saw a way out of this. 'All right. I accept it was unusual. But Richard led an unusual life. You are probably already aware that he had enemies: I certainly was. When he collapsed for no apparent reason, I must have assumed that one of them was responsible.'

'You say that we must be aware that he had enemies. At this early stage, we know little about our victim. Perhaps you can—'

'You know that he was accused of rape. That he was interviewed last week in connection with that.'

'Yes, we do. I interviewed him myself about the allegation. Perhaps I should tell you that at the time of his death the Crown Prosecution Service had decided not to bring a rape case against him.'

Lambert watched her carefully, wondering if this information might be of solace to her, wondering whether, in the onset of guilt which normally follows the death of someone close, it would be a comfort to know that her husband was not to be accused of what many people find the most despicable of crimes.

He had his answer very quickly. Her features twisted into a sneer of derision and she said, 'He bought himself the best lawyers, I expect. Richard Cullis would, once he knew it mattered. I suppose your people were frightened off.'

She might have been a cynical policeman decrying the short-comings of the legal system, so exactly did she echo the CID reaction to the failure to proceed with a case which had cost them much labour. Lambert said. 'You consider that your husband was capable of rape?'

'I know that he was capable of most things, Superintendent Lambert. I know among other things that he couldn't keep his prick in his trousers for any length of time. It surprises me that he would be foolish enough to land himself with a rape case – I did not think he would have been stupid enough to lay himself open to a charge like that. Richard was a bastard, but not usually a stupid bastard.' She repeated the harsh word as if she enjoyed saying it.

'Did you know that the woman who had accused him of raping her was sitting at the table with you last night?'

'I divined that during the evening. Priscilla Godwin. I've met her a couple of times, as I've met most of the people who work in the research laboratories in Richard's section. Until very recently, I was in and out of the place quite frequently: he liked to preserve the fiction of a happy marriage to his staff. I'd met Miss Godwin, but I hardly knew her. She wasn't near me at the table and I didn't have to speak to her last night. I'm glad of that, because I've no idea what I would have said to her. I expect I would have offered her my sympathy, which she probably wouldn't have welcomed.'

A wife would normally have wondered about how this other woman had got herself involved with her husband. Even if she accepted that in the end he had attempted an ugly attack, she would have speculated about what kind of relationship there had been before that attack and how much encouragement he had received from the woman concerned. But it was already clear to them that Alison Cullis was no ordinary wife.

It was Bert Hook who now said to her, 'It is helpful to us to find a wife who makes no secret of her enmity towards her husband.'

Alison glanced at his broad-featured, open face and relaxed a little: this didn't look like a man capable of setting traps. She allowed herself a small, rather grim smile. 'I don't enjoy hypocrisy and I don't suppose you do. In any case, I expect you'll quickly find out just how much I despised Richard, when you talk to other people who were at the table last night. Detection is your business, and that won't be difficult detection.'

Hook gave her an answering smile. 'It is much better to be

honest, I agree. We see people who are not honest with us getting themselves into all sorts of difficulties. Mrs Cullis, you have made no secret of your dislike for your husband. Just now you said that you despised him. That sounds like a marriage which is past redemption. Were you planning a divorce?'

'No.' She paused for a moment on the negative, marshalling her thoughts to it, wondering why she had said this. The denial had been instinctive; perhaps it was the habits of childhood religion which had spoken for her. 'Richard didn't want a divorce. He said he was still in love with me, that we could "reassemble the parts". That was the phrase he used.' For the first time, Alison felt a sudden, unexpected pang of regret that the man was dead, that he would not be able to make one more appeal to her. To shut out that shaft of weakness, she said waspishly, 'Divorce wouldn't have suited Richard's image as a member of the board at Gloucester Chemicals. He was very conscious of that image.'

Hook studied her for a moment with his head a little on one side, as intently as his chief had done before him. She found it even more disturbing in this comfortable, unthreatening face. Eventually he said, 'Wasn't that a rather out-of-date attitude, Mrs Cullis? There are many prominent and highly successful industrialists who have been divorced.'

He was right, of course. She had taken a false step in asserting that. It would be safer as well as more honest to concentrate on her own background. 'I am a practising Catholic, Sergeant Hook. Some people think that is a rather out-of-date Church.' She allowed herself a rueful smile, to show Hook that he had not caught her out and that she was not ruffled. 'My Church does not approve of divorce. Some people think that attitude is unrealistic in the twenty-first century. Others think that it is an example of moral canons which cannot be changed. When I married and made solemn vows, I married for life.'

That at any rate was true, she told herself. She had intended that, all those years ago, in what now seemed a different world: it was the experience of marriage with Richard Cullis which had changed her view. She tried not to think of that dark, high-vaulted church with the candles winking in the shadows, where she thought she had resolved to break her ties with

Richard. Then an idea struck her and she voiced it before she could prevent herself from doing so. 'This gives me a motive for killing him, doesn't it? Murder might have been the only way out of a marriage that had failed.'

Hook smiled at her. In that moment, he was his old reassuring, disarming self. 'Most people, including those with religious scruples, would consider murder a greater sin than divorce.'

She smiled back at him. He didn't seem at all like any of the few policemen she had met in her life. 'Those people include me, Sergeant Hook. When you live with someone and things go wrong, you can cheerfully contemplate murder at times. But it is never a serious proposition. On purely rational grounds – and I think I am a rational person, despite my religious preferences – one would have to reject that solution to one's troubles. As you have just suggested, murder is a very serious crime, whereas divorce is permitted by the law of the land – indeed, sometimes even encouraged, it seems to some of us.'

Alison was relishing this little exchange with a man who seemed to be on her side, enjoying demonstrating that her brain was working even under the stress of interview. It was the man she was not looking at who now said quietly and evenly, 'Who do you think killed your husband, Mrs Cullis?'

She was almost tempted into the flip reply that it was their job and not hers to decide that. But as she transferred her attention to the long, lined face and the unblinking grey eyes, she thought better of it. 'I don't know. I suspect Richard had many enemies among those who worked with him. You hear of people who make friends easily. Richard was the sort of man who made enemies easily.'

It was a little too glib, Lambert thought. It smacked of a prepared statement. At this moment, he did not like this woman he had never met before today. Perhaps he was prejudiced, he thought. He preferred grief in a widow, even when the deceased husband did not really merit it. Perhaps his bias against her self-control was largely a CID man's reaction: people who were in the grip of any sort of emotion were always more vulnerable as interviewees. Anger or jealousy, love or hate, invariably upset their judgement when they were being questioned. It was always embarrassing to have to press for answers from a wife stricken with grief on the day after her husband's death, but it was usually productive: you learned more than you did from someone as composed and aware of herself as this woman.

Yet he could not say that she seemed dishonest. She had made no real secret of the fact that she had thoroughly disliked, even despised, her husband; she had even acknowledged that she expected to be treated as a suspect in the initial stages of their investigation. Lambert wondered if he was trying to needle her a little as he said, 'So it's your opinion that the people who worked with Richard might have had reasons to kill him. But couldn't this also have been a crime of passion?'

Alison was a little shocked at his directness, at his daring to suggest that some other woman might have been sufficiently involved with Richard to want to kill him. But she had a sense that she was winning this little contest. 'It could indeed. There'd be me for one. I've already indicated that I was thoroughly pissed off with the man. Perhaps I should now tell you formally that I didn't kill him.'

She glanced at Hook making notes in his notebook, then gave Lambert a small, slightly mocking, smile. 'There was of course another woman sitting at the table who had a reason to commit what you call a "crime passionnel". The woman whom he had recently raped. You tell me that there was to be no prosecution, but my money would be on the woman in the case to be telling the truth about it. And once she knew he was going to get away with it, the sense of injustice was no doubt very great. I would certainly have felt murderous intent, in her place.'

'Ms Godwin will be questioned in due course, along with the other people at your table last night, as you would no doubt expect. Do you know of anyone else who might have been emotionally involved with your husband?'

'No. But as I told you earlier, I have not given much heed to his movements in the last few months.'

There was no need for her to sound so satisfied about that, Lambert thought. He said more stiffly than he intended, 'Is there any other person who you think could be responsible for this death?'

Alison paused, confident now that they must be near the end and that she had acquitted herself well. 'No, I don't think so. Those All God's Creatures idiots had threatened him, but they weren't near him when he died, were they, so I don't see how it could have been one of them.'

'We shall certainly be investigating that line. At the moment, as you indicate, it seems that whatever their intentions, the animal rights protesters can scarcely have had the opportunity to harm Mr Cullis.' He stood up. 'For the moment, that is all, Mrs Cullis. If you think of anything at all which might have a bearing on this case, you should get in touch with us immediately.' He handed her his card with the Oldford CID number on it. 'With apologies again for our intrusion, we shall now leave you alone with your grief.'

Alison wondered if he intended an irony in that last sentence, but it was delivered so evenly that she could not be certain. She made herself tea when they had gone and sat with her hands round the china beaker in her favourite armchair, finding both the drink and the familiar, enclosing feel of the chair surprisingly comforting. It had gone well, she decided. It had largely followed the lines she had expected and she had been able to give them only what she had planned.

One thing rather surprised her about herself. She had stuck to the line that she had never had any intention of divorcing Richard. Now she wondered why she had done that. It had come naturally to her lips, even when she knew that she had given serious thought to divorce. Her initial intention had been to disguise the degree of acrimony between herself and Richard, so as to diminish the suspicion which must always attach to the spouse when a man is murdered.

But when it had come to it, she had not troubled to minimize that acrimony. She didn't really regret that. It would have felt like a betrayal of herself to pretend that she had been close to her husband, that she had been devastated by his death. And the real state of their relationship would surely come out when they questioned others. But she could reasonably have pretended to be at least in shock, to be fragile, even devastated, by the suddenness of Richard's removal from her life.

She could see why Chief Superintendent Lambert had made his reputation and got results, why he was a man to be feared in her situation. She could even see now in retrospect how that stolid Sergeant Hook complemented his more intense chief, how that man with the weather-beaten countenance should not be underestimated. She frowned at the thought. She had done well, but they would still have her down as a suspect. It would be well to proceed carefully.

In the car making its way back to Oldford CID, Lambert was reflecting on one indication of her innocence which she had curiously failed to stress.

Fourteen

Detective Inspector Rushton switched off his computer with some relief.

He enjoyed collating the various strands of a murder inquiry, building up the files and looking for significant similarities and discrepancies in the accounts people gave. Cross-referencing was the thing: several times in the last three years he had managed to throw up anomalies in the statements witnesses had given which had been the keys to solving the crime involved. He was quite content to let that old dinosaur Lambert go out and question people, to pick and probe a crime until he came up with interesting facts and dishonesties.

In most CID sections the chief superintendent would have been sitting behind a desk and coordinating whilst his inspectors and sergeants and DCs were out at the crime-face. But each to his own strength was a good rule, if one which the police service rarely acknowledged. Chris was prepared to admit that John Lambert was a more subtle and imaginative assessor of people and of what they said than he was. Perhaps in turn he was more competent at the business of collecting and regulating the mass of information which a murder hunt throws up than his chief: certainly John Lambert and Bert Hook assured him that he was.

Yet on this particular Wednesday evening, Chris Rushton was glad to switch off his computer and leave the confusing case of Richard Cullis behind. He had worked for nine hours at classifying and recording the numerous statements which had come pouring in from the people who had been present at that fatal dinner. The staff of the Belmont Golf and Country Club, as well as the laboratory workers at Gloucester Chemicals, had provided him with a welter of material, much of it repetitive; most of it would no doubt prove to be irrelevant, but no one could be certain yet just what was important.

Enough was enough. It was no use becoming obsessive, as he had sometimes been in danger of doing in the last few years. Switch off your mind and come back refreshed to the task tomorrow morning.

This was an eminently sensible attitude. Whether it had anything to do with the fact that Christopher Rushton now had a social life was another matter entirely, which Chris did not want to discuss with himself.

To whit, a lady almost ten years younger than himself called Anne Jackson. Whether she would have been flattered to be described as a social life is another matter, but one Chris fortunately did not have to debate with her.

He was later home than he had expected, so that Anne was waiting for him in his neat little flat. It had been an import-ant stage in the rituals of intimacy when he had offered her the key to his rather sterile little home and she had solemnly accepted it with a chaste kiss upon his brow. One of the things both of them liked about the relationship was that he was never quite sure when Anne was teasing him and when she was absolutely serious.

She had a gin and tonic waiting for him. 'Rest your old bones whilst I cook,' she said as he subsided on to the sofa. Chris was thirty-two.

'I should be doing that.' He made the ritual protest, but remained sitting.

'It's highly demanding stuff, this.' She read the instructions on the packet and switched on the microwave. 'It will be ready in ten minutes. I thought we'd both worked hard enough for one day, so I popped into Tesco's like the slut I am and did the easy thing.'

Anne Jackson was in her first year in teaching. She finished exhausted but happy on most nights. 'It's half term next week. We could go away together for a day or two if you can manage it.' She busied herself with the clatter of plates and the tinkle of cutlery. They had been sleeping together for two months now, but it would be the first time they had been away together, and thus another step towards long-term involvement. She was determinedly casual about this suggestion, shy enough to think she might blush if she looked at him.

He was silent for so long that she had completed the settings for two on his neat little kitchen table before he spoke. 'I'd like to. Of course I'd like to. That goes without saying.' Chris cursed himself for his stiffness. 'But this murder case we've just started on looks set to run for some time. I can't be certain it will be over with by next week.'

'That's all right! It was only a thought.' Her answer came almost before he had finished speaking, showing her that she was much more nervous than she had thought she would be.

He came up and stood behind her, clasping his hands round her waist, holding her against him, in the simple, spontaneous movement which he would have found difficult only a few weeks ago. 'I'm sorry, Anne. I'd love to go away with you. But I don't want to say yes and then have to let you down.'

'It doesn't matter. Really it doesn't. We'll still be able to spend some time together. Perhaps we could play golf again, if you can drag John Lambert and Bert Hook away from the job for a few hours.'

He was irrationally pleased that she should remember their names. She had played golf with them two months earlier, when she had surprised the older men with the standard of her game and Chris had been immensely proud of her. He had originally met her when she was one of the innocent people involved in a previous murder investigation. Now he said impulsively, 'You don't seem to mind the job. It was one of the things which broke up ex-Anne and me.'

One of the things a divorced man should never do is to find a new woman with the same name as his ex-wife. Lambert and Hook would have backed DI Rushton to do it, and sure enough Chris had achieved the unlikely feat. The new lady and he had fixed upon 'ex-Anne' for the vanished former wife, managed to laugh about the unfortunate coincidence, and were now easy with the idea.

Anne Jackson was careful not to show the curiosity she inevitably felt about this woman she had never seen, but she was grateful now for the opportunity to assert an advantage over her. She shrugged extravagantly. 'Everyone has to work. Your particular job makes its own demands: that's all right by me. You'll have to accept that my job makes its own demands as well. Like being far too tired to go out tonight, when you want to go out clubbing.' She yawned extravagantly, then scrambled to her feet as the bell on the cooker timer summoned her to inspect the progress of their food.

Chris was delighted. There was nothing he wanted more than a quiet night in, but he always feared that a twenty-two-year-old must be anxious to be out on the town. When he voiced this thought, Anne said that he had no idea of the amount of energy expended in a day with thirty eight-year-olds. They discussed the murder which had taken place twenty-four hours earlier in general terms. She was wary of treading on delicate ground and knew he could not discuss confidential details of the case, but the death of what the press called a 'prominent industrialist' in front of over eighty witnesses was already established as a local sensation.

Chris told her that ricin was suspected as the instrument of death, since he knew that the press officer had released this information to the media an hour ago. 'It's apparently one of the swiftest and most deadly poisons known to man,' he said, hoping she would be as impressed as he had been by that information. 'Unfortunately, it looks as though almost everyone who was at Richard Cullis's table was a research chemist with access to ricin, so I can't see this being a straight-forward arrest. That's why I'm doubtful about getting away next week.'

It was still early enough in their relationship for Anne Jackson to feel careful about upstaging him, but she still enjoyed giving him little shocks. 'Yes. I know the son of someone who was at that table. A boy called Young – he seems quite upset. Do you want ice cream with your strawberries?'

Chris had never had any problem in thrusting aside his private life once he entered the station at Oldford and became Detective Inspector Rushton.

According to ex-Anne, that was one of the reasons for their marriage break-up. Chris had been so wrapped up in his job and his successive promotions that they had taken precedence over other and more important things. The familiar complaint of the policeman's wife. The concentration which had twenty years earlier threatened to destroy even the marriage of that CID elder statesman John Lambert, whose marriage was now seen as the rock-solid product of an earlier era by the younger members of his team.

The delights of the previous evening with Anne Jackson

were instantly and automatically dismissed as DI Rushton turned to the problems of the morning. There was more information coming in from the murder team assigned to the Richard Cullis investigation, but there was another task to be undertaken before he could get back to his computer and the problems of cross-referencing his files. It was a very necessary problem, Chris told himself firmly. It might even in the end prove to have a connection with the Cullis case.

Scott Kennedy had to be interviewed.

The hunt saboteur had got away with his attempts to disrupt Lord Elton's hunt. Much to Chris's disgust, there were to be no charges. But in the last stages of his questioning in connection with that skirmish he had revealed something much more serious and much more interesting. Bert Hook had trapped Kennedy into an admission that he had been responsible for the abduction of Richard Cullis a few weeks before his murder. Now DS Hook was to assist DI Rushton with the interview with Scott Kennedy, in the presence of his lawyer.

Like all policemen and a goodly proportion of the public they served, DI Rushton did not like lawyers. They were an obstruction to justice, not a protection for innocence, in Chris's heavily biased view. The aggressive newly qualified man who accompanied Kennedy this morning seemed to him a particularly obnoxious specimen of the species.

Tim Cohen was smartly dressed in suit and tie and had encouraged his client to present himself similarly. Scott Kennedy claimed he didn't possess a suit, but he had discarded his jeans for trousers and wore a light blue leisure shirt with a neat collar. In the warm little box of interview room number two at Oldford police station, he was the only one who looked comfortable. He was perky and alert as he came into the room and accepted the seat offered to him beside his lawyer. Only the way that he suddenly ran a hand through brown hair which was too short to need such attention showed that he was nervous.

'Let's have this over with quickly, pigs, and let me get on my way. I don't like the smell round here.' He looked aggressively at the cool, clear-cut features of Rushton, found no reaction there, tried a little contempt on the less threatening face of Hook, and was equally unsuccessful.

Rushton gave him an acid smile. 'I think we'd like to have

whatever you say here on record, Mr Kennedy.' He switched on the cassette tape recorder, announced that it was nine twelve a.m., and gave the names of the officers who were about to interview Scott Alfred Kennedy in the presence of his lawyer.

Tim Cohen raised a hand to prevent his too-impulsive client from speaking and said with his most winning smile, 'I hope there is room for compromise here. You have already indicated that you do not intend to proffer any charges against my client in connection with our disruption of the local hunt. We recognize that you have to enforce the law, however mistaken that may seem to those of us with the interests of helpless creatures at heart. In turn, we hope that you recognize that we have conscientious concerns of our own.'

Rushton kept his attention upon Scott Kennedy as he answered his lawyer. 'Conscientious concerns are one thing, Mr Cohen. Serious criminal actions are quite another.'

Kennedy was now plainly nervous. He folded his arms, then unfolded them again quickly, finding he could not keep as still as the men on the other side of the small square table. He licked his lips and made a final attempt at bravado. 'Let's have this over and get us all out of here. I don't suppose you enjoy wasting time any more than I do.'

'You may not be going anywhere, Mr Kennedy. What you admitted to DS Hook in a previous interview is a very serious offence. Far more serious than inciting violence at a drag-hunt meeting.'

Cohen raised his slim hand again within Kennedy's peripheral vision. 'My client is admitting nothing. It is our belief that you do not have the evidence to warrant a prosecution against him.'

Bert Hook inched himself three inches nearer to the edgy young man in front of him. 'Mr Kennedy has already admitted in a formal interview with PC Stanley and myself that he abducted a citizen, using an offensive weapon. Unless he proposes to tell us that he was lying and provide us with—'

'I wasn't lying!' Kennedy spat out the denial before he considered any consequences.

Hook's experienced, revealing features creased into a smile. 'Good! Then we'll get on with this quickly, as you suggest.'

This time the lawyer's restraining hand had no effect on his overexcited client. 'All right. I admit I took Cullis away and we told him what we thought of him and his firm's activities. It wasn't personal. He was the Director of Research and Development, the man in charge of those laboratories where they torture innocent creatures and claim it's for our benefit! The man who could stop the experiments and the tests on animals at Gloucester Chemicals.'

Rushton said coldly, 'That is how you see it, Mr Kennedy. It is our job to enforce the law and the law sees your actions quite differently. You abducted an innocent citizen by threatening him with a lethal instrument, namely a knife, and made him drive his own car to a point determined by you, where you met your accomplices in this crime. In the course of this episode, you held a knife at his throat and repeatedly threatened to injure him.'

'So get on with it and charge me. I'll pay your bloody fine.'

This time it was Rushton who smiled, his more intense features now matching the satisfaction of Hook beside him. 'Not a fine, Mr Kennedy. You are facing very serious charges. Mr Cohen here knows much more than me about the law, but I know quite enough to tell you that you are facing a custodial sentence here. Probably rather a substantial one.' He nodded happily.

Kennedy glanced apprehensively at his brief, then immediately regretted this obvious gesture of weakness. He said sullenly, 'We were trying to protect innocent creatures. We'd nothing against Cullis personally. You make it sound much worse than it was.'

'I recount the facts. And you do not seem to be disputing them, Mr Kennedy. You would be most unwise to do so, if they are correct.'

Tim Cohen knew that as a lawyer he should not sound desperate, though it was difficult not to do so with this young fool seemingly intent on self-destruction. 'Mr Kennedy has admitted more than I would have advised him to do, as his lawyer. I hope you will not now penalize him for his honesty.' He knew that his words were no more than a rhetorical flourish. He was driven to playing a card he had planned to keep in reserve. 'You will in my opinion have the greatest difficulty in preparing a case against him, in the absence of your chief witness.'

Rushton said drily, 'The judge will no doubt wish to take

Mr Kennedy's honesty into account when it comes to passing sentence. Along with his repeated threats of violence and even death to his victim. I do not think you should rely on the unfortunate death of that victim to extricate your client from charges. Mr Richard Cullis was interviewed by our officers about this incident on the day after it occurred and made a detailed statement. I think you'll find that the CPS feel they have quite enough evidence to bring this to court.'

Bert Hook had not taken his eyes from Kennedy's pale, apprehensive face during Rushton's exchanges with the lawyer. He now said abruptly, 'So what do you know about Mr Cullis's death, Scott?'

'Nothing. I didn't kill him.'

'I didn't accuse you of that, Scott. I suggested that you might know something which could help us to find his killer.'

Kennedy's chastened face now set into a mask. 'I don't know anything that could help you. I don't know why you—'

'You would be most unwise to conceal anything, Scott. You are already facing very serious charges. If you add concealing evidence in a murder inquiry to those offences, you might be banged up for a very long time indeed.'

Tim Cohen spoke quickly, anxious to prevent the impulsive young man at his side from further incriminating himself. 'My client is not concealing anything. I agree with you that it would be most unwise to do so, but he has no connection with this murder.' He tried to recover a little lost ground. 'In my opinion, you would be most unwise to suggest that he does.'

Still Hook did not look at the lawyer, did not take his steady gaze from the face of Cohen's young client. Kennedy was in his view a fool rather than a genuine villain, a young man whose mistaken principles were going to land him in even deeper trouble if someone did not show him the error of his ways. But there was a murder to be solved and anything this young fool knew must be out in the open. 'You told Mr Cullis that your group All God's Creatures had someone working in the laboratories at Gloucester Chemicals. In view of the sudden death of Mr Cullis, this person is obviously going to be investigated.'

Cohen said immediately, 'I need a few minutes to confer with my client. I am making a formal request to that effect.'

Rushton silently cursed all lawyers. He gave the pair on the other side of the table the briefest of nods, then announced, 'Interview suspended at nine twenty-eight,' and switched off the cassette recorder.

Left alone in the windowless box of the interview room, Cohen watched the door close behind their questioners and said, 'I told you before we came in here to let me do the talking. Keep quiet and give them nothing was supposed to be the tactic. If in doubt, leave it to your brief. That's what I'm here for.'

Kennedy glanced round the room. 'Can they still hear us? Will this place be bugged?'

'No. They can't do that.'

'We both know who our man at Gloucester Chemicals is. He announced it at our last meeting.'

'We know but they don't. Keep shtum, Scott.'

'I'm not going to tell them. I should never have told Cullis we had a man in those labs.'

It was a rare admission of weakness; Cohen's impulse was to tell him it wasn't the only occasion when he should have kept his mouth shut. Instead, he said, 'Ben Paddon should never have told the meeting about where he worked: the fewer people who know about these things, the greater the security. But he's done it now and he has to be protected. The only witness to your indiscretion about us having a mole in the labs is Richard Cullis himself, and he's dead. If you now deny that you ever said anything about having a man under cover at Gloucester Chemicals, I don't see that they can do a thing about it.'

'Did Ben Paddon kill Cullis?'

'I don't know. Neither do you, and you don't want to know. Ignorance is bliss here, believe me. Try to forget even the man's name. That's the best way of convincing these buggers that you know nothing.'

It didn't take long to conclude matters when the interview was resumed and the tape was running again. In answer to Rushton's renewed inquiry, Kennedy said woodenly, 'I do not recall saying anything about an All God's Creatures person in the Gloucester Chemicals factory.'

Cohen came in quickly on the heels of this prepared sentence. 'It seems probable that the late Mr Cullis was enlarging the exchange – embroidering it, as he no doubt did other words and actions of Mr Kennedy.'

Bert Hook looked steadily into the eyes of the young man whose presence here seemed to him to represent a warning to anyone with sons approaching adolescence. 'It's rather late to start withholding information, Scott.' He glanced for the first time at Cohen and did not trouble to conceal his disgust.

Then he turned back to the wretched young man in front of him and spoke more formally. 'You've already confirmed much of what Mr Cullis told us about his abduction, Mr Kennedy. You will be charged in court tomorrow morning with abduction and with threatening with an offensive weapon. I advise you to consider your position. If you do know of anything which might have a bearing on the death of Mr Richard Cullis, you should certainly reveal it. By doing so, you might protect yourself from the even more serious charges which will inevitably follow for anyone aiding and abetting a murderer.'

Fifteen

Lucy Dimmock received the phone call she was expecting whilst her husband was still in the house. It was eight twenty-five and they were just finishing their breakfast. The cool, impersonal female voice said that Chief Superintendent Lambert would like to talk with her informally about the death of Richard Cullis thirty-six hours earlier. He would come and see her at work or she could come into the station. It should not take very long.

Lucy reviewed her options rapidly. 'It's difficult to ensure privacy at work: our premises aren't extensive. But we can meet here. That way, we shan't be disturbed.' The calm voice told her that she already had the address and that the CID visitors wouldn't need any guidance to find it. Lucy was a little disturbed to find she was to have more than one visitor.

She waited until Jason left the house, then rang the office and told her partner that she wouldn't be in until around midday. She did not give the reason, though she had no doubt that Lesley would divine a connection with the death which was already a local cause célèbre. At least when you owned the business you could come and go as you pleased. She and Lesley ran a secretarial agency, supplying reliable temporary staff for emergencies and occasionally helping with more permanent appointments. They did not need extensive premises, but their success meant that the small office premises which a year ago they had thought would be more than adequate were already fully stretched.

The CID men came exactly at half-past ten, the time she had arranged. She was already aware of the local reputation of Detective Chief Superintendent John Lambert, whom the press had taken to designating 'the Gloucestershire supersleuth'. She had seen both these men from a distance in the hours after the murder at Belmont, but at close quarters

Lambert was older than she had expected from his dynamic reputation: a tall, lean, intense man who was immediately intimidating. She was pleased to find that the Detective Sergeant Hook who was going to take notes on this conversation was a pleasant, burly figure who seemed anxious only to reassure her about what was to come.

Lucy took them into the drawing room and sat them down on the leather Chesterfield sofa. They looked at the oil paintings on the wall and at the silver in her cabinet; probably it was their habit to observe everything, but she found the way they took in every detail of their surroundings rather unnerving. 'I collect silver,' she explained with a nervous laugh. 'I think the insurance is fully paid up and we updated the security system last year.'

Lambert gave her a grim smile. 'We aren't here to check on your valuables, Mrs Dimmock. We are concerned with a much greater crime than burglary.'

Lucy told herself to stop being overawed like an impressionable schoolgirl and behave like the shrewd businesswoman she was. 'I obviously want to help in any way I can. But I shall be surprised if I can add anything to what Jason told you on Tuesday night. I'm sure he told you as much or more than I can. He pulled himself together faster than the rest of us – we were all in shock at the time.'

'One person wasn't. One person sitting very near to Mr Cullis knew exactly what was going to happen to him.'

She looked into the long, grave face and decided that she did not much like the man. 'Well, it wasn't me, Mr Lambert!' She looked at Hook and found his attention upon his notebook. 'That's a formal denial, if you need one.'

Hook looked up at her and gave her a friendly smile. 'We shall be interviewing everyone who was at that table, Mrs Dimmock, and getting them to sign statements in due course. It's part of the routine. Perhaps someone will confess. As no one has done that so far, I expect everyone will deny committing the crime, just as you have. As DCS Lambert has said, it is almost certain that one of the people who sat with you will be lying, because we think Mr Cullis's killer was at that table. It's a disturbing thought for you, but one you can best dispel by being totally honest with us this morning.'

'I've no intention of being anything but honest.'

'Mrs Dimmock, how well did you know Mr Cullis?' Lambert had the air of a man impatient with preliminaries.

'I'd met him on social occasions. I'd never worked with him, like most of the other people at the table.' She looked him boldly in the face.

'That doesn't really tell us how well you knew him, does it? Did you see him once a year? Two or three times a year? A dozen times a year? Did you know him just as your husband's boss, or was there a closer acquaintance than that? Was there a real friendship between the two of you? Were you on first name terms?'

Lucy forced herself to smile. They had moved straight on to dangerous ground, but she told herself that she had expected that and prepared for it. 'I met him as Jason's boss, but he was a friendly and informal man, so we were soon on first-name terms. I suppose I must have known Richard and his wife for about three years.' It was more or less what she had planned to tell them, though she hadn't expected to be challenged so directly about it.

She waited for a reaction, but Lambert merely nodded, with his head a little on one side, as if he expected more. She knew they would be talking to other people, so she must give them enough to be convincing and yet pick her way carefully. 'We were certainly on first-name terms. I suppose we saw each other on average four or five times a year, but at irregular intervals, mostly in connection with company gatherings. The research scientists who work in the labs are quite a small group, so they and their wives get to know each other fairly well.'

Lambert studied her with no hint of embarrassment. Thirty years of experience rather than anything specific in her tone or movement told him that this woman was holding something back, was proceeding with caution in answering a straightforward question. 'Did you and the Cullises see much of each other?'

Lucy smiled and relaxed a little. Here was an opportunity to divert attention from herself to another woman. 'Not lately. You may already know that Richard and Alison Cullis had their problems.' She smiled at the euphemism. 'I should be surprised if they'd done much entertaining at home over the last two or three years.'

'Mrs Cullis has already been very frank with us over the state of their relationship.' Lambert looked around again at the large, well-furnished room, with its low window which looked down a large lawn to a shrub border beyond it, where the autumn crimson and gold of maple leaves dominated the quiet scene. 'Mr Cullis hadn't been in this house recently, then?'

She smiled away the directness of his question, trying to convince him that she had nothing to hide, that he was probing areas which would prove quite irrelevant to his investigation. 'I think he was last here some years ago for some sort of business exchange with my husband. I think Richard visited most of the laboratory scientists at home after he had been appointed Director of Research and Development, to discuss their roles in the lab work. He could have seen them in his office, but I think he thought he'd find out more about his staff if he saw where they lived. But we have never entertained the Cullises here. All our meetings have been on what I suppose you would call neutral ground.'

'Thank you. I'm sorry if we seem unnecessarily inquisitive, but you will probably understand that we need to establish exactly what sort of relationship Mr Cullis had with everyone who was around that table on Tuesday night.'

She was glad she was able to smile. 'What you really mean is that we're all suspects.'

'If you like. We prefer to think in terms of eliminating people from our inquiry. Of people becoming non-suspects as a result of what they and other people tell us. The more honest people are, even about things they may find embarrassing, the more quickly we can complete that process.'

'That sounds perfectly logical to me. My problem is that I haven't anything useful to tell you, embarrassing or not.'

Lambert looked at her without blinking for what seemed to Lucy a very long time. 'Mrs Dimmock, who do you think killed Richard Cullis?'

She almost flared out in anger and told them that detection was their job, that she didn't know and didn't care and wasn't going to speculate. But she knew that it would not be wise to antagonize this man she now disliked, that this formidable, watchful presence would make an even more formidable enemy. Moreover, this was an opportunity to divert attention from what she was concealing to other aspects of the case, to other people who had had good reason to wish Richard Cullis off the scene. She said carefully, 'I'm sure several people who were sitting at that table on Tuesday night are glad he's gone.'

Lambert nodded, as if that was the reply he had expected. 'And why do you say that?'

She took a moment to think, feeling for the first time that she was controlling the direction of these exchanges. 'I don't know how much you know about Richard's lifestyle. It was – well, colourful.'

'You mean he was a womanizer.'

'Yes, I suppose I do. I've already told you that his marriage was struggling. I imagine that was the reason. I also think that men must make themselves a lot of enemies when they philander.' She was glad she had come up with that rather old-fashioned word: it seemed somehow to distance herself nicely from the man.

'Indeed. Cuckolded husbands are capable of violent re-actions, in our experience.'

Lambert responded with an old-fashioned word of his own, almost as if they were rallying across a net. For a moment of panic, Lucy saw Jason's thunderous, hate-filled face and thought that Lambert must know about them, must be taunting her with what he had learned. But the moment passed and she picked up the rally. 'You have far more experience of such things than I have, Mr Lambert. I bow to your superior knowledge.'

'Our knowledge is general, yours is more specific. Which of the people at that table had suffered from Richard Cullis's pursuit of women?'

'You would need to ask them yourselves.'

'Which we shall do. At the moment I'm asking you.'

'You should ask Priscilla Godwin. She wasn't speaking to Cullis during the meal. There was something between them. Hostility, I mean. Perhaps he'd had an affair with her and let her down. That's the sort of thing he did, I believe. But apart from one or two things my husband's told me, it's all hearsay. I've already told you that I didn't know Richard particularly well. I'm only speculating because you asked me to.'

She was almost coy, almost taunting them, now that the centre of interest had moved away from her. Lambert said suddenly, 'You say you didn't know him well, but I get the impression that you didn't particularly like him. Had you any particular reason for that?'

Lucy Dimmock paused for a moment, gathering her resources, wondering just how much she could afford to reveal. 'I didn't particularly like him or dislike him, Superintendent. I suppose that when I heard of his lifestyle, I felt for his wife, being a married woman myself. There may have been a certain female solidarity colouring my reactions. But I saw very little of Richard Cullis, so I can't say I was very passionate about my disapproval of him.'

She looked at the two men with her head tilted a little backwards, her black hair framing her intelligent, interested, face, making her wide dark eyes seem even larger. Despite her confidence, there was something curiously brittle about her, as if she were challenging them and expecting at any moment to be defeated. Lambert gave the briefest of nods to Hook, who said, 'I believe you are a university graduate, Mrs Dimmock.'

'I have a chemistry degree. I do not use it in my present work.'

'But you understand your husband's work at Gloucester Chemicals.'

'I retain enough from my university days to follow what he is about there, yes. We're lucky in that he can talk to me about his work.'

'So you have a knowledge of poisons?'

She understood now where this was going. For a moment, she wondered if she could disclaim all knowledge of what had killed Cullis. Then she decided she had gone too far for that. 'I know quite a lot about toxic substances, Sergeant Hook. As a matter of fact, it used to be a special interest of mine, some years ago.'

'You know about ricin, then.'

She smiled, perfectly at ease with herself and them now that she had determined what to say. 'The sensational assassination of Georgi Markov in 1978 ensured that everyone with an interest in poisons knows about ricin. There is no simple analytical test for it, I believe: you have to diagnose its presence from certain symptoms in the victim.' She paused, then let enlightenment glow on her face. 'Was it ricin that killed Richard Cullis?'

'That is the conclusion of the pathologists, yes. I think tests have become a little more sophisticated in the thirty years since Markov's death. But you would know more about that than either of us ignorant CID men, I'm sure.'

Hook gave her a wide, encouraging smile, and she divined in that moment that he was more dangerous to her than she had thought him to be. She beamed back at him. 'This is really quite exciting, isn't it? Professionally speaking, I mean. If someone who runs a secretarial agency may be allowed to have a professional interest in poisons.'

'You know that ricin is produced in the laboratories where your husband works.'

It was delivered as a statement, not a question, and she could hardly deny it, having confessed to discussing Jason's work with him at home. 'Yes, I do. I understand that government contracts demand some very dangerous substances are produced and stored in those laboratories.'

'So your husband would obviously have had access to ricin. What about you, Mrs Dimmock?'

She smiled at him, feeling the adrenalin raising her acuity, positively enjoying this little game she was playing with them. 'This is rather exciting, isn't it? You must forgive me, gentlemen: you've no doubt been involved in lots of murder investigations, but this is my first one. Jason doesn't often bring anything like that home, though he does have his own little experimental workshop in the attic of our house. But I suppose if we were in it together, I could have got him to supply me with ricin, couldn't I?'

Lambert was not smiling. He said tersely, 'Did you or did you not have access to this poison, Mrs Dimmock?'

'Not at home, no. But I have been into the laboratories to meet my husband there – not frequently, but often enough for me to have access, I suppose. Other people are going to tell you this, so there's no use me denying it. And as I've already indicated, I know enough about the subject to know exactly what I was looking for.' She nodded a couple of times to herself, as if checking on her facts. 'Perhaps I should now deny formally that I have ever had any contact with ricin.'

Lambert did not answer the bright smile with which she tried to convey the ridiculous nature of that idea. 'Someone who sat at that table with you on Tuesday night had ensured that Richard Cullis was going to die, probably by planting ricin in his food or drink. You appear to be telling us that in the day and a half since the man's death, you have had no thoughts as to who that might be.'

'No. I have thought about it. I have some knowledge of poisons, as you have already established. But apart from my husband, I do not have detailed knowledge of the lives of the people who sat with me. Still less do I know about their relationships with the man who was killed.'

'Yet you have already indicated that you thought Ms Godwin saw him as an enemy.'

Lucy paused, nodded, appeared to come to a decision. 'All right. I've heard certain rumours over the last few days, about an accusation by Priscilla of some sort of sexual harassment. I don't know how much substance there is in them. But I did see that the two of them were strained with each other: that they weren't even speaking, in fact. I merely reported that fact to you.'

'As a good citizen helping the police in a murder inquiry should. If you have any further thoughts on the people who dined with you, please ring this number immediately. Anything you tell us will be treated in confidence. Unless it proves to be evidence in a murder trial, it will never be revealed by us. Good morning to you, Mrs Dimmock.'

He placed the card on her coffee table and swept out with no more than a nod to her, leaving Bert Hook to thank her for her help.

Alison Cullis hadn't asked the priest to come to her house. But her Catholic upbringing had taught her what to do when she opened the door and found him on the step, and she did it automatically.

You took the priest into the best room in the house, the one reserved for important visitors. You sent any noisy children out of the building or, if the hour or the weather made this impossible, made sure that their anarchy was at the furthest possible point of the house from the man in the cassock. You told them to sit still and read, with the severest punishments threatened for any transgression, any fracturing of the rule of silence. Then you offered your honoured visitor refreshment: tea and cake if it was during the day; whisky, preferably Irish, if the priest came during the evening.

Life in that cramped terraced cottage was a distant memory for Alison Cullis. In the big detached house at Cheltenham, she had no children to banish. She also had much disillusionment about her own beliefs and the efficacy of a celibate clergy. But childhood habits are bred deep and die hard. She led her visitor into the little-used dining room at the front of her big detached house, took her best china from the cupboard, brewed a pot of tea, and slid ginger biscuits on to a plate. She did not welcome this visit, did not know what she was going to say to the priest, but she did all of these things without even thinking about them.

The man settling himself comfortably into the armchair immediately irritated her. 'This is a time of great sorrow, my child,' he said comfortably. It was the delivery rather than the sentiment which annoyed Alison: it was so obviously a standard opening, without emotion or any genuine feeling. Father Driscoll was into his sixties: he should do better than this, with the experience he must have had. She nodded, not trusting herself with words, noting against her will the food stains on the chest of the black cassock.

'Holy Mother Church will be a consolation to you in this time of grief.' The priest dunked his second ginger biscuit into his tea and nodded his certainty about that.

'There can't be a funeral yet. The police won't release the body.' Alison looked into the complacent face and wondered how to shock it into some genuine emotion. 'They say the defence counsel for the murderer has the right to a second, independent post-mortem if they request one. That's if they ever manage to decide who killed him.'

'You husband wasn't of our faith, but I'll be happy to arrange a service for him, when you require it. Ecumenism has led to a great relaxation in such things.' Father Driscoll spoke as if he regretted that.

'I shan't be having a service for Richard, Father. Your ministrations will not be required.'

'Ah, you shouldn't make such decisions in a time of grief, my child. Maybe when you've had time to get used to the idea of—'

'I'm not grieving, Father. I'm glad Richard's out of my life.'

For the first time, the priest showed real distress. 'That is a hard thing to hear you say, my child. It might indeed be sinful. Even in a time of stress like this, you should consider the welfare of your immortal soul.'

Alison found herself wondering why people in clerical garb allowed themselves the sort of clichés which would have been risible in politicians. 'I'm more concerned at the moment with my life on earth, Father Driscoll. What's left of it will be a lot happier without my late husband.'

'I'm sad to hear you speaking like this, Mrs Cullis. I haven't seen you at Mass in the last few weeks. And I have to say that—'

'Richard was a consistent and random adulterer. He did not even trouble to disguise the fact. He was a cruel, shallow, man. I am well rid of him.'

'Sure you mustn't be unchristian, Mrs Cullis.' The priest's Irish brogue came out when he was confused.

'I suppose that is how I am behaving. But you didn't have to live with him, Father Driscoll.'

'That I didn't, I know, Mrs Cullis. But you'd bound your-selves in the holy sacrament of matrimony, and I'm thinking that—'

'If Richard had lived, I'd have divorced him.' She was suddenly sick of the charade he was compelling upon her.

'Ah, ye say that now, Mrs Cullis, because you're upset. Sure it's understandable that you wouldn't be thinking straight in your grief. I'm hoping that when your mind's a little more at rest you won't be after telling people—'

'I'd have got rid of him through the law. He was a bastard, Father, if you'll excuse the language – I'm sure you've heard worse, in your time. I'd had enough. I was determined to be rid of him. This has saved me the trouble. So you see, I don't need your pity or the consolation of your religion.'

Alison wondered why she was telling him this, when she had denied such an intention to the police. It was the desire to shock him, she supposed, to have some revenge on the people like this who had cheated her out of so much of her life. She reached over and poured him more tea, noticing how brown and strong it was now, how steady her hand was as she held the pot.

She thrust the biscuits at Father Driscoll, was surprised when he took two more of them. She had thought he would have been embarrassed now, glad to make his escape from her house as quickly as he could. Instead, he dunked the biscuits in his tea and ate them silently. His ill-fitting false teeth slipped a little as he raised the elegant china cup, causing him to slurp a little as he drank. The sound made her for the first time sorry for the isolation of this forlorn figure, whose offers of comfort she had rejected. It wasn't entirely his fault that he was out of his depth. The religion with which he grew up in Ireland had been overtaken by the ways and thoughts of the twenty-first century.

Father Driscoll finished his tea before he spoke. He forced himself to raise his eyes from the table to this troubled woman before he said, 'Another one of our seven sacraments still has a great deal to offer you, my child. That is the sacrament of penance. You may be absolved from any sin you have committed, however grave it might be, provided that you are truly repentant. And the secrets of the confessional remain with the priest. There is no power on earth which can force him to divulge them. I urge you to give some thought to that, my child.'

The shabby, ageing figure acquired a strange dignity with his determined recital of dogma. It was only when she had shown him out of her house that Alison realized that Father Driscoll seemed to have decided that she had murdered her husband.

Sixteen

B en Paddon found a morning spent working in the laboratories surprisingly therapeutic. He had feared going in
there after Tuesday night's murder. He had thought that
everyone's eyes would be upon him, that it would only be a
matter of time before his position as an All God's Creatures
infiltrator and enemy of Richard Cullis would be exposed.
After that, his arrest could surely only be a matter of time.

Instead, he found that other people as well as him were
responding to the rhythms of work, to the triumph of routine
over outlandish speculation. Most people in the labs were
not golfers and had thus not been at the Belmont dinner
where their boss had died. But there were others who had
sat down to that fatal meal: Jason Dimmock and Debbie
Young and Priscilla Godwin were all questioned excitedly
by those who had not been there. The other three all seemed
calmer than him about the excitement they met among their
colleagues, but their coolness was in itself a help to Ben,
who found himself taking his cue from the composure of
the other three.

All four had made brief statements to the police about what
they had seen and heard at Belmont on Tuesday night. Ben
had kept his replies non-committal and the junior police officer
who had taken the statement had merely recorded them, not
pressed him for detail as he had expected. It was likely that
more senior officers would need to question him in due course,
the young woman explained, and Ben had nodded sagely, as
if he took part in murder inquiries every month.

So far, these more senior officers had not appeared. Ben
wondered whom they were questioning and what they were
discovering about him. The factory wasn't buzzing with CID
activity as he had expected. He waited, watched his colleagues,
and speculated about what they were thinking. This was the

period of the phoney war, when you waited for the real hostilities to begin.

He knew that Jason Dimmock had talked to the man in charge of the case immediately after Cullis's death. At coffee break, Jason announced that he thought the police were probably talking to his wife at that very moment: he seemed unnaturally relaxed about it, to Ben's mind, behaving as if the whole thing was rather a joke. Ben got nothing out of Priscilla Godwin, who replied to people mainly in monosyllables; she seemed preoccupied but calm. Debbie Young, on the other hand, was as talkative as ever, and positively cheerful about the demise of their chief. The behaviour of the other three helped to clear Ben's mind, as did the mundane but demanding piece of research he was conducting.

This involved the recording of detailed figures about the behaviour at different temperatures and over several hours of a new chemical compound. It wasn't difficult, because he knew exactly what he was doing and how to do it. But the task required his full concentration, which he soon decided was a good thing.

He noted down his final figures at midday, then found tension building within him as he waited for people to go to lunch. They departed in ones and twos, and seemed to him to take a very long time over it. It was twenty to one before he was left on his own and could slip into the little office at the end of the long, low laboratory room. He knew the number, but he still checked it nervously in his diary before he made the call.

Ben hardly recognized Scott Kennedy's voice at first: it was high-pitched because of his nervousness. 'They said I could go to prison,' he said.

Ben didn't want to know about that, didn't really care what happened to Kennedy. But he said, 'I expect they were trying to scare you. To get all the information they could out of you. They work like that, the police. Was Tim Cohen there?'

'Yes. He helped me, I suppose. They must have been more careful, when they saw I had a lawyer with me. It didn't seem like that at the time, though.'

Ben was suddenly impatient with this brash, rather silly, young man. He had always thought that kidnapping Cullis was an act of bravado which couldn't bring any real benefits to animal rights. Kennedy had wanted the publicity and the personal glory, without any consideration of the implications of his actions for others who were pursuing more subtle paths. This was the man who had had been foolish enough to brag to Cullis that All God's Creatures had a man in his laboratories. Ben said, 'Did they ask you anything about this place?'

'They asked me about us having someone under cover. I told them I didn't know anything about that and they didn't pursue it.'

That was contradicting his original boast, but he was probably speaking the truth. The police would have been round here double quick if Ben's cover had been blown. He said, 'All right. If they come back to you, don't give them anything you don't have to. In fact, don't give them anything at all.'

'You're safe with me, Mr Paddon. Don't worry about that.'

It was the first time Kennedy, who was only three or four years younger than Ben, had ever called him 'Mister'. Perhaps he thought he was giving the respect due to a murderer.

Ben had no time to think about that. He had scarcely put the phone down when it rang again, making him jump with the shock. The calm female voice on the other end of the line told him that Chief Superintendent Lambert would like to see him as soon as possible.

Paul Young said, 'I've a job interview tomorrow. I don't expect to be out of work for long. Not at all, if things go well. I'm still serving notice at Gloucester Chemicals, but they've said I needn't go in for the last few days, to enable me to secure other employment.'

He wondered why he was telling the two men in plain clothes this. Was it just nervousness, or was he anxious to emphasize the severance of his ties with the place where Richard Cullis had worked?

John Lambert, however, saw the chance to go straight for an area he wanted to explore. They were sitting in the big, well-fitted kitchen of the Youngs' modern house; he thought the man looked apprehensive. 'I gathered from the employee files that you were leaving the company. Was that your own decision?'

'I thought those files were confidential.' The words were

out before he could check them: it had shaken him to know that they had been studying such things.

Lambert gave him the reassuring smile he normally retained for the anxious elderly. 'They are, in the normal way of things, Mr Young. Murder opens doors which would in other circumstances remain firmly shut. We shan't reveal any of the personal information involved.'

Paul Young tried to lighten the atmosphere with an exaggerated grin of his own. 'That's all right, then. No, I didn't leave of my own accord. Not to put too fine a point on it, I was sacked. I was told very politely that my work wasn't up to scratch and that I must be on my way.'

'I see. I'm sorry about that. I also noticed in your file that you are very well qualified.'

Paul wondered if they were trying to mollify him. 'I have a 2.1 degree in chemistry, if that's what you mean. I've never used it directly in my working life. Perhaps I should have done. My wife's done well enough as a research scientist.' It came out almost as if he was jealous of Debbie, which he had never intended.

'You didn't work in the laboratories at Gloucester Chemicals?'

'No. I was a sales rep. They thought when I was appointed that my technical knowledge of the products would be an advantage in sales, but it didn't work out that way.'

'Who took the decision to get rid of you?'

It was direct, even aggressive. But they'd already indicated to him that they didn't pull punches in a murder investigation. No use trying to disguise things, then. 'It was Richard Cullis. Oh, he said it was a joint decision, that he was sorry things hadn't worked out, but I'm quite sure he was the motivating force.'

It was the shorter, burlier man with the weather-beaten face, who had been introduced as Detective Sergeant Hook, who now spoke unexpectedly. 'You must have resented that, Mr Young.'

'It was a bit of a shock at the time. But to be perfectly honest, it's a relief, now that I've got used to the idea. I don't think I have the qualities to be a good salesman. I'm not applying for sales posts now.'

He half-hoped they would ask him about what sort of work

he was now pursuing and thus allow a diversion from the
event which had brought them here. Instead, Hook nodded
thoughtfully, apparently accepting what he had said. 'No bitterness against Mr Cullis, then.'

Paul frowned. 'I'm trying to be as honest as I can. I knew
Richard fairly well, because my wife was working at
Gloucester Chemicals before he was put in charge of research.
We've known him for years: he may even have helped to get
me appointed to the sales job. I'm not sure about that, but I
can't say I ever liked the man or that we were ever very close.
We were different types, with different interests.'

'Apart from golf.'

'Apart from golf, yes. But we've never even played a lot
of that together. I'm not really much of a golfer – I almost
didn't play on Tuesday, as a matter of fact. But Debbie thought
I should show the flag, not hide away because I'd been made
redundant.'

'I see. For the last few years, your wife has worked in the
laboratories at Gloucester Chemicals under Mr Cullis's direction, hasn't she?'

This harmless-looking figure had zoomed in on to the very
subject he had been determined to avoid. 'She has, yes.'

'And how did she get on with Mr Cullis?'

Paul made himself pause before he replied. This needed
careful handling. He wondered exactly how much his wife's
file would have told them about her career. 'I never saw them
actually working together, so I couldn't tell you much about
their working relationship. Socially, I think Debbie felt as I
did about Richard. No open hostility, but she didn't approve
of the way he treated his wife and she wasn't particularly
close to the man.' Paul tried to develop this in an innocent
way. 'You must understand that we have two boisterous children who occupy much of our lives. Richard – well, he had
a very different lifestyle.'

Lambert said drily, 'So we have been informed. But you
surprise me when you say you don't know much about your
wife's working relationship with Mr Cullis. Surely she must
have talked at home about her working day? Particularly as
you have the scientific background to follow any of the issues
involved.'

Paul felt himself reddening. 'We don't discuss work much

at home. We're both happy to switch off – me in particular, since work hasn't been going very well over the last year or two. And we have the children to keep us busy. We really don't have much time to talk about work.'

It was too much talk to cover a trivial omission. Lambert made a mental note to explore the matter with the lady in question in due course. 'I see. You have a chemistry degree. How much do you know about poisons?'

'Enough. More than the average layman. Less than the people who work all day in the research and development of drugs.' It was the answer he had prepared and he delivered it easily enough.

Lambert smiled, digesting the idea. 'Enough, you say. What exactly would you mean by that?'

'I know about ricin.'

'I see. Very frank of you, that. I think you'll find that frankness is much the best policy. Do you also know who used ricin?'

'I meant I know all about its deadliness as a poison. About how difficult it is to counteract, or even detect. Most chemists with any sense of curiosity are aware of ricin, because of the case of Georgi Markov. I was only a child at the time, but I still remember the excitement that case caused.'

'So I expect you knew it was available in the laboratories where your wife worked.'

'Debbie had nothing to do with this, Superintendent Lambert.'

He had suddenly become tight-lipped and tense. This was a welcome development to Lambert, who had long since learned that all successful CID men must be predators. 'I didn't suggest that she had, Mr Young. All that I know is that it is almost certainly one of the people sitting with you at that table on Tuesday night who committed a premeditated murder. If you're now telling me that you can prove that person wasn't your wife, I shall be very grateful for the information.'

'I can't do that. I just know that Debbie wouldn't do such a thing. Couldn't do such a thing.' He sought desperately for words which would convince them, would convince himself.

'Your conviction about that is admirable. But you will understand that we must be sceptical, until we have some definite proof.'

'I can't give you that. But I know she didn't do it.'

Hook smiled at him, relaxing the tension. 'They say that poisoning is a woman's crime, Mr Young. There is a certain amount of statistical evidence to support the view.'

'Debbie didn't do it,' Paul said desperately. 'I could have got hold of ricin as easily as she could. I go into the laboratories sometimes. Fairly often, really.'

'And did you do that?'

'No. But I'm just saying, I could have done. Or Debbie could have given me the ricin to administer.'

'Which would have made her an accessory to murder. Is that what happened, Paul?'

'No, of course it isn't. Debbie had nothing to do with this death.' He glared at Hook, trying to convince him. It was only as an afterthought that he added, 'And neither did I!'

Lambert had been studying the vehemence with which he defended his wife. It might mean merely that he loved her and found it inconceivable that she could commit murder, or it might mean something very different. 'So who did murder Richard Cullis, Mr Young?'

Paul realized for the first time that he was breathing deeply and irregularly. 'I don't know. Priscilla Godwin, perhaps, if you think it's a woman. From what I've heard, she had good reason. But I'm not accusing her: I'm just telling you that it wasn't Debbie.'

Lambert studied him for a moment. Then he stood up abruptly. 'I hope you secure suitable new employment quickly, Mr Young. Please don't leave the area without notifying us about your movements.'

Lambert felt a deep weariness at the end of a long day. He was getting old: the days when he could work for sixteen hours without noticing the passage of time were gone now. He drove the old Vauxhall Senator which he stubbornly refused to relinquish into the garage and paused to smell the roses which were still flowering freely on his way to the door of the house. The scent was best at this time, on the edge of darkness.

Christine opened the door before he could insert his key. 'Jacky's here,' she said softly.

John Lambert's first feeling was of pleasure that his elder daughter should be here. The bond went back to those distant days which still felt to him very near, when he had dandled her on his knee and coaxed her into her first words. Then a more selfish feeling took over, as his weariness reminded him that he had been looking forward to a quiet meal and drowsy hours in front of the television, not breezy attempts to cheer up a woman who had recently endured a bruising divorce. There were only so many times that you could remind yourself and your daughter that it could have been worse, that at least there were no children involved.

Christine knew her husband well – too well, John often thought ruefully. She waited for his mental sigh, then spoke in short, rapid sentences, needing to get all her information out without interruption. 'She rang at lunchtime. She was quite excited. She told me there's a new man. He's here with her tonight. I suggested they came for dinner.'

Lambert made quite a business of putting his short coat upon a hanger in the cloaks cupboard, giving himself time to think. 'What does he do?'

Christine grinned indulgently. 'Shouldn't you be asking whether I like him first?'

He grinned back, enjoying the moment of mutual self-knowledge they could not have savoured in their younger days. 'You'll tell me he seems quite nice, which will mean absolutely nothing. You'll be determined to see the best in him, for your daughter's sake.'

She didn't trouble to deny it. 'If that's your attitude, you grumpy sod, you'd better come and meet him! For your information, I think he's a solicitor.'

'Not a bloody lawyer!' Lambert displayed the policeman's ritual horror of the species.

His outrage lacked impact, since the whole of this brief exchange had been conducted in hushed tones. Now Lambert braced himself mentally and physically and went into the sitting room with his shoulders thrown back and a determined smile. Jacky was already standing; the slim man beside her wore collar and tie and a well-fitting suit. She gave her father the bright, brittle smile of a daughter bringing a man forward for her father's scrutiny. 'This is Tim Cohen, Dad.'

They shook hands. Lambert caught a whiff of aftershave.

The man was clean-shaven and his expensive shirt and tie were impeccably clean. You had to be thankful for such things nowadays, John told himself, though he had known hundreds of clean villains and a few dirty saints in his time. Cohen had a short, well-trimmed beard, which was unusual among lawyers. Not a conformist then, which was no doubt an excellent thing as far as Jacky was concerned. He was a few years younger than her, Lambert's expert eye told him.

'We're having fish pie,' said Christine as they moved towards the dining room a few moments later. She fixed her husband with a basilisk eye for an instant, warning him not to query the change of menu.

'Tim's a vegetarian,' said Jacky rather too quickly.

'Not a vegan or anything too severe,' said Cohen nervously. 'I'm always willing to enjoy fish.'

'I like fish pie,' said John Lambert determinedly.

They disposed of the weather quickly, congratulating themselves on the calm, mild October days and the absence as yet of much autumn colour. Then Tim spoke as if making a confession. 'I was in the station at Oldford today. We do quite a bit of legal-aid work. I saw Detective Inspector Rushton and a detective sergeant, whose name I forget.'

'Probably Bert Hook. I expect they made you very welcome.'

For the first time, the two women felt the air crackling above the dining table. Christine said, 'No shop at meal times. It's one of the rules of the house.'

Lambert grinned apologetically at Cohen, making them for a moment two helpless males conforming to the domestic rules of the distaff. Rushton had actually given him a brief report on the meeting with Scott Kennedy. Cohen's vegetarianism fell into place now: he must be an All God's Creatures supporter. He tried not to feel a prejudice against this connection, telling himself that it was nice to meet a lawyer with moral convictions.

He was aware of Jacky watching him, measuring his reactions to this new presence in her life. He watched her too, wondering just how serious the relationship was, whether Jacky had taken the initiative in bringing Tim Cohen here or whether it was Christine's anxiety to see the new man which had brought this tension to his evening meal. Was Jacky, even at what seemed to him her tender age, flattered by the attentions of a younger man? How much was she just welcoming male attention after the shattered confidence which always follows a rejection by a long-term partner? How well did she actually know Cohen? How much of this new liaison depended on the strength of pure sexual attraction?

He wondered about these things, but came up with few answers. After thirty years of analysing people and their motives, he was normally adept at such insights, but tonight he discovered little. He was much too close to the woman he was studying to be objective.

Cohen excused himself at the end of the meal and went to the bathroom. Lambert insisted on going to his bedroom to change into the more comfortable clothes he would have donned as soon as he came into the house had it not been for this unheralded visitor. Thinking that the bathroom would now be empty, he tried the door on his way back to join the company.

The door opened, but the room was not empty. Lambert said, 'I'm sorry. That lock doesn't always catch. I really must get round to . . . '

Cohen looked up from the washbasin with a face full of guilt. 'I was nervous. I don't usually—'

'Not here you don't.' Lambert's voice was harsh with shock. He stared at the banknote in Cohen's hand, at the few grains of white powder which were still on the porcelain at the edge of the washbasin.

'It's only a snort of coke. You must understand that the evening has been something of an ordeal for me, Mr Lambert, that—'

'I should arrest you, here and now.' They stared at each other for a moment, with Lambert's shock and anger matched by the fear and defiance in the younger man's face. 'Have you offered drugs to my daughter? I advise you not to lie to me about this.'

'No. It's a social habit, that's all. Everyone in my circle—'

'You're a fool, Mr Cohen. I shall say nothing downstairs, for the moment. Get out of my house as quickly as politeness allows. Kick this bloody "social habit". If you ever introduce my daughter to it, you can forget a career in the law. Now get out!'

Lambert did not move until he heard the sound of Cohen's voice with the two women downstairs, telling them that he had to go, that he hadn't realized how the time had passed. He was doing it too well, almost glibly. What other deceptions had he practised upon Jacky?

When Lambert finally moved, he washed the tiny vestiges of cocaine away three times, wondering what he should do about Jacky, wondering whether there could even be room for diplomacy in a situation like this.

Seventeen

B en Paddon, who was normally a sound sleeper, spent a very disturbed night. He woke after only an hour from a rest beset by confusing dreams. For a long time, he could not sleep again. At five o'clock, his fevered mind was rehearsing for the tenth time what he would say to the CID officers he was to see in the morning. At half-past seven, the alarm he normally switched off before it sounded startled him back into the consciousness he had lost less than an hour earlier.

The staff files in the hands of the CID revealed that Paddon had been working at Gloucester Chemicals for two years and was twenty-seven. To Lambert he looked younger than that, an impression which was reinforced by his obvious apprehension and his rather gauche manner. He was tall and gangling, already developing the slight stoop which was the bane of tall men; he strode cautiously across the small, low-ceilinged room, as if he feared to damage things by more rapid movement. His dark hair would have benefited from a skilled trim; he had a nose which seemed longer because of its thinness and restless blue eyes behind large-lensed glasses.

He had said that he would rather see them in his flat than at work. Lambert and Hook looked round the combined living room and kitchen with their normal swift, unembarrassed observation. There were the standard television and DVD player and a hi-fi tower which was flanked by a large collection of CDs and DVDs, classical and popular. There were family photographs on top of a bookcase which threatened to overflow with paperbacks, but the walls were crowded with pictures of modern landscapes, African and Asian as well as British. Photographs were mixed with paintings, with mountain scenes prominent. There were pictures of Kilimanjaro and of the great Himalayan panoramas alongside Snowdonia and the Western Highlands. Some of the more intimate pictures had animals within the scenes; there were tigers and cougars as well as native birds and red squirrels. There was scarcely a foot of wall without a picture. A print of Landseer's *Monarch of the Glen* struck an inappropriate Victorian note among the more modern pictures.

They took him through his unremarkable statement about the sudden collapse and death of Richard Cullis, confirming his determined assertion that both had been a complete surprise to him. Then Lambert said unexpectedly, 'Good golfer, are you, Mr Paddon?'

'Not bad. I'm better than people expect me to be, I think. I'm twelve handicap and I usually manage to get somewhere near it.' He smiled deprecatingly as his scientist's objectivity led him into this un-English lack of modesty. 'People tell me I could be quite good, if I played more.'

'Yes. One or two of the other statements indicate that people were surprised to find you playing on Tuesday.'

'I was a little surprised myself, as a matter of fact. But Richard was anxious to have everyone out who played at all. It was the first company golf day and he wanted it to be a bonding exercise.' There was a hint of derision in the way he pronounced the phrase.

'So you didn't play just to have the opportunity of getting close to Mr Cullis?'

Ben felt a sudden stab of alarm at the way the older man had led him into this. 'So that I could poison his food, you mean? No. The impetus came from Richard, as I said, not from me. In any case, I had plenty of opportunities at work, if I had intended him any serious harm.'

'But few of them with a group of other suspects conveniently gathered around him, I should think.' Lambert found unexpectedly that he rather liked this loose-jointed young man who looked so vulnerable but so far seemed quite able to hold his own in their exchanges. 'Which of those people do you think killed your boss, Mr Paddon?'

'I can't help you there, I'm afraid. But I can tell you one thing I did notice: no one seemed to be riven with grief. The death was a shock, of course, but after the initial consternation, no one seemed to be desolated. Richard Cullis had a lot of enemies around that table, you know – sorry, I'm sure you do know that, by this time. It's your business to find out these things, isn't it?' He smiled deprecatingly at Hook, who was taking notes.

Lambert's smile was much grimmer. 'We're building up a picture of the dead man and his friends and enemies, yes, Mr Paddon. We have to do that from scratch, because a murder victim can never speak for himself. We need to know about your own relationship with him.'

'Almost purely professional, Superintendent. I've been at Gloucester Chemicals for four years and Richard was my boss for the last two of them. He encouraged me in my work and congratulated me upon my small successes. I knew him through our almost daily exchanges in the labs. I hardly ever saw him after work, except on company occasions. The golf day at Belmont was really one of those.' This was what he had planned to say and it came out quite well, he thought. That was probably because it was true. Ben was sure that he'd read somewhere that the best liars always told the truth whenever it couldn't hurt them.

'Tell us about your work in the laboratories, Mr Paddon.'

'I do the work I'm given. It's mostly experimental, but that isn't as exciting as it sounds. You go down a lot of blind alleys, reaching the conclusions you expect to find, but that's because all new drugs have to be thoroughly tested before they can be released for use on the public.'

'This includes tests on animals?'

'It does, yes. We are careful to use animals as infrequently as possible and to ensure that the minimum of discomfort is occasioned, but the public has to be safeguarded: occasionally the use of the animals is the only way to ensure that.' It was the company line; he had mouthed it at interview to secure his job in the first place, and often enough since to keep up his front with Cullis and his colleagues.

Perhaps he had delivered it a little too glibly, for instead of accepting it and moving on, Hook said, 'You don't find the use of helpless animals difficult, Mr Paddon? I think I should.'

Ben smiled the practised, superior smile of the specialist. 'I think all of us who work with small mammals find it difficult, DS Hook. The difference between scientists and the often very sentimental public we serve is that we accept the inevitability of a certain amount of animal testing. I think that there are certain small sections of our laboratory work which none of us enjoys, but we get on with it because there is as yet no reasonable alternative.'

It sounded very stiff and mechanical, but Lambert decided that Paddon had probably delivered the same thoughts very often before. Animal experiments had had a lot of publicity and no doubt anyone involved in them was often called upon to state his case. 'We don't indulge in idle gossip, Mr Paddon. But when someone questioned in connection with a murder case tells us that the victim had lots of enemies, we have to follow that up. You said that no one round that table on Tuesday night was very upset at the sudden death of the man presiding over the occasion.'

'I said that that was my impression, Superintendent.'

'Indeed. And you showed commendable honesty in doing so. I should think the impressions of a scientist are more valid in such circumstances than those of less precise people.' Lambert allowed himself his sliver of irony at the expense of this earnest young man, then spoke more sternly. 'One of those people killed Richard Cullis. Which of them do you think it was?'

Ben, in his relief at moving away from the subject of animals, found himself beset by an overwhelming urge to direct suspicion away from himself. 'I don't know: I should make that quite clear to you. But what I do know is that the women there all had good reason to dislike him.'

His pale, unlined face suddenly had the eagerness of the gossip-monger. Lambert, who had picked up much useful information in his early CID days from elderly ladies observing from behind lace curtains, prompted him eagerly enough. 'We had better have your thoughts on this, Mr Paddon, in the interests of furthering our inquiry.'

'Well, there's Priscilla Godwin, for a start.' Ben stopped for a moment, feeling guilty because Priscilla had been unexpectedly pleasant to him on the course during the golf day, had even told him to call her Pris. And he liked her, perhaps more than just liked her, now that she had given him a little encouragement. But you had to safeguard yourself: that had become a watchword to him, during the years he had spent concealing his All God's Creatures background from everyone who worked with him. Ben put his elbows upon his kitchen table and leaned forward a little. 'She'd been assaulted by Richard, you know – perhaps even raped – a week or two before the golf day.'

'We do know that there had been a serious incident, yes, Ben.'

He felt a little deflated, as well as disloyal to the woman he liked, and moved on quickly. 'Debbie Young has never liked him, you know.' He looked into their non-committal faces. 'She was passed over for promotion when Richard got the job. And last month Richard was the man behind the decision to make her husband redundant: I'm sure she didn't like that.'

Ben waited for the questioning that did not come and was drawn on. 'Lucy Dimmock didn't seem to like or dislike Richard.' He seemed disappointed by that. Then his face brightened. 'But I'm pretty sure that she used to be more friendly towards him at one time. And Alison Cullis didn't like her husband: that was patently obvious at the dinner, when he expected her to be the company wife and she wouldn't play his game. But to tell you the truth, I'm surprised they were still married. From what I've heard, Richard had given her ample grounds for divorce, over the last few years.'

Bert Hook leaned forward, encouraging the almost spinsterish figure on the other side of the table. 'This is all valuable information for us. As Chief Superintendent Lambert told you, we're trying to build up a picture of a dead man who cannot speak for himself. From what you say, the men at that table were not overfond of Richard Cullis, either.'

'They certainly weren't. Paul Young had just been sacked by him, in effect. I'd have felt pretty murderous myself, in his shoes.'

'I expect most of us would.'

'And Jason Dimmock has been very off with him over the last few months. They used to be quite close, but they've hardly spoken, outside the needs of the work in the labs.'

'And why would that be, Ben?' Bert Hook's face was filled with an innocent curiosity.

Ben was intelligent enough to know that the question could not be as innocent as Hook made it sound, but he was filled with the self-release of diverting their questions away from himself. 'I don't know, but it's not my imagination. There's been something between them: I imagine they must have had a major row about something – perhaps something to do with work.'

Bert Hook nodded, apparently accepting and valuing everything Ben said. Then he said, as if it were an afterthought, 'And then there's you, of course. I don't suppose you liked him any more than the others at that table on Tuesday night.' He nodded slowly, leaving the thought hanging in the air.

'I'd nothing personal against him.' That was maintaining the policy of giving them the truth whenever it was possible. 'I've already told you that we weren't close friends, but we had a good working relationship. I'd no reason to wish him dead. I didn't hate Richard as some of the others round that table did.'

Hook nodded, made a note, gave him a smile which Ben thought was encouraging. They took him through the routine stuff about knowledge of poisons and access to them, which he handled well because he'd expected it. He managed to convey that everyone at the fatal meal had knowledge of ricin and either direct or indirect access to it. Even the spouses of the people employed there came in and out of the laboratories on occasions. He intimated to them that he had reluctantly accepted that one of those people must have killed the Director of Research and Development at Gloucester Chemicals.

He made himself a cup of coffee when the CID men had gone and reviewed the interview. It had gone rather well, he decided. He seemed to have created a good impression with them, without giving away anything he had wished to conceal. Perhaps the years of living a lie as he worked in the labs and waited his chance had prepared him for this.

If you found yourself a patch of sun, it was still warm enough to sit outside at lunchtime, even in late October. They watched the waters of the Wye moving serenely below the patio outside the pub, eddying pleasantly as they reached the bend in the river a hundred yards below them.

Jason Dimmock congratulated himself openly on his decision to bring his wife out for lunch. 'There won't be many more days like this before the winter.' He took a pull at his pint of bitter, savoured the taste of it on his tongue and its passage through his throat. He glanced up at the motionless oak tree on the bank of the river, with its leaves still virtually untouched by autumn decay, then at the attractive, intelligent features of his wife in their frame of black hair. 'It's good to get away from the others for a little while, on a day like this.'

Lucy smiled down at the table, saying nothing until the waiter had deposited their food and left. 'We're lucky with the day and this is a nice spot. I suspect you would have abstracted me from the works cafeteria whatever the weather.'

Jason smiled wryly and took another drink. 'How well you know me, Lucy Dimmock. Other men tell women that their wives don't understand them. My problem is that my wife understands me all too well!'

'And just you remember it!' said Lucy heartily.

'Did Cullis tell you that his wife didn't understand him?'

The words were out before he could suppress them, almost before he knew the thought had been formed. He regretted it immediately and stared for a second at his wife and then, unable to meet her eyes, at the river. She said with immense weariness, 'You can't let it go, can you? Even with his corpse cut up and stowed away in the morgue, you can't let it go.'

'I'm sorry.'

'It's not a matter of being sorry. It's a matter of letting go. I've told you a hundred times that it was all over months ago. The truth is that it was for me, but not for you.'

'We have to be careful, that's all. We must be suspects. However innocent we may be, it's important that we don't make mistakes, in the circumstances.'

'The circumstances being that I had an affair with him and you were and still are insanely jealous about it.'

'All right. As a summary, I accept that. I don't mean to be jealous, but it still comes out and surprises me. I still don't know how—'

'Leave it! If you don't want to attract police attention, for God's sake leave it!' Lucy's voice was harsh with strain.

'You're right. Of course you're right. I know you're right. Intellectually, I accept everything you say. It's just that emotion still breaks out, sometimes when I least expect it and least want it.' He took a bite of his sandwich, found it like ashes in his mouth. 'They'll want to speak to me again, you know, the police. I want to prepare myself for it.'

She gave him a look which mixed anger with concern. 'You mean you want to know what I said to them, don't you? That's why you brought me out here. That's the reason for this charade.'

'I do need to know. It's for both our sakes. I mustn't contradict anything you said when they speak to me. That's the way they work, exploiting discrepancies between what people say to them. They won't believe anything we say, if they catch us out in one thing.'

She wanted to ask him bitchily how he came to be such an expert in police methods. But she controlled himself and said between clenched teeth, 'You needn't worry. I didn't tell them anything. I was just your dutiful wife, who was shocked and bewildered by this murder. I played what you men would call a straight bat.'

He didn't think he'd ever used that particular cliché to her. The part of his brain which he wanted to suppress asked if it was Richard Cullis who had used that phrase. He reached out and placed his hand on top of hers. 'It's a bad time, this, Lucy. But we'll come through it all right, won't we? With him out of the way, we can get on with our lives.'

He sounded as if he was trying to convince himself, she thought.

Soon it was time to return to work. They did not speak much on the way back into Gloucester. Though the October sun blazed down with uncharacteristic warmth on postcard scenes, their minds were occupied with darker thoughts. Each of the pair was reviewing the other's motive for murder, trying to answer the question neither of them dared to put into words.

Eighteen

The managing director of Gloucester Chemicals was an American with English habits. He wore a dark blue Savile Row suit and shirt and a dark red silk tie. He was polite with all of his staff in public and he listened carefully to their concerns in private.

Yet no one underestimated his clear-sightedness, his willingness to make even unpopular decisions swiftly, his ruthlessness in the pursuit of his goals. Marvin Hestler had been brought in to increase the international sales and presence of a company which had good products but which was only a sprightly minnow in the big pool of the major drug companies. Sales had trebled since his arrival in Gloucester three years ago and profits had quadrupled. The share price was now quoted in the FT top hundred on the London Stock Exchange. The board of Gloucester Chemicals was concerned not with the survival of the company, as it had been a decade earlier, but with protecting itself from takeover bids from the world players in the drugs field like Glaxo and Pfizer.

One of the consequences of this success was that the death of the company's Director of Research and Development made news in the financial press. This could have been an irritation for the managing director, but he shrugged it off with characteristic positivism: the paragraphs in the financial sections of the broadsheets were further evidence that the company had arrived.

This was the reaction which Marvin Hestler conveyed to Debbie Young as she sat in his office. The room had prints of Braque and Modigliani; a portrait of the young Marie Curie was balanced by the standard Annigoni depiction of the young Elizabeth II, hung here as an assurance that this presence from across the pond was not about to jettison all things British.

The room had a massive desk, but Hestler had come round

it to sit in an armchair opposite the woman he had summoned to discuss the impact of this death upon the company. They had a tea tray with Worcester china on it on the low table between them; in the subtle ordinances of industrial procedure, this meant that this was an important meeting and Mrs Young a welcome presence here. The MD poured the tea carefully and offered Debbie the shortbread which he eschewed himself.

'Richard will be a loss to us, there's no doubt of that.' Marvin knew the ritual which must be gone through, however truncated: in Britain, as in most other places in the world, you did not speak ill of the recently dead.

'He knew what he was doing,' said Debbie Young cautiously.

Hestler divined that this muted phrase meant that she hadn't liked her late boss. Nothing wrong with that. You didn't have to like people to work efficiently with them: that was one of the mantras he regularly and breezily delivered to his staff. The absence of grief in this efficient woman could be a positive advantage to him. 'It's a tragedy, of course, and inconvenient for the company in this time of growth. But it's our job to cope with things like this. And you're going to be a key person in that process.'

Debbie gave him an acid smile. 'I'm prepared for that. I've done the job before.' No harm in reminding him of that.

'Indeed you have. And by all accounts you got good work out of the research scientists. That was before my time, of course. And before the research laboratories were thought to warrant a director's post.'

'Yes. I'm aware that you had no part in the appointment of Richard Cullis.'

'No. I understand, though, that you were considered for the post at the time. It was a close call, but the then board considered that a candidate with more varied experience would be an advantage to the company.'

'And is the present board likely to replicate that view?'

She was coming at him directly, telling him that she wanted to be considered, that it had been a mistake to bring in Cullis over her head two years ago. He doubted that: Cullis had been excellent at perceiving the connections between research and commercial success, at spotting those products which would have international possibilities. But Marvin Hestler was a

forthright man himself; that made him respond to this directness in her. He also liked feisty women, and Debbie Young
promised to be one.

'I've noted your work. It's been consistently good.'

Debbie knew exactly what that meant. A managing director
with a company-wide brief hadn't time for detail. 'I'm
surprised that you've had the opportunity to look at what I
do.'

'I haven't the technical expertise to estimate it, even if I
had the time. But I got regular reports from Richard. He was
impressed with what you were doing. The new Aids drug in
particular has great potential.'

One up to him in this little game: she hadn't expected him
to know about her work on the Aids remedy. 'It still has a
long way to go. But the early evidence is positive, as you say.
I'm hoping it could alleviate a great deal of suffering, particularly in Africa. It also has the potential to make a great deal
of money for the company.'

They smiled at each other, two professionals together.
Marvin said, 'The two go hand in hand, you know. It's the
success of the drugs we market today which fund the research
of today and tomorrow. The budget for research is in my view
the most important budget in the company, but it is dependent
on commercial success.'

'I appreciate that. It's one of the things I constantly emphasize to people who come into the labs clutching their PhDs.
Realism was one of the things I used to check out carefully
when making appointments.'

Marvin nodded amiably, aware that she was reminding him
again of her claims to take over Cullis's role. 'Research and
development is a much bigger department now than in the
days when you were in unofficial control.'

She didn't like that word 'unofficial', but she could not
dispute it. 'Bigger but not essentially different. We do the
same kind of work; we conduct the same kind of intensive
research and testing, on a wider range of products; we have
to resist the same kind of idiot opposition from the animal
rights lobby.'

'And you now have representation on the board of the
company, which you didn't have then. Success brings its
rewards and its extra pressures, Debbie.'

'Exactly. And I've been a part of that success and I appreciate exactly what is required in the new director.'

'I'm sure you do.' He rose with the ease of a very fit man from his armchair and looked her straight in the face as she followed him. 'This has been a most useful conversation, Debbie. I have registered your interest in the replacement appointment compelled upon us by this unfortunate death. The decision will be the board's, not that of any particular individual. If it is advertised externally, we shall of course have to consider the quality of the applicants we attract. But within those parameters, I am happy to assure you of my personal support.'

He had fenced it about with the necessary jargon to protect himself, as he nowadays did automatically. But he was genuine about his support. Everything about her work and her attitude suggested that she could make the step up to director. But no one would expect the post to be filled immediately.

There would be time to make sure that Mrs Young was not the murderer of the previous incumbent.

Priscilla Godwin had been smiling ever since Tuesday night. That's how it felt to her, anyway. She hadn't troubled to disguise her delight in Cullis's death. Most people seemed to know what he had done to her, so they should expect her to be pleased, shouldn't they? Even when she had met Alison Cullis when they were finally allowed to leave the building at Belmont on Tuesday night, she had not been able to conceal her satisfaction in the justice of this death. Neither of them had spoken, but Priscilla was sure that her feelings had shown in her face. Come to think of it, she hadn't noticed the bereaved wife shedding any tears.

Two days later, Priscilla still felt as if a great weight had been lifted from her shoulders. She knew she must be a suspect, but the police hadn't spoken to her since the young uniformed officer had taken her initial statement on Tuesday night. Perhaps even the police had sympathy with her situation, after what Cullis had done to her; perhaps that motherly Sergeant Fox who had been so embarrassed that it wasn't going to court had leant on the CID people a little on her behalf.

She was in this buoyant mood when she met Ben Paddon as they were both leaving work at the end of the day. He gave her the slightly uncertain smile that had so attracted her on Tuesday. 'I enjoyed the golf,' he said. 'Pity the day had to end like that.'

'I enjoyed the whole of the day,' Priscilla asserted robustly.

'Even the death at the end of it?'

'Even the death at the end of it. I'm not going to pretend I feel anything else. I've no reason to regret what happened. I expect you heard what Richard Cullis did to me.'

'I heard something about it, yes. None of the details, of course.' Ben was glad to reach the door and pass into the twilight outside it. He had a horrid feeling that he might be blushing.

'He was going to get away with it, you know. The police knew that he was as guilty as hell, but the Crown Prosecution Service was afraid of his lawyers. So I see a sort of justice in this.'

'Yes, I can see that you would. You didn't kill him, did you?'

His hand flew to his mouth. It was the sort of gauche question which always seemed to get him off on the wrong foot with women, and this time the subject was surely too serious to be swept away.

But she laughed, throwing her head back as she did so, looking much younger than her thirty years in the relief of her release from Cullis. 'I didn't, no. But I might have done, if I'd had the opportunity.'

Ben reflected as they walked through the car park that Priscilla Godwin had had the same opportunity as everyone else to kill their leader, along with a stronger, more immediate and more personal motive than anyone else at that table. But this time he had more sense than to point that out. Instead, he said, 'The police talked to me about it this morning.'

'Really? I didn't see them come into the labs.'

Ben wanted to call her Pris, as she had invited him to do during the golf on Tuesday, but he couldn't quite bring himself to do so. 'No. They saw me at my flat. I thought it would be more private there.'

'How exciting!' She stood by her car, looking up into his diffident, unguarded face. 'Look, why don't we go for a drink. Then you can tell me all about it.'

*   *   *

It was six o'clock. Debbie Young was waiting in the deserted office at the end of the long laboratory when her CID visitors arrived. They noted the single light in the room as Hook parked the police Mondeo in a car park which had almost emptied during the previous hour.

'We shan't be disturbed here. I didn't want teenagers interrupting us at home.' She sounded nervous, making them wonder if this was her real reason. They took her through the statement she had given immediately after the murder: she answered them mostly in monosyllables, as if waiting nervously for some greater challenge.

Lambert was prepared to offer that. 'Richard Cullis was demonstrably a successful man. Would you say that he was also a popular one?'

'No. I would say that he was anything but that. Oh, Richard had a surface charm all right. He wouldn't have lined up a stream of women without that, I suppose. But I doubt whether anyone who knew him well liked him. That would certainly include his wife.'

Lambert nodded. 'We've already spoken to Mrs Cullis. She made no secret of her feelings.'

'I can't understand why Alison didn't divorce him years ago. She's a Catholic, I believe, but even so!' Debbie threw back her head in a gesture of impatience that someone of her own sex should be so accommodating. 'I suppose you keep hoping for better things, but that was flying in the face of the facts. I don't know how much Alison knew about the way Richard behaved, but she isn't stupid. If I'd been her, I'd have kicked him out years ago.'

'And the others who were at your table on Tuesday night?'

'It's not my job to put the boot into anyone, is it?' Debbie was already regretting the vehemence with which she had spoken about Alison Cullis. If she was equally forthright about the others, they might question her motives.

Lambert looked at her for a moment before he spoke. She was blonde, blue-eyed, buxom: the little extra weight she had put on in her thirties suited her, making her look younger than her forty years. But this was no Hollywood dumb blonde: she was weighing her words and conscious of whatever impact she was making. 'It is your duty to give us every help you can, in a murder inquiry,' he pointed out gently.

'I appreciate that. But most of these people are my colleagues. You can't expect me to implicate them.' She waited for some emollient phrase of understanding, but Lambert remained silent and Hook was conveniently occupied with his notebook. 'Priscilla Godwin was accusing him of rape. I don't know any details. I'd have thought Cullis was too cute to get caught out pushing things as far as that, but if Priscilla says it happened, it probably did. Mind you, she's worked with him for two years and should have known all about Richard Cullis. I can't believe she was stupid enough to get involved with the bastard.'

The last thought was a mistake: it told them the depth of her own hate for the dead man. Hook looked up from his notes and said mildly, 'You didn't like Richard Cullis very much yourself, did you, Mrs Young?'

'No. For one thing, he'd just made my husband redundant.'

'I thought that was a company decision, not one taken by Mr Cullis alone.'

'Richard was the driving force. He enjoyed telling Paul he had to go.' She was tight-lipped, determined, gazing not at Hook but at some point beyond him.

Lambert saw a woman determined not to listen to other arguments, a scientist who was at this moment in the grip of emotion. 'Your husband told us that he felt he was not cut out for a career in sales. Mr Young said he did not plan to apply for sales posts in the future.'

Her face flashed anger for an instant, but when she spoke she was in control of herself. 'Paul is too fair-minded for his own good. It was Richard Cullis who recruited him: he told him then that his scientific background and knowledge of our products would be an advantage in selling them. It was also Richard Cullis who took the decision to fire Paul. I'm quite sure he enjoyed taking that decision, enjoyed telling Paul he was for the chop.'

Lambert raised his eyebrows. 'You're saying that he had some personal grudge against your husband?'

She had led herself here; she couldn't see a way out of it. 'Cullis enjoyed humiliating people.' She knew that wasn't true: the man wouldn't have been as successful in his work as he had been if he'd indulged in petty feuds. His delight in getting rid of Paul had been the humiliation it had caused to her, but she couldn't tell them that without drawing attention to herself. 'Sometimes I think he only took Paul on a couple of years ago with a view to sacking him now.'

'And yet your husband thinks that his redundancy was justified by his record over those years.'

'I told you: Paul is too hard on himself and too anxious to make excuses for others.'

Now for the first time she was looking her age and more. The colour had drained beneath the fair skin and the round, pale face looked taut and apprehensive. Lambert said quietly, 'I'm sure that's true. But your husband also concealed certain facts from us.'

'I'm sure he didn't. Paul's a very honest man. Too honest for his own good, sometimes.'

'Which makes cynical policemen quite suspicious when this sort of thing happens. It makes us ask why such a habitually honest person would be concealing facts from us during a murder inquiry. Mrs Young, why haven't you told us today that you were interviewed with Richard Cullis for the post of Director of Research and Development?'

'It didn't seem relevant.' Her voice was dull with defeat: the argument didn't seem convincing, even to her.

'I'm sure you don't believe that. We've been discussing why you and others didn't like a murder victim. Are you saying that you had no resentment at all about being passed over for Mr Cullis?'

For a moment, Debbie was tempted to take the bait and say that yes, she had accepted the appointment without rancour. But these men were skilled interrogators, who were talking to other people as well as her. Indeed, someone had already told them about the circumstances of Cullis's appointment, and probably added that she was enduringly bitter about it. Fleetingly, she wondered who that person might be: she knew that they hadn't got the information from Paul, who had kept to his brief and told them nothing about it. She said evenly, 'I didn't tell you because I thought you'd suspect me of murder. And I've no doubt Paul, as a protective husband, concealed the fact that I'd been passed over for exactly the same reason. That's understandable, isn't it?'

Lambert wasn't going to comment on that. 'The way to make yourself a prime suspect is to conceal facts like this.

Your resentment over the appointment must have been considerable, if you think it needed to be hidden.'

'I hated Richard Cullis.' She was suddenly weary of concealment. 'He took the job that should have been mine and he reminded me of the fact at every opportunity. Sacking Paul was just one in a long line of moves to inflame me. He wanted me out of the place.'

If that was true, it wasn't unusual: it was an embarrassment to someone appointed in these circumstances to have the person who had been passed over working under his command, watching his every move, possibly making critical comments about the way he was running things. Richard Cullis seemed to have been an efficient and imaginative director, judging by the way things under his control had burgeoned during his two years in charge. But that hardly mattered: whether Debbie Young's resentment of him was justified or not, she was clearly a bitter woman, perhaps even a paranoid woman.

'You had access to ricin as part of your job?'

'Everyone around that table on Tuesday night had access to it, directly or indirectly. Even Cullis himself took drugs out of the labs, on occasions, when he needed to talk about their possibilities to the board and to customers. And everyone around that table hated Richard Cullis.'

'As much as you did, Mrs Young?'

For the first time in many minutes, she smiled. 'Maybe, maybe not. I wouldn't speculate on the degrees of antipathy they felt. I might well have hated him as much as anyone. But I didn't kill him.'

'Then who do you think did administer that ricin?'

'I don't know. I probably wouldn't help you if I did, because I think the world will be a better place without Richard Cullis. I'm glad he's dead.'

Nineteen

Chris Rushton was feeling very tired. Working up to twelve hours a day on coordinating the mass of material from a murder investigation he could take in his stride. Occupying a lively five-year-old girl for a whole day was another thing altogether. He was very glad when Anne Jackson arrived fresh and cheerful in the late afternoon.

She took over little Kirstie, who had been getting increasingly fractious, played with her, talked to her, persuaded her to eat her tea, read her a story from the book she had brought in her car. The little girl, who had been wanting her mother during the afternoon, was actually quite sorry when the time came round for Daddy to take her home.

'I don't know how you do it. I was at my wits' end,' whispered Chris after he had watched her performance admiringly.

'Kirstie's a nice kid. She was getting tired and overexcited, that's all. You should try coping with thirty of them for five days a week!' said Anne Jackson grimly. Secretly, she was delighted to have made such a good impression with the daughter of whom her man was so fond. She thought of him rather possessively as 'her man' now, she noticed.

In the early evening darkness, Chris buckled Kirstie carefully into the car seat. His daughter gave impatient instruction to his unpractised, clumsy hands whilst Anne watched from a distance. 'I should be back in about forty minutes,' he called as he went round to the driver's seat.

Anne called him back to her and spoke in a low voice so that the child would not hear her. 'You'll need to tell ex-Anne about me, you know. Kirstie's enjoyed herself, so she's going to chatter about her day when she gets home. It will be much better if you tell her yourself that you have a new woman in your life than let her hear it from Kirstie.'

He nodded agreement. Inside, he was exultant that Anne

Jackson thought of herself as the new woman in his life. Chris Rushton was a shy and diffident man, whose confidence had been dented far more than he had ever admitted by the break-up of his marriage. For weeks he had been putting off telling his former wife about this new relationship, first because he found it difficult, but secondly because he feared that it would come to nothing.

Ex-Anne had had a new man for ages; he was sure that it wouldn't be long before she was telling him that she planned to remarry. Of course, it was inevitable that life should move on: any civilized person should rejoice in the happiness of a former partner. But he remembered the feeling of desolation with which he had heard the news of ex-Anne's new liaison, the raw pain which he had felt at the thought of a new man in her bed. He would tell her about Anne Jackson carefully, not with the pride and even arrogance with which he had once planned to announce that an intelligent and lively young woman thought that he was worth her time and effort.

Anne Jackson, tidying the toys and books away in Chris's flat, knew Chris in some respects better than he knew himself. She knew that he would keep his revelation low-key, that both Chris and his ex-wife would have a moment at least of sadness, of regret for times past and happiness spent together, for the tiny, incidental joys of intimacy which now could be no more. She even had a quickly passing moment of jealousy for those years which she could never share with her man.

Then she collected the dishes, washed up sturdily, and rejoiced that another stage in their relationship had been successfully accomplished.

On Saturday morning, Bert Hook was at his books by six. The gap between now and the final Open University examinations in November was narrowing with alarming speed. He had completed his coursework assignments. Now he began a belated attempt at revision and tried not to panic at the number of days left.

At eight o'clock, he sighed, shut his books and addressed himself to the demands of his family. The boisterous breakfast chatter of his boys left him little room for reflection. He tried to present himself as the calm, paternal figure all the experts said they needed for security. 'Dad's quiet this morning,' said Jack to Eleanor as he gave himself a generous second helping of cornflakes. 'Go easy on him, Mum. He's probably beginning to get worried about his exams.'

'Mrs Fogarty says older people get much more worried about exams. It's because they've more at stake, you see.' Luke nodded sagely. Bert's smouldering looks were wasted on subjects who were studiously avoiding eye contact.

By half-past nine, Bert was addressing himself to the altogether more serious subject of Jason Dimmock.

He had expected to sit on the same Chesterfield leather sofa he had occupied when they had spoken to Lucy Dimmock. Instead, Jason Dimmock chose to see them in his office at Gloucester Chemicals. He explained logically enough that they would not be disturbed there on a Saturday morning. CID men are trained to weigh every move in their suspects; they wondered if he wished to obviate any possibility of his wife listening in on their exchanges.

It was a featureless room, overcrowded with chairs, a small desk, and four filing cabinets. A door in the corner led into a small storage area. Save for a rather dusty black-and-white photograph of Marie Curie which some earlier incumbent had installed, there was not a single picture on the walls. Perhaps Dimmock noted their examination of the room, for he explained nervously that this was a communal office, at the disposal of anyone who needed a little temporary privacy or a place to meet a visitor. 'Only Richard Cullis had his own exclusive office,' he explained in a carefully neutral tone.

Lambert cut through the preliminaries with a challenging, 'We've interviewed most of the people who were eating at your table since we saw you on Tuesday night, Mr Dimmock.'

Jason knew that: he'd gathered what little he could from his colleagues and his wife. Lucy had told him that she hadn't liked this tall, intimidating figure and Jason thought he could see why. For his part, Hook thought it was curious that the man should seem more apprehensive now on his own ground than he had in the aftermath of a shocking murder at Belmont on Tuesday night.

Dimmock said edgily, 'I expect you've found that not many people liked Cullis. Frankly, I haven't seen many of the people who worked with him shedding tears over this death.'

'That includes you, Mr Dimmock.'

It was said so quietly that Jason was not certain whether it was a question or a statement. He wondered what they had picked up from others. Lucy had assured him that she'd given nothing away, but he wasn't sure how much others knew and what they might have said to these persistent, clever men. He said carefully, 'Richard was all right to work with. He was fair. He knew what he wanted and he explained his decisions clearly to us. I believe he represented the interests of the research and development department ably to the rest of the board.'

Lambert looked at him hard. 'What you're describing are professional qualities. You're confirming what I said: you didn't like the man.'

'That's fair. I didn't like the way he conducted his private life. But that wasn't my business, was it?'

'I don't know. Was it? Did his conduct offend you? Did the way he conducted his life impinge on yours? We're here to gather information, Mr Dimmock. You seem to me very cautious. Your wife also seemed extremely careful when she spoke to us. That makes us wonder if you're concealing something. You could say that it's our job to think in that way.'

'I kept my distance from Cullis, that's all.' He sought desperately for a rationalization of his conduct and thought he saw one. 'The other staff knew I didn't really like him. I'm a senior member of the laboratory team: they would have seen it as creeping if I'd pursued more than a professional relationship with Richard.'

Lambert smiled. 'Yet it seems that you were once closer to him than you were in the weeks immediately before his death. Perhaps you fell out over something.'

Now Jason was rattled. He'd felt confident before they came that he could fend them off, but to do that he needed to know exactly where he stood. What had other people told them? Was this man Lambert leading him on, encouraging him to pile deceit on deceit, lie on lie, so that he would incriminate himself irretrievably? He said stiffly, 'Perhaps we were more friendly, at one time. Perhaps we became less close as I saw more details of the way he lived his life.'

'What sort of detail, Mr Dimmock?'

He said priggishly, 'I don't wish to talk about that. I don't wish to speak evil of the dead.'

'How honourable and how unselfish!' Lambert's voice hardened. 'You don't have a choice, Mr Dimmock. You're supposed to be assisting the pursuit and arrest of a cold-blooded murderer.'

'You should ask Priscilla Godwin what she thinks of him!'

'We're asking you, Mr Dimmock.'

'The talk is that Pris was raped by him. So she'd every reason to hate him, hadn't she?' He could hear his own voice rising, the capacity he had always had to pick his words deserting him.

'I'm asking for *your* reasons, Mr Dimmock. A moment ago, you told us that there were details of Cullis's life you didn't approve of.' Lambert, sensing a weakness, was at his most ruthless.

'I've told you I didn't like him. There's nothing more than that to tell.'

Jason was thoroughly disconcerted by his own weakness. Normally his mind worked swiftly and the precise words to express his thoughts came easily to him: now both skills seemed to have deserted him. His senses reeled with an overwhelming sense of unfairness. He didn't know how much they knew, what other people had told them in the last three days: this wasn't an equal contest.

It was at this point that the stolid, unthreatening Bert Hook looked up from his notes and smiled at him. 'And yet others tell us that you were apparently quite friendly with Richard Cullis at one time.' Hook's voice was as gentle and persuasive as a therapist's. Jason felt his head nodding, as if jerked by strings which someone else was controlling. 'But by the time of his death you plainly disliked him intensely. I think you should tell us the reason for the change.'

'I hated him.' It seemed to Jason necessary to correct that word 'dislike', which was so neutral and so inadequate a word for the way he had felt about Cullis. 'He'd given me every reason to hate him.' He looked into the earnest, understanding, unthreatening face. 'You know about this, don't you?'

'We need to hear it from you. We need to hear your version of events, you see.' Hook was as inscrutable as an amiable Buddha.

Jason nodded, almost eagerly. 'He should never have done it. "Don't shit on your own doorstep." That's one of the rules of the game for the wandering shagger, isn't it?' He gave a curious, mirthless giggle, finding that the obscenities were a sort of release for a man who normally avoided them. 'Cullis should have kept his fucking away from work, shouldn't he? That's one of the rules to avoid trouble; everyone knows that. I know Lucy didn't work here, but I did. If he'd kept his hands off Lucy, he'd have been all right.'

Hook nodded: not a line on his face gave away the fact that this was new information. 'When did this relationship between your wife and Mr Cullis begin, Jason?'

This use of his first name would normally have made him suspicious: it was evidence of how far he had lost control of himself and the situation that he now leaned forward eagerly and said, 'A year or so ago, I think. You'd have to ask Lucy, to be certain. They say the husband is always the last to know, don't they?' Again he followed his question with that odd mirthless giggle; it made a very odd sound in this quiet room with its dull office furniture.

'Was it still going on at the time of Cullis's death?'

'No!' The cry was more dismay than simple negative. It was followed by a look of horror on the normally quiet face. 'Lucy has assured me time and again that it was over months ago. Are you telling me that she was lying, that she was still seeing the man right up to—'

'I'm telling you nothing, Jason. I'm gathering information during the course of a murder inquiry. Mrs Dimmock gave us no details of this herself. Therefore I am asking you: when did this affair end?'

'Yes. Yes, I see. Well, three months ago, I think.'

'You think?'

'Yes, I'm certain. I'm sorry for the confusion. Lucy wouldn't lie to me. I'm sorry if I gave you the impression that she might.'

Lambert had watched Bert Hook's probing with admiration. He now said, 'Let's be clear about this. Your wife began an affair with our murder victim one year ago. This lasted for nine months. You are confident that it ended then.'

'Yes, that's right.'

'And why did you conceal this information from us?'

'It – it's embarrassing, isn't it? No man wants to announce to the world that he's been cuckolded.' Jason felt better now that the secret was out. He even enjoyed using the old-fashioned word he had never spoken before: perhaps the return of his vocabulary showed that he had a measure of control again.

'Did you kill Richard Cullis?'

'No. No, of course I didn't.' He tried desperately to put an edge of ridicule into his tone, feeling his senses beginning to reel again.

'You've just outlined a motive for yourself. Cuckolds commit murders. The fact that you attempted to conceal both your wife's affair and your own reaction to it reinforces the case against you.'

'I shouldn't have concealed it. My wife asked me to do it. For obvious reasons – Lucy isn't proud of what she did.' He wondered if she would be willing to bear him out, if they went back to her. He must get to her before they did.

'Did Mrs Dimmock kill Cullis?'

'No. That's a preposterous idea.' Again Jason could not summon the indignation and outrage he wanted.

'You know that isn't true, Mr Dimmock. Lovers who have been cast aside are usually afflicted by strong emotions. They often behave irrationally. Murder is an irrational crime.'

Not so irrational when you stood where he did, Jason wanted to say: he bit back the words just in time. 'She wasn't "cast aside", as you call it. It was Lucy who ended their affair.'

Even as he said it, the old, wounding fear struck back at him. She had told him that, again and again, but was it really true? Hadn't Cullis left a trail of angry women behind him, moving on to the next one as the fancy took him? For almost the first time, he wondered how the termination of this coupling which had caused him so much pain had affected Lucy.

Lambert's grey, searching, unblinking eyes seemed to Jason to be all-seeing. They studied his face for seconds now before the superintendent made one of his disconcerting switches. 'Mr Dimmock, your wife told us that you have a small laboratory in your own house.'

'Yes. I have the facilities to do minor experiments. We have no children, so it seemed a sensible use of one of the rooms. It's been useful over the years: I do minor research there, which sometimes suggests a line of more complicated experiments to be pursued with the infinitely greater facilities of the research labs at work. It's prompted a few things like that, and saved a lot of time we might have spent going down blind alleys. It's an example of using what was originally a hobby to provide useful pointers in working life.' He was talking too much, trying to explain himself to scientific novices like them. He forced a smile. 'Sorry, my enthusiasm's getting the better of me. Would you like to see the place?'

'Not at present, thank you.' Lambert returned his smile. 'I'm sure anything significant to our inquiry would long since have been removed, if it had ever existed. Does your wife have access to that room?'

'Of course she does. But she doesn't use it. I find I use it myself less frequently than in my early years at Gloucester Chemicals.'

'And who do you think killed Mr Cullis?'

Another of those abrupt questions. But a welcome one, this time, switching attention away from him and Lucy at last. He smiled again, flicked a finger down the side of the nose which was a little too long, telling his inquisitor that he knew the game they were playing. 'Detection is your job, not mine, Mr Lambert.'

'And you know the principal suspects as well as anyone, and far better than DS Hook and I do. You promised to give the matter some thought when we left you on Tuesday evening.'

Jason nodded two or three times, checking his stance like the competent golfer he was before he committed himself. 'And I have thought about it, without reaching firm conclusions. If I'd been Alison Cullis, I'd have wanted to kill him, I think: he was a rotten husband. If the rumours about what he did to Priscilla Godwin have any truth, she'd also have good reason for revenge. Debbie Young never liked him: she has never been able to accept that he was appointed to his job over her head. And Cullis had just been instrumental in firing Paul Young, which hadn't left him very happy. Either or both of the Youngs could have planned that death.'

'As could either or both of the Dimmocks. The forsaken woman and the cuckolded husband inflamed with jealousy,' Lambert reminded him. He allowed himself a grim smile, watching the man's reactions. 'The other man at that table was Ben Paddon. I'm rather surprised that you haven't found a motive for him.'

Jason didn't rise to the bait. 'He's a quiet young man. A likeable young man, from what little I know of him. He does his work competently enough. He's a bright boy, or he wouldn't have got a job in our research labs, but something of an introvert. He doesn't socialize much: I wouldn't say I know him much better now than when he came here. He seems to me neither an admirer of Richard Cullis nor an enemy of his. I can think of no reason why he should kill him.'

He said it with an air of regret, but Lambert did not comment on that. He was impressed by the scientist's precise use of words. Bert Hook had got through his defences and exposed raw emotions for a moment or two, but otherwise he felt the man had delivered to them no more than he had planned. A coolly competent man this, as he had appeared when he had talked to them on Tuesday night, just after the murder.

A man clearly seared by the thing he had attempted to conceal from them, his wife's affair with Cullis. A man who clearly had the capacity to plan and execute a murder like this one.

Ben Paddon took a long time to make a decision. Even when he had done that, he spent a good ten minutes pacing restlessly about his flat, wondering what words he should use. Eventually, he almost leapt at the phone, then tapped in the number with furious speed, before his nerve could break.

It rang several times, until he thought she must be out. He was wondering how to phrase his message for the answering machine when a cool voice said, 'Priscilla Godwin speaking.'

'Pris, it's me. Ben. Ben Paddon.'

'Hello, Ben. What a relief to find it's you – I thought it might be those CID men who've been prying around at the works over the last three days. What can I do for you?'

She sounded genuinely pleased. He said, 'I was wondering if you'd like to go out this evening. Perhaps to the cinema.'

There was a pause, whilst he waited with heavy resignation for her rejection. Whatever excuse she made, he would help her out with it, saying that it had just been a spur-of-the-moment idea and absurdly short notice anyway. Then her voice said, 'That's a lovely idea. I'd be delighted to go with you. You choose the film. I'll just be relieved to get out of this place.'

He suggested *Atonement* and she accepted immediately, before he could explain that he'd read the book and enjoyed it: he'd hoped she might be impressed by that. She suggested that she'd pick him up in her car, and when he demurred, she said quickly, 'I have my reasons. I prefer it that way.'

Ben accepted immediately, then ate his sandwich lunch with a sly, private smile. It had all been much easier than he'd anticipated it would be.

Twenty

The weather was good, for late October. But there was still quite a nip in the air after sundown; there might even be a frost, before the night was out, if the sky remained as clear of cloud as it was now.

Paul Young liked this spot at the bottom of his long garden. You could see May Hill from here; the Gloucestershire rise was of no great height, but it was visible from many points in the county. It obscured the greater and more impressive heights of the Welsh hills beyond it, but it gave intimacy and definition to the ancient landscape around it. It was a natural, permanent feature, a landmark which brought consolation to those residents of the area who thought the world was changing too rapidly.

It was almost six o'clock now, and there was not much light left in the silent landscape. Paul's bonfire of autumn rubbish from his garden had been sending a thin column of grey smoke into the windless air. Now it blazed into sudden life, its intense light denying the view not only of May Hill but of anything more than a few yards away. He watched the dead wood he had placed at the centre glowing red, until the heat made him step back a pace. He looked towards the black outline of his house, where the orange lights were now dimmed by curtains. No curious eyes were following his movements.

He waited another minute, checking that the cheerful blaze was at its most fierce. Then he took out the pages of the diary which he had shredded earlier in the house and placed them swiftly in the very centre of his blaze. He had to leap back quickly from the heat, but he pushed more wood around the fire with his rake, watching the tongues of flame lick around and then quickly swallow the curling worms of paper.

He was leaning on his rake with satisfaction when he was startled to hear his wife's voice calling to him from the house, telling him that they were almost ready to eat. 'I'll be there in five minutes, Debbie,' he called back to his invisible informant. 'I just want to make sure this fire is safe before I leave it!'

He pushed the remaining garden detritus to the spot where the paper had vanished with the back of his rake, watching his blaze subside to a tiny, smouldering pyre, checking that there was now no remaining sign of the pages he had first shredded and then burnt.

You could not be too careful, when the stakes were as high as this.

Priscilla Godwin enjoyed her Saturday-night outing.

The multi-screen cinema in Gloucester was crowded, giving her a pleasing sense of anonymity within a public place, a feeling she had not enjoyed since first the rape and then the murder of the rapist had dominated her world. The heterogeneous bustle of a weekend crowd, largely of noisy young people full of their own concerns, was just what she needed.

Her escort became more attractive to her as he grew in confidence. It had been an awkward moment when she collected him from his flat; the reversal of normal roles seemed absurd and neither of them knew quite how to carry it off. The conversation was stilted in the car and in the cinema queue; then they made forced and not at all funny remarks to each other during the seemingly interminable series of adverts which prefaced the screening of *Atonement*. She accepted an ice cream she did not want just to have something to do with her hands and something to obviate the need for conversation.

But the film was good, when it at last began, and the themes of childish betrayal and suffering in war were so far from what they had experienced in the last week that both of them were absorbed. An hour into the film, Priscilla let her hand steal gently sideways until it found Ben's. He grasped it eagerly and she was surprised how much she welcomed the soft, reassuring, unthreatening squeeze of his fingers on hers. For a woman who had a week ago been abjuring any contact with men for the rest of her life, this was quite a turn-up, she admitted to herself wryly. He kept her hand in his for the rest of the film, but did not attempt to take matters any further.

They chatted more naturally as they walked the two hundred yards to where she had parked the car. Beneath a sky now sprinkled with stars, there was a bite in the night air, and after a moment, she slipped her arm through Ben's and walked with her side against his; she could feel the warmth of his tall, rather gangling frame as he held her lightly against him. They did not speak a lot, and it was mostly about the film, but the silences were easier between them now.

'I'll drop you off at your flat,' she said unnecessarily as they eased themselves into the damp cold of her car. Lay down your own rules and make sure you stick to them, she had told herself before she set out.

Yet when she got there, she was reluctant to leave him. Ben Paddon sat very still for a moment in the passenger seat, making no move towards her, yet unwilling to get out of the car and leave the evening incomplete. Eventually he said, 'I heard what happened to you. I understand how you feel. I'll just say good night and go, if that's what you want. You decide.'

Priscilla gazed straight ahead for what seemed to both of them a long time. Then she said slowly, 'Thank you for being so understanding, Ben. I'd like to come in for a coffee, I think, if that's all right with you. Just a coffee.' She laughed at herself for the last phrase, found him joining in, grasped both his hands and pulled him towards her. They kissed each other briefly on the lips.

Ben said, 'I think I've only got instant coffee!' and they both laughed as if it was the wittiest rejoinder he could have made. She turned the car off the road and into the space he directed her to in the car park for the block of flats.

He was glad he had left the heating on. His flat was warm and welcoming. She walked around the big living room and studied his photographs and paintings of animals, whilst he busied himself with coffee and made sure that the china cups and saucers he rarely used were perfectly clean.

They sat and talked on his sofa for a long time after the coffee was finished. He had his arm round her, holding her comfortably against him, but he made no move to kiss her again. He was conscious of that other man, now dead, and what he had done to her, desperately afraid of appearing insensitive. Priscilla knew this, but was too unsure of her own reactions to help him.

She persuaded him to talk to her about his successes at cricket and golf and his interest in animals: he told her how he had come to buy most of the pictures in his flat. He enjoyed telling her these things: for the first time in years, he was finding it easy to talk to a young woman. Ben did not learn very much about her, though he divined that she was actually very fond of the mother she humorously affected to find a burden.

It was after a comfortable pause that she said suddenly, 'Do you want me to stay the night?'

He pulled away from her, turned sideways to look into her face. 'Do you really want to do that?'

She grinned at him: he looked absurdly young and in-experienced in his earnestness. 'I wouldn't have asked if I hadn't wanted to, would I, you goon?'

'I'd love you to stay. It – it wasn't expected, you know.'

'If it had been, I wouldn't be here. And I'll quite under-stand it if you want to send a nutcase on her way.'

'And why would I want to do that?' Ben was suddenly smiling, confident, immensely pleased with himself and with her.

As she saw his pleasure, her own fragile well-being was affected. 'I'm nervous because of what you know happened to me. Ben, I'll stay, but don't expect much. I won't be very good. And please understand that it won't be your fault if I can't . . . '

He put both arms round her now, held her against him for a moment, whilst both their brains raced. At length he said softly, 'It will be all right, Pris.'

It was much later, when they lay relaxed in his bed, that she told him all about Richard Cullis. He listened without inter-rupting, staring at the ceiling of his room. Then, without talk and with a minimum of fuss, they made love, and fell asleep in each other's arms.

In the morning, Ben brought beakers of tea to the bed and they watched the day brightening beyond the cotton curtains of his bedroom. For both of them, the world beyond those curtains seemed less threatening than it had done on the previous day, but they were in no hurry to rejoin it. She told him more about herself than she had told anyone else for years and he listened with an earnest appreciation of the privilege she was according him.

It was then that Ben quietly told her about himself.

John Lambert eyed his daughter warily over the top of the Sunday paper.

Jacky had stayed the night with them, as she had done periodically since the break-up of her marriage and the departure of her husband. It was good for you to have an unchanging welcome when your world and your confidence had been battered; Christine Lambert understood this as clearly as Jacky herself, though neither of them had ever framed the thought in words.

Mothers and daughters are almost always close in times of crisis. Yet in this household, Jacky had always chosen her father when she felt the need to confide. Even as a teenager, she had sometimes done that rarest and most difficult of adolescent things: she had asked her father for advice. Now he wondered if the bond between them had been shattered by what he had done on Thursday night. He had in effect thrown the man she had brought here out of the house; Jacky was far too intelligent to see it as anything other than that.

She looked at him with that half-humorous, half-serious, expression with which she had always introduced her intimacies to him. 'What did you think of Tim Cohen, Dad?'

'Shouldn't I be asking you that? Your feelings are far more important than mine.'

'Ah, but I was in first. Do tell!' She used the phrases which might have come from her many years earlier, when she had been young enough to sit on his knee and test him with a barrage of childish questions: the old tricks are the best ones, with parents who love you.

'He's a well-qualified young man, who will no doubt have a successful career,' John Lambert said carefully.

'You didn't like him, then.' There was a humorous triumph in the way she so effortlessly cut through his cautious phrases.

'I didn't think he was right for you.'

'And why would that be?'

Her father noted the edge entering her voice with the challenge. 'Do you like lawyers?'

'Do you always answer a question with a question? Is that part of the CID technique taught on courses?'

He didn't think any of his techniques were taught on courses. His first maxim would be to get yourself a Bert Hook, and he was sure that wouldn't feature in any of the manuals. You were supposed to direct investigations from behind a desk nowadays, but he had also acquired a Chris Rushton to co-ordinate the masses of information for him. He put the sports section of the newspaper down on the table and said doggedly, 'I think he'll be successful. I didn't take to him as a partner for you, but you must make the decision on that, as I think you're telling me.'

She looked at him very seriously for a moment. Then her face cracked into a broad smile and she said, 'Relax, Dad. He's not my type. I wouldn't even have brought him here, if Mum hadn't been so anxious to see him.'

Lambert's long, lined face looked suddenly ten years younger as he smiled. 'You young minx! You enjoy winding me up.'

'Always did, Dad. It's not as easy as it used to be, but I can still do it.'

'I'm sure to meet Tim Cohen professionally, you know. He acts as legal adviser to All God's Creatures, who are quite strong around here. I don't know if he's got any strong convictions about hunting or animal drug-testing himself.'

'He hasn't.'

He was encouraged by her prompt, slightly contemptuous dismissal of that thought. It made him ask the question he knew he should avoid but could not resist. 'Did Cohen offer you drugs?'

There was a long pause before she decided that she must answer him. 'He asked if I used coke. I suppose you could call that an offer. It's one of the reasons why I decided not to pursue things with him.'

'He was taking coke here. I walked in on him taking a snort.'

She looked at him hard for a moment, then burst into giggles. 'So that's why he shot away so quickly on Thursday night. There's no way he'll want to see me again, after that.'

'I'm sorry. I couldn't just let it go.' He didn't want to tell her that his first reactions had been those of a protective father, not a senior policeman.

'I'm glad you didn't. You've saved me the small embarrassment of refusing any future invitations from Tim. There won't be any.'

Jacky spent the morning in the family home before going back to her ancient cottage. Christine Lambert wondered what shared secret made father and daughter so at ease with each other.

Priscilla Godwin relished the autumn sun and the glorious autumn leaf shades as she drove the few miles from Ben Paddon's flat to her own. There was still warmth in the sun. On impulse, she slid open the sunroof of her small car, a facility she rarely used, and enjoyed the breeze in her hair. There was no need to cocoon herself away from the world on a day like this.

She crossed a bridge over the Wye, glimpsing its waters flowing placidly at the end of an October when it had hardly rained. She had not been so happy for months, not since well before the episode with Richard Cullis. That was how she could and would regard it: an episode, unsavoury but now completed, not a trauma that was going to ruin the rest of her life.

She told herself that a thirty-year-old woman should not be humming like a self-satisfied teenager after her first night of sex. This was surely an adolescent overreaction, this feeling that all was now well with the world, that she could make it spin to her wishes, rather than being whirled round helplessly on an alien planet. This rebuke did not affect her mood at all. All was indeed well with the world, now that Cullis was out of it and Ben Paddon emphatically within it.

She would pursue a new and intriguing relationship with this naive but sensitive young man who seemed so ready and able to attune himself to the needs of her mind and her body. Where this would lead her, she was not quite sure, but she found that she could even welcome that uncertainty. In the weeks to come, she would no longer have to drive herself through the motions of existence at home and at work. Life was back there before her, waiting to be explored.

Even the flat she had recently dreaded to enter had no fears for her, in this mood and on this bright morning. She opened the windows to let in the midday sunshine. Priscilla decided that she would make herself a snack and then sit down with the Sunday paper she had bought on the way home. It seemed a long time since she had allowed herself such innocent indulgence.

She went to the phone to check if there were any messages. The impersonal voice told her that Chief Superintendent Lambert would like to see her as soon as possible, in connection with his investigation of the suspicious death of Mr Richard Cullis.

Twenty-One

It was Sunday afternoon. Paul Young's son was playing football with the local club's junior side. Normally he would have liked it if his daughter had also been out with her friends, because he liked to have his wife to himself for an hour or two. In the days before the death of Richard Cullis, they had even sometimes made love on afternoons like this. Debbie had laughed with him, and teased him, and taken him up to the bedroom, and said that it was good sometimes to feel like a mistress rather than a wife.

Yet since that death a curtain had fallen between them. It was not a curtain of silence: they still spoke, and strangers who were not familiar with their normal exchanges might scarcely have registered that anything serious was wrong. Yet they were guarded with each other, so guarded that laughter and warmth and love seemed to have deserted them. The children had noticed it; even those teenagers so preoccupied with their developing selves had noticed it. An air of mutual suspicion hung over the husband and wife who were normally so close. They watched each other and wondered, knowing the strength of their feelings against the dead man, knowing that love as well as hate can sometimes lead to violence.

Paul Young, stacking the crockery into the dishwasher after Sunday lunch, was glad today that his daughter was in the house, glad of the cheerful cacophony of music from the room above his head. He moved around the kitchen slowly, wondering what other household chores he could find to avoid contact with his wife.

He heard the unexpected sound of voices in the hall. One of them was Debbie's, but he could not distinguish a single word of the conversation because of the noise from upstairs.

Then the kitchen door opened and Debbie said with a bright, false smile, 'We have a visitor, Paul.' He wiped his hands hurriedly on the kitchen towel and followed her into the hall. 'Alison Cullis has popped in to see us.' She gave him the full name, as if she feared he would not recognize the woman behind her with the pale oval face and the attractive dark hair. 'Do take Alison into the sitting room and I'll make us a cup of tea.'

Paul did not quite know what to say, so he called up the stairs to his invisible daughter, 'Turn that down, will you, Zoe? We can hardly hear ourselves think down here.' He waited until the volume minimally decreased, then shrugged the word 'Teenagers!' at his visitor and led her into the sitting room.

His visitor seemed nearly as embarrassed to be here as he was to receive her. She said, 'I hope I'm not interrupting anything. I probably shouldn't be here, but you get to thinking all kind of strange thoughts when you're in that big house on your own.'

'You're very welcome!' said Paul, as heartily as he could. Suddenly, he found that he meant it. He'd always liked what little he'd seen of Alison Cullis in the past, and anyone married to that monster Richard deserved every sympathy. And she was surely right: being isolated in that big house after a partner's death must be an eerie experience, leading to a sense of isolation, even if you'd long since ceased to love the man who had died. The widow had a strange sort of serenity about her, but it must be a very odd feeling, sitting in that house and wondering who had killed your husband.

As if she read his thoughts, Alison said, 'I've been wondering how the police are getting on with their investigation. They didn't tell me much about it when I saw them: I suppose you wouldn't expect them to. I expect you two exchange notes with other people at Gloucester Chemicals about what the police have said. I haven't got anyone to exchange notes with.'

'Actually, I'm not there any more. I've been busy finding myself a new job.'

She nodded thoughtfully. 'Richard sacked you, didn't he? I'd forgotten about that. I'm sorry.'

'It wasn't your doing, was it? And he might have done me a favour: I wasn't cut out for sales and I think I'll be much happier in a different sort of work.' Paul wondered if Cullis had aired his dismissal to other people as well as his wife, whether his humiliation had been common knowledge at the works. He was glad when Debbie came in with the tea and some of her home-made cake.

Alison looked up at his wife and said, 'It's good of you to invite me into your house like this, after what Richard did to you.' Her smile was as wide and as brittle as Debbie's own.

Paul wondered for a moment what she meant, but Debbie was so obsessed with the injustice in being passed over for Cullis that she responded immediately. 'It's not your fault, is it? I shouldn't think you had any more time for Richard's dirty tricks than we have.'

'No, I didn't.' Alison's dark eyes glittered with the sincerity of her hatred. 'He was a rotten husband. I don't have to disguise that any longer, do I? I expect you could cheerfully have killed him, after what he did to the two of you.'

Paul was taken aback by this vehemence in a widow, but Debbie accepted it as natural. 'You've hit the nail right on the head there, Alison.' She handed a slice of fruit cake to her guest, then took a small, fierce bite at her own piece. 'I shan't be at all sorry if the police don't feel able to arrest anyone for this. They don't seem to be making much progress.'

'That doesn't worry me. I agree with you, Richard had it coming to him and I hope whoever did it gets away with it.' Alison nodded calmly, as if she were merely confirming her agreement on some small point of fashion.

Paul Young, a fundamentally decent and conventional man, was shocked by this feverish compact between the two women in his sitting room. He found that the muted sound of pop music from his daughter's bedroom was now a reassuring assertion of normality in a world which seemed in danger of running out of control. He was more than ever disturbed by an awful intuition of his wife's guilt. Was the woman who shared his bed and his children the demented perpetrator of the death of this man who had so unbalanced her judgement? Paul was trying to convince himself rather than the women as he said diffidently, 'It must be difficult for the police. Everyone at that table on Tuesday night seems to have had a reason to wish ill upon Richard.'

'To kill him, you mean.' Debbie was like Lady Macbeth in her contemptuous dismissal of his evasion.

'He was bedding Lucy Dimmock, you know.' Alison Cullis

sipped her tea with quiet satisfaction, like one of the women she had known as a child announcing a minor piece of parish gossip.

Debbie nodded her satisfaction. 'I always suspected that. They were too discreet about it for me to be certain.' She refilled Alison's cup, then waved the teapot vaguely over the full one, which her appalled husband had not touched. 'Was it still going on when he died?'

'I don't know. It was months ago that I caught him out making a telephone call. I'd ceased to care about what he was up to long before Tuesday night.'

Debbie pursed her lips thoughtfully. 'It's my guess that he ditched Lucy a while back. But I think Jason Dimmock had found out about it. He used to be quite thick with Richard at one time, but they were hardly speaking at the time of this death.'

'So either of them could have done it, couldn't they? The rejected mistress and the wronged husband.' The thought seemed to give Alison Cullis considerable satisfaction. 'I never knew Lucy very well, but she struck me as a resourceful lady.' There was a hint of bitterness in the phrase, as if she felt a belated resentment of the woman who had betrayed her, even with this despised husband.

Debbie said, 'Jason wouldn't take kindly to an affair like that. He's well capable of planning that sort of murder.' It was the first time the word had been mentioned.

Paul caught a whiff of his wife's lingering resentment for Dimmock: she had regarded it as a betrayal when Jason had offered friendship to the man who had taken what she had always seen as her post. He said rather feebly, 'I expect the police are well aware of these things, by now.'

As if she took that as a dismissal, Alison Cullis glanced at her watch and said, 'Well, I must be off. Thanks for entertaining the harmless ramblings of a confused woman. I feel much better now, really I do. As I say, it's lonely sitting in a big house on your own and wondering quite what's happening outside it.' In the hall, she looked up towards the bedroom and the invisible presence behind the noise, as if registering it for the first time. She said bleakly, 'I wish we'd had children. At least I'd have been left with something then, wouldn't I?'

They watched her car until it disappeared at the end of their cul-de-sac. 'That was an odd visit,' said Paul.

'I'm glad she came,' said Debbie firmly.

Paul looked directly at her for the first time in minutes. She seemed to him to have a strange excitement in her eyes. He said slowly, 'I burned your diary yesterday.'

'Did you? Why did you do that?'

He had thought she would be bewildered, would ask him which diary he meant, but she had known immediately. 'I burned it with the garden rubbish. It's gone now. I didn't think it was a good idea to have the record of how you hated Cullis over the last few months hanging around the place. Not with a police murder investigation going on.'

He willed her to laugh at him, to declare that it was an absurd overreaction. Even anger would have been welcome. But Debbie nodded and said, 'You're probably right.'

Priscilla Godwin's first reaction to the phone message from Oldford CID was to ignore it for the moment and enjoy the rest of a day which had started so well. She could easily say that she had been out for the whole of Sunday and not picked up the request for an interview until late in the evening. Then she decided that she had much better have this meeting as soon as possible: she wouldn't get much sleep if she left it until Monday.

Before her resolution could falter, she picked up the phone and said that she was available for the rest of the day, though she didn't suppose they would want to speak to her on a Sunday afternoon. Within minutes, the phone rang and the calm female voice told her that Chief Superintendent Lambert and Detective Sergeant Hook would visit her at three o'clock.

The CID top brass, then. She had seen them after the murder and in the labs, heard other people talking about their meetings with the man whom the local press called the 'super-sleuth'. Now she wished she had listened a little harder to their impressions. She watched from the window of her flat as he climbed a little stiffly out of his old Vauxhall Senator, then looked up at the sky and around at the buildings rising above him, as if he could gather fragments of information even from bricks and glass and tarmac.

This fanciful thought was not diminished when the lined

face looked down at her in the doorway of her flat. The grey
eyes seemed to take in every detail of her appearance, until
she felt that the make-up she had applied and the hair she had
carefully combed for this meeting were artifices which were
immediately apparent to him. Then the tall man said unexpectedly, 'I'm sorry about the rape case. It was the Crown
Prosecution Service which wouldn't take it on. It often seems
to us that people who can employ expensive barristers have
a decided advantage.'

'It hardly matters, now that the man is dead.' She was amused
and slightly touched by the man's awkward apology for the
shortcomings of the system in which he operated. In the last
twenty-four hours, it had become easier for her to get things
in perspective. 'I'm trying to move on. It's probably a good
thing I don't have the ordeal of a court case like that to look
forward to.'

'I'm sure you're right there. Well, we've studied your preliminary statement about the events of last Tuesday night. We
left it as long as possible before coming to speak to you
because our colleagues in the Sapphire Unit told us that you
were understandably very upset about the CPS decision not
to prosecute in the rape issue.'

'That was very considerate of you.'

Lambert smiled gravely. 'It was also common sense from
our point of view. It is difficult for someone in a highly
emotional state to be objective about what she saw in the
hours before a murder.'

Priscilla nodded. 'For at least a day after the murder, all I
could do was rejoice that Richard Cullis was dead and out of
my life for ever.'

They took her through that fatal hour at the top table at the
Belmont, traced the course of the meal and the speech which
had been Cullis's swan song, confirmed that she was adding
nothing to what they already knew. Then Lambert said, 'I
want you to go back to events earlier in the day, to see if we
can tease out anything which might have a bearing on what
happened later.'

'The golf competition, you mean? Well, the weather was
splendid: you couldn't have had a better day, in October. I
was playing with Ben. Ben Paddon. He's a surprisingly good
golfer.'

'Surprisingly?'

She smiled. 'He's tall and a little gangly. You wouldn't expect Ben to be a good sportsman. But he's amazingly well coordinated in his movements.' She hoped that she wasn't blushing.

'I see. Did Mr Paddon give you any reason to think he was planning to harm Richard Cullis?'

'He certainly did not!' She was over-emphatic in her rejection of the suggestion. But she knew Ben as they surely couldn't know him.

The four practised eyes which were studying her reactions noted her instinctive springing to Paddon's defence. It was Hook who said gently, 'Is Mr Paddon a particular friend of yours, Ms Godwin?'

'I scarcely knew him, before the golf day. We've worked together in the labs for two years, but not in the same areas. He tends to confine himself to the early research on new drugs, whilst I'm more concerned with the final testing of products before they are released for human use. We saw each other on most days, I suppose, but scarcely exchanged more than polite greetings.' She tried to keep the puzzlement out of her voice. It now seemed to her very odd that Ben and she should have known each other for so long without becoming friendlier with each other. 'Ben is a man who keeps himself very much to himself. He's rather shy, not too sure of himself in social situations.' That was the phrase he had used about himself to her last night, before everything changed.

'But you obviously got on well last Tuesday.'

Priscilla did not know what quite to deduce from Hook's 'obviously'. She smiled a little at herself, trying to relax. 'We did, yes. It was probably partly the splendid weather: it was almost the first time I'd been out in the fresh air since – since the rape episode. And Ben was a good companion; I liked the way he played the game well without seeming to take it too seriously.' She wanted to say this wasn't their business, but she couldn't summon the will to do it. 'I'm afraid I can't provide you with any information about who killed Cullis.'

'Any thoughts about the people who were at that table with him when he died are welcome. Ben Paddon is one of those people.' Hook smiled, reminding Priscilla suddenly of her father, who had died three years ago. 'You won't be surprised to learn that Richard Cullis was a man who had made many enemies: almost everyone around that table seems to have had a motive for murder.'

'And I had the strongest one of all.'

'The most obvious and recently acquired one, certainly.'

She realized that she had been hoping that this avuncular figure would reassure her, rather than reinforce her position as a suspect. She had to tell them things about Ben, things which might shatter her relationship with him when it had scarcely begun. She had no idea how to go about it, but she needed to protect herself.

Priscilla said suddenly, without knowing the words were coming, 'I went out with Ben Paddon last night.'

Hook raised his eyebrows only minimally. 'I'm happy to hear you're picking up the pieces after your experience with Cullis.'

'Ben was a perfect gentleman.' Even through her tension, she smiled at the old-fashioned phrase she had never thought she would use. 'We got on very well, partly as a result of that.'

Hook smiled. 'Priscilla, there's clearly something you need to tell us.'

She wondered how he knew that, but she was grateful for his prompting. 'I think Ben is the mole you were looking for at Gloucester Chemicals – the undercover person in the labs whom you were searching for last week, after Richard Cullis had been kidnapped. I – I spent last night with him. He opened up, the way he had never done before: he told me about his sympathies with the group. I realize now why he always does purely experimental work and has always kept away from animal testing. He's a very bright man and I thought he was just pursuing his interests, but I believe that there's an issue of principle involved.'

She had delivered the whole thing quickly, with scarcely a pause, fearing that if she stopped she would never complete her thoughts. As if he understood all of this, Bert Hook said quietly, 'You were right to tell us about this, you know.'

'It doesn't mean that he killed Cullis. I'm quite sure he didn't.' Belatedly, Priscilla tried to mitigate her treachery.

Lambert said decisively, 'If he didn't, he has nothing to fear from us. The company may of course wish to review the situation and decide whether they wish to employ a man with such beliefs in their research laboratories.'

'But he wouldn't have killed Richard.' To her horror, Priscilla heard the fear and the uncertainty in her own voice.

Lambert said rather wearily, 'He must have felt very near to being unmasked when we questioned all the laboratory staff last week after Cullis had been kidnapped. You must be aware that some animal rights protesters resort to violence in pursuit of their ends. We have to consider it possible that he might have wanted to make the big gesture and cut down the person officially in charge of experiments on animals. There are certain people in the movement who have already proclaimed the death of your Research and Development Director as an example of what will happen to people who conduct tests on animals.'

'I read that. I despise people who hold back their names. These anonymous cranks are just opportunists who have seized on this death to claim it for themselves.'

'Maybe. There is also the possibility that they have to keep things vague to avoid dumping Paddon into court on a murder charge. Ms Godwin, did Ben Paddon give you any reason to think that he might have committed such a crime?'

'No. I'm sure he didn't.' She was suddenly struck by the incongruous image of Ben over a golf ball, striking it with smooth and surprisingly well-directed violence. A man capable of murder?

Lambert was right about the extremism of the animal rights movement: she had always taken care not to talk openly about exactly what she did at Gloucester Chemicals in case she was targeted. She felt affection towards Ben certainly, and possibly even the beginnings of love. But she knew very little about him, even after last night. She wondered for the first time what other shocks were concealed beneath his unthreatening and diffident appearance. She said feebly, 'Ben's not the murdering type.'

Lambert refrained from telling her that there was no such thing as a murdering type. He said grimly to Bert Hook as he levered himself back into the driving seat of the Senator, 'The one person at that table who didn't seem to have a motive now has one.'

'At least we've unearthed the All God's Creatures undercover man,' said Hook. 'I wonder how much Priscilla Godwin was trying to divert us away from her own more obvious motive.'

'I told ex-Anne about us.' Chris Rushton was surprised how relieved he had been to have that conversation out of the way. 'It was just as well I got in first, because you were right about Kirstie. She was full of you and how much she'd enjoyed her day.'

'How did she take it?' Anne Jackson was studiously casual.

'She was all right. Sort of quiet. I didn't rub her nose in it.' He didn't tell Anne Jackson that when the moment came he would have liked to have done just that. He'd felt a surprising and unbecoming inclination to boast. He'd wanted to tell ex-Anne and her new man that he'd attracted a new and vibrant younger woman into his life, that his new Anne was impossibly pretty and impossibly understanding and impossibly good with children, as Kirstie would witness. He'd resisted the temptation, fortunately, and merely announced woodenly to his former wife that he thought she ought to know about this new development.

Ex-Anne had professed herself pleased for him, in an equally conventional and equally wooden way. Her new man had said, 'Good on yer, Chris,' and gone back to his wrestlings with eBay and the computer.

'She's got herself a new partner, who was there when I told her. She couldn't be other than accommodating, could she?' said Chris.

'I suppose not. But I'm glad you've told her. I didn't want her hearing about us from someone else.' Anne Jackson wondered how she would feel in the ex-wife's shoes, then shrugged and hoped that would be a position in which she would never find herself. Without knowing quite what she was about, she went up to Chris, put her arms round his neck, and kissed him briefly on the lips. 'I've prepared my lessons for the coming week. We've got the evening to ourselves.'

They ate comfortably together. Chris was a surprisingly good cook of simple food, and the bottle of Merlot went down smoothly with it. He had his arm round her on the sofa when she said, 'You're tired, aren't you?'

'It's this murder we had at Belmont. Unless it's a domestic with a quick arrest, you work long hours on a murder.'

'It affects a lot of people. I told you, I know one of the Youngs' children; they live in the same village as my parents. I met him in the park yesterday, and even he seemed upset by it, poor kid.'

Chris cast thoughts of the case resolutely aside. 'I'll arrange a game of golf for us with John Lambert and Bert Hook, when this murder case is over. You can take them to the cleaners again.'

She grinned, stroking the back of his wrist. 'We won't have the surprise factor on our side, this time. They assumed that I'd be useless.'

'There aren't many four-handicap women about; I'm sure neither of those two had ever played against one before!' said Chris, stretching his legs in happy reminiscence. 'Next time, I'll have to play better.'

'You will indeed.'

Golf is plainly a more dangerous game than even its enthusiasts appreciate. For it was not long after this that Chris Rushton asked Anne Jackson to marry him.

She stared at his flickering gas fire for many seconds before she said, 'It's too early yet, Chris. Let's not take things too quickly.' Then, as disappointment welled within him, she turned her hazel-coloured eyes up towards his and said quietly, 'I'm not saying no, mind. You're not to snatch the offer away from me!' and kissed him again, before snuggling down into the crook of his arm.

Chris had never intended to propose when they had sat down together on his sofa. He felt a strange mixture of achievement and relief.

Twenty-Two

Eleanor Hook knew that her husband had put in two hours of work before his eight o'clock breakfast. She would be glad when this Open University studying was over. Bert had found it enormously stimulating and she was immensely proud of his efforts and his results so far, but with a demanding job and a family he was determined not to neglect there just weren't enough hours in the day.

She said as much to Bert. He nodded ruefully and said, 'And not enough weeks in the year. There aren't many left now before the final exams in November.'

'Can't you get any time off?'

'John Lambert says I must take a week before the finals. He'll insist on it, I fancy.' Lambert had followed Bert's progress with almost as much interest and pride as Eleanor; he was anxious that the sergeant who had refused to become an inspector should do himself justice in the last stretch of this long academic pilgrimage. 'I expect we shall have this Belmont murder case wrapped up by then.'

'You'll need that time to recharge your batteries,' said Eleanor firmly.

'Mrs Fogarty says life's made too easy for older students nowadays,' said Luke, arriving unexpectedly with a bright and innocent smile.

'Mrs Fogarty should keep her opinions on these things to herself,' said his mother grimly. She'd met the famous Mrs Fogarty at a parents–teachers evening: an earnest young woman with small-lensed glasses on a thin nose and a mouth which did not smile much. She'd said what a bright and industrious boy Luke was and Eleanor had been overcome by maternal pride. Now she found herself contrasting young Mrs Fogarty's education at an expensive private school with the robust teenage years of Bert Hook as a Barnardo's boy.

'She says older people are feather-bedded with degrees they can bite off in lumps,' said Luke. The Hooks' younger son had a habit of delivering ideas he did not understand with ringing authority. His mother had a secret fear that he might become a politician.

'Dad's looking worried again.' Jack entered the kitchen as abruptly as his younger brother before him. He flung a protective arm around his father's shoulders. 'Final exams looming even closer, are they, Dad?' he added with exaggerated sympathy.

'I'm quietly confident,' said Bert firmly. He felt anything but that.

It was almost a relief to arrive at the station for a Monday morning conference with his chief and Chris Rushton on the progress of the Cullis inquiry. Bert felt he'd already been up for half the day; his mood was not improved by Rushton's mysterious air of secret satisfaction with himself. Bert had grown used to Chris being both slightly overawed by John Lambert and at the mercy of the humorous sallies of the two older men who had worked together for so long.

Rushton said briskly, 'We have gathered a lot of information in the last five days, but we haven't yet been able to eliminate anyone who sat at that table with Richard Cullis. Normally the use of ricin would rule out most people, but in this case everyone seems to have had access to the poison. There are two husband-and-wife pairings involved: all four of them have plausible motives. Paul Young had recently been sacked from his job at Gloucester Chemicals, seemingly at the behest of Cullis. Debbie Young was passed over for promotion when Cullis got the job of Director of Research and Development; by all accounts she took it very badly and was still very bitter about it when Cullis was killed. Neither of these things seems like a motive for murder to me, but you two have seen these people.'

Lambert nodded. 'Debbie Young is resentful to the point of paranoia about Cullis taking what she saw as her job. Her husband says he accepted his redundancy philosophically, but he's a great supporter of his wife. I wouldn't rule either of them out.'

Rushton said, 'For what it's worth, Anne knows one of the Youngs' children. She says he's been quite disturbed since Cullis's death. But I suppose there could be all sorts of reasons for that.'

Lambert smiled. 'There could indeed. The Dimmocks had very different reasons for hating Cullis. Lucy Dimmock has confessed to what seems to have been a pretty torrid affair with Cullis. The man seems to have left a trail of disappointed women behind him: I think it's very possible that she took the affair more seriously than he did, in which case she would be extremely bitter. Jason Dimmock is a cool customer in most things, but he was clearly very disturbed by this liaison. Both of them concealed the affair during our first interviews with them, which might be significant.'

Chris Rushton flashed up names on his computer. 'There are two other women involved. We haven't been able to rule out the wife yet. Alison Cullis makes no secret of the fact that their marriage was on the rocks. Divorce might not seem the natural way out for her, because she's a Catholic. She also says that Cullis was resistant to the idea. In any case, she strikes me as a woman who might have been prepared to dispatch him rather than divorce him; she clearly felt very embittered about the way he'd treated her.'

Bert Hook spoke up as Lambert nodded to him. 'Priscilla Godwin is the most obvious of suspects. I think all of us believe that she was raped by Cullis shortly before his death, even though the CPS refused to take it to court. Her distress and frustration no doubt made her feel tempted to murder. There would have been a degree of public sympathy for her if she'd taken her own retribution, and I've known women to react in that way. When we saw her, she seemed relatively calm and objective; on the night of the murder, she might have been feeling and behaving differently.'

Lambert was privately amused by his old ally's attempts to be objective: he knew enough of Hook to divine that he didn't think the vulnerable but resourceful Priscilla Godwin had done this. He pointed out, 'Ms Godwin understands the situation and her position within it. She did point us towards a man whom she'd just slept with. According to her, Ben Paddon is the mole at Gloucester Chemicals. As she clearly understood, that gives him a motive we weren't aware of until yesterday afternoon.'

'Would he go as far as murder?' said Rushton, making a note to enter on this man's file.

'Remains to be seen,' said Lambert tersely. 'Bert and I

are seeing him this morning. Paddon is clearly a naturally secretive young man – successfully secretive. He's managed to watch and observe in the research labs at Gloucester Chemicals for two years without being exposed as an animal rights mole. That's why the local group's been so well informed about developments there. We know that there's a dangerously violent element within the movement. It wasn't long ago that they dug up the body of an elderly lady and treated it appallingly in a warped attempt to make some sort of point. The local group is numerous and strong: we've already seen them kidnap Cullis because they saw him as a figurehead; to people like that, murder might be the next logical step. All fanatics are capable of murder, especially when they think they are acting not for themselves but a cause. Martyrdom is a very persuasive concept, for people who combine quiet, undistinguished lives with blazing beliefs. Almost all terrorists are fanatics.'

It was a long speech for Lambert, who usually left much unsaid with his experienced CID colleagues. Perhaps he had been clarifying his own thoughts as he spoke. There were a few seconds of silence before Hook said, 'Perhaps we may know a little more after we've seen Paddon again and confronted him with what we now know about him.'

Ben Paddon took Lambert and Hook into the office room at the end of the labs where they had seen Jason Dimmock.

The movements of his long body seemed even more jerky and uncoordinated than when they had seen him in his flat: the man was plainly nervous. He acknowledged this with his first abrupt statement to them. 'Pris spoke to me this morning. I know that she told you about my All God's Creatures membership.'

'Which you carefully concealed from us when we met on Friday,' Lambert pointed out.

'She should never have told you. I spoke to her in confidence.'

'On the contrary, she did exactly the right thing. In a murder investigation, anyone who conceals information about a suspect runs the risk of becoming an accessory after the fact.'

'So I'm a murder suspect, now, am I?'

'You have made yourself one, by concealing information. You deliberately hid your association with the movement, both from our officers a few weeks ago and from DS Hook and me on Friday.'

'In that case, I insist on having my lawyer present for this conversation.' Paddon walked over to the door of the store-room at the back of the office and flung it open with a stage magician's gesture. The man standing within the cramped space emerged with an air of embarrassment, holding a document case in front of his chest as if it were a necessary shield. It was Tim Cohen.

The brash young man whom Lambert had dispatched from his house three days earlier now studiously avoided eye contact with him. Cohen announced stiffly to the filing cabinets behind the superintendent, 'I must remind you that Mr Paddon is a citizen who is voluntarily assisting you with your inquiry. He has been charged with nothing: he is not under arrest.'

'If he is not cooperative this morning, he may very well find himself under arrest, on suspicion of murder. If he is not guilty of that crime, he would do well to give us all the assistance he can, in view of what he has concealed from us in the last few days.' Lambert gave Paddon a sour smile and added without looking at Cohen, 'I am sure that would be your advice to him as his legal consultant.'

Cohen weighed this for a moment, then nodded quickly. 'Mr Paddon is innocent of this crime. He has nothing to fear.' He made himself smile. 'The most you could accuse him of is wasting police time, and I'm sure you wouldn't wish to dissipate the resources of the police machine on such a minor charge. It would make you look rather silly.'

Cohen still wouldn't look at John Lambert. He directed his supercilious smile at Hook, who said with some relish, 'I'm not sure the public would think concealing information during a murder hunt was a minor offence. Any more than I'm sure they'd approve of a lawyer who tried to divert us from the truth.' He turned to Paddon. 'Why did you conceal your All God's Creatures affiliations when our officers questioned you about the matter last week?'

'I saw no reason to reveal views which are my own concern.'

'You didn't just conceal things. You lied quite deliberately about the matter.'

Ben decided to play the only card he had left. 'My job was at stake.'

'You're a member of a group which has broken the law of the land on numerous occasions. A group which has perpetrated serious violence and boasted that it would do more. One of these enlightened thinkers kidnapped a member of the public who had offered them no aggression, Richard Cullis. They boasted to him of the man they had working under his direction in the labs at Gloucester Chemicals. Richard Cullis is now dead. You need to explain to us not only why you lied to us about your views on animal testing but why we should not consider you a prime suspect for murder.'

'I didn't do it.'

'So convince me.'

'My client doesn't have to do that, DS Hook,' said Tim Cohen smoothly. 'Innocent until proven guilty is fortunately still one of the principles on which our law functions.'

'So convince us you're innocent, Mr Paddon.' Hook's eyes had never switched from Paddon's face to Cohen's.

'He doesn't need to do that. He merely has to—'

'Mr Paddon will no doubt speak for himself. He is here, as you pointed out, to help us with our inquiry.'

Ben had not been prepared for this aggression from such an unexpected source. He said almost wonderingly, 'I don't approve of the testing carried out on animals at Gloucester Chemicals. I've been watching things happen for too long, biding my time and waiting for the opportunity to make some big gesture about it which would draw the public's attention to what goes on there. But I didn't want Cullis to be kidnapped. That only drew attention to my situation at work, especially when that idiot Scott Kennedy boasted that we had someone under cover in the research laboratories.'

Hook nodded, shrugging away his aggression, dropping into his favourite role of the understanding older man. 'So you thought you must act quickly. You got yourself involved in the golf day, because you saw that it would give you the opportunity to get close to Richard Cullis, alongside other people who would be as suspect as you of causing his death. And you took advantage of that opportunity to kill him last Tuesday night. You made the "big gesture" you just mentioned.'

'I didn't. I didn't kill him. It was someone else who put that ricin in his food.' Ben thought hopelessly that however often he repeated that idea he would not convince them. Hook's account of his thinking in the lead-up to this death was so accurate that Ben's phrases didn't even convince himself.

He could think of nothing else to add in the pause before Lambert said quietly, 'Do you have access to ricin, Mr Paddon?'

'Yes. But everyone who works on research and development does. Everyone at that table on Tuesday could have got hold of it, either directly or through a partner.'

'So who killed Richard Cullis?'

Ben felt a surge of hope that they were even allowing the possibility of someone other than him having done this. He'd had visions of them leading him out of here, past dozens of curious eyes, and pushing him with head bowed into the back of the police car. He felt an absurd urge to help them with their work, to get himself off the hook by presenting them with a better candidate for murder. 'Alison Cullis. She hated Richard. He'd raped Pris Godwin only a few days earlier. I reckon Alison had found out about it and it was the last straw.'

Lambert looked with distaste at the animated, excited face. 'That's a motive. Have you a shred of evidence to support it? Have you a single fact to offer us in support of your accusation?'

'Well, no. Not really. But you asked me who had done it, and I thought she was the most likely candidate.'

'More likely than the woman who spent Saturday night in your bed? More likely than the victim of this rape?'

Ben tried to make his racing mind work as quickly and clearly as it usually did. Pris had shopped him, hadn't she? She had blown his cover, revealed to them things which he had told her in confidence. She didn't deserve to be protected. But perhaps she'd been put under pressure by these ruthless men, who were so much more formidable than he'd expected. The memory of his night with Pris, of what they had started and what he wanted to continue, held him back. 'Priscilla didn't do it. She's not the type.' How trite that sounded! What a fool he would be, if it emerged that she had been stringing him along! He heard the doubt in his voice as he said, 'Pris would have told me if she'd done it.'

'I wish I could share your confidence,' said Lambert drily. 'Don't leave the area without giving us the details of your movements, please, Mr Paddon.' He gave Tim Cohen a long, assessing look before he left the room.

Cohen shut the office door carefully. 'They can't touch you for anything you said today,' he told his shaken client, with more assurance than he felt.

Ben put his hands together in front of him on the desk and realized that they were shaking. He couldn't remember that ever happening to him before. 'I didn't think Pris would have told them,' he said dully.

'People do what they need to do to protect themselves. They're cleverer than you think they are, these plods.'

Ben nodded. 'You weren't much use.'

'I did what I could.' Tim didn't want to tell Paddon how much he'd been shaken by the presence of Chief Superintendent Lambert, the man from whose house he had recently been forced to beat such an ignominious retreat. He told Ben to keep a low profile, to contact him immediately if he felt the need of his services. 'If the firm wants to get rid of you, tell them you haven't broken the law. You may have concealed your animal rights sympathies, but tell them your private opinions are your affair and not theirs. Is that understood?'

'I lied about it at interview,' said Ben dully.

'That's a long time ago. Some of the people involved won't be around any longer, and the ones who are still here probably won't remember.'

'I'm not sure I'll be able to work here any longer. Not if everyone in the labs knows about my beliefs.'

'That's up to you. But do what I said and you'll be able to leave on your own terms, not theirs.'

Cohen got out as quickly as he could. He'd been happy to divert Paddon on the lesser issue of his position at Gloucester Chemicals. He didn't want him coming out with a confession of murder. The English legal system didn't allow you to defend people if you knew for certain they were guilty.

Twenty-Three

O n the following morning, the weather was fine and clear, but a white frost sparkled on the lawn outside John Lambert's bungalow as he backed out the car. He drove east, peering into a sun which was low and dazzling beneath a brilliant blue sky. He picked Bert Hook up after a few miles, but they did not speak as they drove towards Cheltenham. It was a benefit of working together for so many years that each was content to let the other pursue his own train of thought.

The big house in the suburbs looked even more imposing with the clear morning light upon its front elevation. But the flowers on the dahlias alongside the long drive, which had been so colourful on their last visit, now hung black and limp after the winter's first frost. The leaves of the maples still made their brilliant crimson show, but they carpeted the ground beneath the plants, which had been stripped bare by the night's cold.

Alison Cullis had the big front door open before Hook had finished ringing the bell. She stood above the big men at the top of the three steps, bathing them in a smile of false welcome, looking beyond them to the deserted road and the other big houses on the other side of it, where there was no sign of life. 'It won't be long now before winter is here!' she said clearly over their heads, directing her words towards the leafless maples in the border beyond the lawn, as if she was enunciating an important line in a play.

She took them into her sitting room, as she had taken Father Driscoll before them when he had come to offer her the solaces of Holy Mother Church. These were also important visitors, though they had not the trappings of childhood reverence you gave to a priest. But she offered them the same hospitality she had offered Father Driscoll: they refused the coffee and shortbread rather curtly, she felt. She gave them her brittle smile again and said, 'It will be a week ago tonight that Richard died.'

'That he was murdered, yes.'

The Lambert man had corrected her like a schoolmaster. She said a little waspishly, 'That's right, yes. Have you found out who killed him yet?'

'I believe we have, yes.' The lawyers would have tut-tutted and said that he hadn't sufficient evidence for a case yet, but Lambert didn't think that this woman was going to conduct the long ritual of denial.

'He had a lot of enemies. We discussed that last time you were here.'

'But only one who killed him. How did you get hold of the ricin, Mrs Cullis?'

'Me? Oh, you must be desperate, Superintendent! I'm the one who isn't a scientist, remember?'

'You're also the one who knew before he hit the floor that it was murder. The one who called for the police before even thinking of a doctor.'

For the first time, she was looking at them and not at some indeterminate area beyond them. 'This is old ground, Mr Lambert. I explained that last time you were here.'

'You didn't, Mrs Cullis. You provided no answer at all to the question. You merely said that your husband had a lot of enemies round that table.'

'Which was true.'

'Of course it was. But it was nevertheless an evasion. You also neglected to emphasize to us essential features which were in your favour: I found that quite significant. In retrospect, it seemed that only someone who knew she was guilty would have made such an omission.'

Alison tried to be haughtily dismissive. 'And what were these mysterious "essential features" which I so conspicuously failed to use?'

'You never asserted to us that you were the only person at that table who was not a scientist. Nor that you were the only person without obvious access to the poison involved in this death.'

'Self-evident, Superintendent.'

'Maybe. I would have expected someone who asserted to

us at the time that she was a suspect to point out things which were in her favour.'

'I took an interest in my husband's work, in the early days. We were not always bitter enemies.' Her eyes were gazing past them again, out over the garden and the trees, towards the sheep dotted on the hill beyond them, recalling another time and another world, where things had been so different.

'And you had access to the laboratories and what went on there. You went in and out of the place.'

She looked at him as if re-registering his presence. 'I didn't need that. Richard brought things home.'

It was the first acceptance of guilt, the beginning of a confession. It was Hook who now said gently, encouragingly, 'We were told that by people who worked in the labs.' By Ben Paddon, that gentle, mistaken, unthreatening figure who had unwittingly revealed so much about his fellow suspects.

'He was a cruel man, Richard. Of course, you know that by now. But you may not know how cruel.'

'How cruel, Mrs Cullis?' Hook was as soothing as a therapist.

Alison looked into the weather-beaten, understanding, persuasive face and wondered why confession to this man should be easy. So much easier than it had been over those many years when she had knelt in the private cells of church confessionals and struggled to recite her sins to those anonymous men in cassocks behind the screens. 'Richard brought home ricin. Months ago, I'm not sure when. Threatened me with it, when I taxed him with his women. Said he could dispatch me with it whenever he chose, that so long as the body wasn't discovered for a few hours no one would know what had killed me.'

'He threatened you?'

'He didn't mean to kill me. He just wanted me in his power. Wanted to see me squirm. Richard enjoyed watching me squirm. He said I was a helpless worm and he would tread on me whenever he chose.'

She paused, seeming to revel for a moment in her pain and humiliation. Hook sought for words, however banal, which might prompt her. 'From what you say, he was indeed a cruel man.'

She nodded several times, as if it was important for her to confirm this to herself. Then the CID men saw that slyness, that delusion of her own cunning, which they had seen before in murderers. 'He was sadistic. Over the years, he got worse. But this time I was a match for him.' She leant forward confidentially towards Hook. 'I went into the study when he was out with his latest floozy, didn't I? Took a little of his precious ricin. He never knew that when he returned it to the labs.'

'But you didn't use it immediately.'

'No. I bided my time. Gave him the chance to mend his ways. There is always hope for those who repent, you know.' She was plainly reciting some tenet of faith from her youth, but it was not clear whether she was thinking at that moment of her victim or herself. 'But he got worse. The final straw was when he raped someone. He went too far then, didn't he?' She looked at Hook with her dark eyes widening moistly in an appeal on behalf of all her sex.

'And the day at Belmont gave you your opportunity.'

She nodded, eagerly accepting this appreciation of her actions. 'He set it up himself. "Hoist with his own petard", you might say. That's Shakespeare, you know.'

'Yes. *Hamlet*, isn't it?'

The oval face filled with delight. 'That's right. Richard wouldn't have known that. He thought that anything but science was so much frippery.'

'But you were too clever for him. You chose an occasion when there would be lots of other people around him. People who might be more obvious suspects than you.'

'Yes.' Again a horrid tremor of her own cleverness shuddered her body for a moment. 'But I don't think I thought of it like that when I planned it. It just seemed to me appropriate that Richard should die in front of his colleagues. Particularly if they could include the woman he'd raped. I wasn't sure until the day that she was going to be at the table, but that seemed very appropriate to me. Doesn't it seem appropriate to you, Detective Sergeant Hook?'

It was Lambert on this occasion who stepped forward and announced the words of arrest. Alison Cullis nodded at the formal phrases she had heard before, as if participating in some familiar religious ritual. 'Amen to that,' she said, almost happily, as she prepared to accompany them to the police car and the cells.